Sorcha

Sorcha

AWAKEN

Susan Alford & Lesley Smith

Illustrated by Candy Alford

ISBN: 069251368X
ISBN 13: 9780692513682
Library of Congress Control Number: 2015949773
Concept III Publishing, Cleveland, TN

Dedication

For Homer & Pearl, our grandparents, who entertained
angels unaware…and for our beautiful children
Kaitlyn, Caroline, Emma, Noah & Ansley

Acknowledgments

• • •

THANK YOU, GOD, FOR YOUR Son, your Spirit and for your incredible blessings to each of us. You are our inspiration and our guide. Our gifts are yours!

Value can be defined as relative worth, merit, or importance. The people who have helped us along our journey have added a value to our lives and to our story that cannot be measured. And for that we are grateful:

Delton & Myrna Alford
Andy Smith
Axel Arzola
Clark Campbell
Richie Hughes
Lucas Hicks
Jacqueline Campbell
Lee University Family
The Crew: Austin, Carly, Kaity, Nick, Devonte, Oto, Tiffany, Ben S., Kenzie, Ben C., Holdan, Devin, Cait, Dylan, Zach, Drew and Olivia

Our families and our friends!

"From within or from behind, a light shines through us upon things, and makes us aware that we are nothing, but the light is all."

~Ralph Waldo Emerson

"And the light shines in the darkness; and the darkness has not overcome it."

~John 1:5 (ESV)

Contents

Prologue

●●●

The past, present and future are links in a chain that cannot be broken.

Nothing happens by chance. We know that now.

If we are to gain any measure at all in this life, you must know the truth.

Time is running out for all of us.

The mask has been removed. We have seen the face of evil and grappled with him.

But evil will not be deterred from its chilling purpose.

He watches...a sentinel in the dark...waiting for one of us to falter.

He will never tire of the hunt. He wants us: our blood, our suffering, our destruction.

Every moment brings us closer to our destiny.

We must find the others quickly for the uniting of the twelve has been foretold.

We must find the key and unlock the secret of the Book.

Our quest has begun.

CHAPTER 1

Senses

• • •

ROCKY MOUNTAINS, COLORADO
December 2007

The heavy snow blew across Lucas's face. It was cold, but he didn't mind.

Even though his ten-year-old twin sister, Lily, was light on her feet, he passed her easily. Up ahead, the path turned deeper into the forest. He and Lily reached the small clearing breathless from their run.

"Your old man's still got it! Beat ya fair and square!" Elijah Quinn's wide mouth split into a smile. His thick brown hair, dusted with falling snow, looked almost grey. Lucas's father's clear green eyes, a perfect match to his, twinkled.

"But I beat Lily!" Lucas shot back proudly.

"Betcha I can make a snow angel better than you," Lily boasted.

Never one to back down from a challenge, he plopped down beside his sister and furiously waved his wiry arms and legs in the snow. He didn't like to lose.

"See, mine's better. Look how big it is," he exclaimed.

"It doesn't even look like an angel! It's just a big mess," Lily retorted.

"I don't know about you two, but I'm starving. Ready to head back for breakfast?" Eli asked.

"Yes!" The twins answered together.

Lily continued, "I hope mom's making pancakes." She grabbed Eli's hand and followed him to the path.

"Come on, Lucas, it's freezing out here," Eli called.

His father was right. His body was so very cold all of a sudden. He felt very strange.

"Lucas, I said, let's go!" his father said.

He willed himself to move but he couldn't. No matter how hard he tried, his body was frozen. He wanted to open his mouth to call out, but it was clamped shut. What was happening to him?

"Stop playing around, Luc," Lily urged, walking back over to him.

He was getting scared. Something wasn't right. Why couldn't he move? Even when Lily pulled his arm he didn't budge. His vision blurred but he could hear the desperation in his father's voice.

"What's wrong, son? Come on, Luc, talk to me."

His heart stopped when a soul-shattering scream rent the air. His senses went into overdrive. A cold vice squeezed his heart. His mouth was dry and burned like fire. Dark shadows enveloped him. Focusing all his energy, he screamed, but no sound was released from his clamped lips.

Without warning, his world turned upside down. His hearing was so acute the falling snow was like a beating of a snare drum as it fell from the angry sky. Cold air stabbed his skin like millions of tiny needles. Gasping for air, he gagged on the most foul and indescribable scent. His lungs burned with it. His vision cleared and honed in on the unearthly silver lights weaving gracefully through the trees. Eli and Lily were totally unaware, panicked, and still trying to shock him from his stupor. Only he saw what was coming.

"Turn around, Dad," his mind pleaded. "Lily, can't you hear them crashing through the trees?"

Almost upon them, the haunting illuminations took form. Figures, men and women with bodies of substance and strength, emerged from the shadows. Time stopped. Unbelievably beautiful and faultless in their appearance, the extraordinary winged creatures were frightening. Clothed in incandescent garments, the commanding figures pulsed with light. Each wore a breastplate of gleaming silver. Fiery crimson hair flowed down their backs. Some wore lustrous diamond masks while others displayed their stunningly perfect countenances. All had the same cold, intense, and smoldering blue eyes.

Their incredibly large leather-like wings were translucent. Lucas could see red blood pulsing through them. Great black beasts, their thick muscled bodies covered with short rough fur, accompanied the beautiful ones. The animals growled and gnashed their razor-sharp teeth, barely restrained by their masters' hold on their resplendent silver collars.

Lucas knew the instant his father became aware. His head whipped around, realization dawning in his eyes. Eli moved in front of him and pushed a fear-stricken Lily, behind him. One of the beautiful winged creatures glided smoothly towards his father while the others kept vigil from the trees. A long hooded cloak billowed behind him. A rich ruby ring on his middle finger was the only sign of warmth on his person. Lucas gagged, so strong was the smell of death that swirled around the hooded figure.

Below his silver faceplate, a calculating smile spread across the figure's full lips. "It's been too long, Elijah. I have truly missed you."

With lightening force, the beautiful creature delivered a backhanded slap, sending his father to his knees. Lucas felt the ferocity of the blow as if he had been hit as well. He willed Eli to get up. When Eli stood slowly and squared his shoulders, Lucas saw the bright red blood trickling from his father's mouth.

"My time is past, Cain," Eli said. "What do you want with me?"

"Still ignorant I see—it's not you I want," Cain said with disdain.

"Even you would not dare to break the covenant!"

"Typical of your kind, blind faith in something you cannot even see—tragic, really. You have no purpose, not any longer. You know death came swiftly for the others, but I have been saving the best for last."

"Your soul is as black as the pit you climbed up from. I don't fear you."

"Of course not! I would be sorely disappointed if you did. I'm not so sure, however, about your children? I believe they are much afraid. Look at the poor souls. Tell me, Elijah, have you ever heard the whimpers of a child when their bones are broken, one by one? When their flesh is gnawed and torn from their pathetic form? Children are very fragile, Eli...so easy to break. When they beg for the pain to stop, you will fear me then. Won't you?"

The taunts proved too much for his father. A roar ripped from Eli's chest and he lunged. But Cain was too quick. He materialized at the other side of the clearing, a faint smile on his face. Eli landed heavily in the snow, his target gone. In the blink of an eye, silver lights exploded all around, and the bright figures that had stood around the far side of the clearing now surrounded Eli. Their unearthly blue eyes were icy flames.

Lucas' ears burned with the hideous chant coming from the beautiful ones. Their words were beyond understanding but he knew it couldn't be good. No longer restrained, the growling black beasts circled him and Lily. Separated from his father, he knew they were going to die. Lily moved closer to him. She must have been scared witless and he was powerless to protect her, locked in his sensory prison.

Lucas searched for Eli across the clearing. His father was absolutely still, head bowed and eyes closed, surrounded on all sides. The palms of the creatures' long-fingered hands now burned with cold blue flames.

"Daddy, please get up," Lily begged.

With all his might, Lucas willed his father to obey his sister's plea. They had to escape, together. But how? His fear was replaced by confused frustration. Why couldn't he make his body obey? Look at me, Dad! What do I do? Help me. He met his father's eyes. His father wasn't scared at all. His eyes were filled with confidence. He was shocked to the core with what happened next.

Eli scooped up a large amount of snow. His hands moved rapidly with a carpenter's precision to craft the icy powder into a shield. When the beautiful ones flung their first fiery darts, he moved to a crouching position and deflected every one. He leapt to his feet and ran towards him and Lily, using the shield to bash the black beasts that stood in his way.

Lucas cringed when one of the beautiful ones pounced on Eli's back. A glittering diamond faceplate covered her face; her long braided hair hung down her back. Her slight wingless form belied her incredible strength. She hoisted Eli into the air and flung him with great force into a tree. She hissed in delight.

"Finish him," Cain ordered.

Helpless, Lucas watched the creature stalk toward Eli. Blood flowed freely from a wide gash across his forehead. The arm that had raised the snow shield now lay at an odd angle against his bruised body. His other arm twitched in the snow. Lucas could see the icy flames burning in her eyes. Lowering herself into a crouch, the creature placed her fiery hand on Eli's chest over his heart.

"Your children will watch you die, light-bearer!" she jeered.

The blue pulse coming from her powerful hand never penetrated his chest. Eli drove a snow sword deeply into the creature's shoulder. He must have fashioned the weapon while the woman was approaching him. Shocked, and momentarily thwarted, she fell back. Lucas watched his father stand and brandish the sword. The beautiful ones writhed in anger.

Suddenly, a warm glowing light burst through the snow-clouds above. Lucas felt the ground tremble like an earthquake when a golden man with glittering wings embedded with deep grey eyes landed next to Eli. Rich warm light surrounded them both. The hideous beasts were paralyzed, whimpering like dogs. Their masters hissed in frustration at the arrival of the man from the sky. The golden man whispered in Eli's ear, then he was gone as quickly as he had appeared.

Eli looked at Lucas with a whisper of a smile in his eyes. The warm glowing light that had enveloped Eli faded away. Her shoulder bleeding from Eli's sword thrust, the beautiful one pounced once again on his father's back, knocking him down. She grabbed Eli's hair and jerked his head from the snow, exposing his neck. Flaming blue darts sizzled through her hands. Eli's body shook violently. The air crackled with electricity. Then, she released him to the frenzied attack of the scavenger beasts.

"No!"

The soul-shattering scream rushing from Lucas's body freed him from his sensory prison. He reached for Lily but she was already running toward Eli's body. He watched in horror as one of the beautiful ones astride a winged horse swept her up. "Lily!"

He started to run after her when a strong clear voice checked him, "Run, Lucas."

He hesitated for a split second. Who had spoken to him?

But the voice returned with its same command. "Move your feet, Lucas."

"I can't leave them."

"Trust me. Now move!"

Instinctively, he ran, moving his feet as fast as they would carry him away from the clearing. He missed his sister's shocked look of betrayal before she disappeared into the fray.

"Faster, Lucas."

Gasping for air, he pumped his legs and arms. He would never outrun them. He stumbled over a tree root and fell hard.

"Get up, Lucas! They're right behind you."

He picked himself up and ran with a speed only fear could induce. They were gaining. He could hear them...smell them. His legs felt so heavy. He could barely see through the hot tears streaming down his face. Still, he pressed on. Silver lights shot through the trees on either side of him. Ahead, two of the beautiful ones astride their winged horses waited with triumphant smiles.

He was trapped. It was no use. There was nowhere else to run. Not knowing what else to do, he yelled into the frigid wind, "Help me!"

CHAPTER 2

Wings

• • •

THE FEAR AND DESPERATION GRIPPING his heart disappeared instantly when the golden man swooped from the sky and enveloped him in his glittering wings. They shot through the air like lightening. Soaring above the death below, Lucas stared in wonder at the myriad of sparkling colors shimmering all around his rescuer. The eyes embedded in the man's majestic wings gazed back at him. He felt like they were looking straight into his soul willing him to be calm.

Was this even happening? When his protector set him down in the snow, he saw that he was home. Smoke curled from the chimney. Eli's work boots sat at the backdoor. He turned around but the glowing man was no longer there. He was alone.

Maybe it really had been a dream. Maybe he would run into the kitchen and find Eli drinking his morning cup of coffee. He would just close his eyes, and when he opened them again it would be like nothing had ever happened.

"Lucas, you are safe now. Go inside."

Obeying the voice, he stumbled across the short distance of the yard and flung open the back door.

"Mama!"

Mia was at the stove flipping pancakes. When she saw him, her spatula clattered to the floor.

"Luc, what's wrong?"

"I left them. I didn't know what to do. They were chasing me. The screams…"

He collapsed on the floor.

"Lucas, you're scaring me. Slow down."

"She killed him, mama…she killed them both."

At a dead run, his little sister slid on sock-covered feet into the kitchen.

"Mama, what is it? What's wrong with Lucas?" Zoe asked, running a hand through her strawberry-blonde hair. She was only eight years old but already taller than her older sister.

"I'm not sure," Mia answered. "Call the park ranger's office. Tell them it's an emergency."

Zoe picked up the phone in the kitchen and called 911.

"I've got to go back out there. I have to look for them," Lucas insisted.

"Lucas, you aren't making any sense. We need to wait on the rangers. It's really coming down out there now. It's too dangerous. Zoe, help me get your brother to the couch."

They helped him into the den where he sat on the worn leather couch. Zoe sat down beside him and put her small hand in his.

"Now, tell me what you saw Luc," Mia urged.

Before he could even begin, a hard rap sounded at the door. Mia ran to open the door. "Lily!"

Two park rangers supported the weight of his very dazed sister. An egg-sized knot marred her forehead and dried blood smeared her face.

"Lily, honey, what happened? Are you okay?"

Mia led her daughter to a chair.

Lily just stared into the distance not saying a word. Lucas could only imagine the horror his sister witnessed after he deserted her. Would she ever be able to forgive him?

"Officers, please come in," Mia urged.

"Mrs. Quinn, I'm Officer Nolan Gable and this is my partner, Sam Asher. Ma'am, we found your daughter unconscious not far from here in the clearing off the Silverdoe Trail. She doesn't remember anything. We were bringing her home when dispatch relayed your emergency call."

"My husband? Where is he?" Mia asked.

"We followed some tracks leading into the forest. We believe bears must have attacked your husband. He was badly wounded. There was nothing we could do. I'm sorry, ma'am, but he's dead."

"Bears don't come down the mountain this far, not this time of year," Lucas whispered under his breath.

"It is unusual but it can happen," Officer Asher offered. "Mrs. Quinn, we would be happy to take you and the children into town. The kids need to see a doctor."

His grief-stricken mother wrapped her arms around herself and hung her head. Zoe whimpered in the seat next to him.

Lucas stared out the window at the darkening sky. He was in a nightmare. His whole life, all that had made him feel safe and secure, had been ripped from him in an instant. Nothing made sense about today...nothing at all.

"Mrs. Quinn," Officer Gable urged, "You and the children don't need to be alone. I think it best you come with us now."

When his mother answered, she echoed Lucas's own dark thoughts. "Yes, you're right. I'm afraid we aren't safe here, anymore."

• • •

*The pleasure was almost more
than she could bear. Desire
pulsed through her, beautiful,
forbidden. So sweet.
Even now she could feel
the softness of his hair,
the muscled strength of his body
under hers, trembling with release.
Her lust was not satisfied.
She supposed it never would be.
It only deepened, reaching the darkest
corners of her sadistic mind.
It wasn't the power wrought
from the killing itself
but the insatiable thrill of the chase.
Today, she had been awakened
from a profound slumber.
He was her first.
The beginning.*

Exit 25

• • •

Cleveland, Tennessee
June 2015

Lucas turned on the blinker of the battered white SUV and veered off the highway toward their destination. All night, mile after mile, he had prayed for their safety. Savannah had become too dangerous for the Quinn family. He wasn't surprised. It was just another city to add to the growing list of failed attempts to put down roots. They had lived in five different states in the last eight years struggling to adjust with each new place. Would he and his family ever find a home? Would he ever close his eyes at night and know peace? After his father died, he had retreated into his music. Alone deep in his dark thoughts, playing his guitar was the only thing that soothed the ache in his soul. He missed Eli. He knew his twin sister did as well but she had chosen to cope with her grief in a different way.

Eighteen-year-old Lily, in the passenger seat beside him, was zoned out. Her honey-blonde hair hung in loose curls past her shoulders. Her eyes were closed and her face was a blank space. Lucas was thankful. Lately, whenever Lily had turned her dark blue eyes on him, all he could see was resentment and anger. He missed his best friend. Lost in the music blasting through her iPod, Lily's legs hadn't stopped their rhythmic bouncing the entire drive from Georgia. Even though she had little memory of the day in the snow, it had changed her. Gone was the energetic happy girl he had known and in her place was an angry rebellious young woman. Emotions were a two-edged sword bringing great joy but also immeasurable pain. He knew his sister wanted neither—so she withdrew within a hard caustic shell. The only sign of her struggle was the nervous bouncing. Lily was petite but her movements were strong enough to make Lucas feel like the car was shaking. He reached over as he often did to still her leg.

His mother, Mia, was quiet as well. Her sketchbook, which was never far from her, lay open on her lap. She was capturing the beautiful summer sunrise. He had grown to deeply respect his mother. She was stronger than he had ever imagined. But living on the run was taking its toll. She was plagued with fear and her beautiful face was too often lined with worry. Only he and Mia knew the truth about the danger that always followed them. He hoped that moving to live with his mom's sister would bring his mother a safety she had not known since Eli was murdered. Maybe, just maybe, his family could put the roots down here in Tennessee that had been torn from the icy ground of Colorado.

"Looks like we made it," Lucas announced to no one in particular.

"I can't wait to see Aunt Audrey. I bet she won't even recognize me it's been so long," Zoe responded.

His adopted sixteen-year old sister grinned at him in the rear view mirror. She was always quick to smile. He watched her pull her curly strawberry-blonde hair into a low ponytail. Zoe was tall, lanky even, with fair skin, freckles sprinkled across her nose, and hazel eyes. When her parents died in a tragic car accident, Zoe had been placed in foster care. Jumping from home to home, she finally landed with the Quinns. And the rest was history! No matter the situation, he could always count on Zoe's positivity. The glass was always half full for her. Instead of withdrawing from the tension, his sister just dived into it. He often thought Zoe would truly wither and die if she ever lost her ability to talk. For the last seven hours, to buoy his mood, she had entertained him singing every song that played on the radio, dishing the latest Hollywood gossip, and discussing all the latest activities and places she had added to her bucket list.

"Do you have the directions, Zoe?"

"Got them," she pulled a piece of paper from her backpack and gave them to Lucas. "Turn left up here and go straight through downtown."

Small businesses and shops lined both sides of street. The summer sun was beaming in the clear blue sky. Brightly colored flowers were blooming in big planters all along the way. Stopping at a traffic light, Lucas watched people strolling down the sidewalks, coming in and out of shops and restaurants. Smiling and talking, it seemed that everyone knew everyone else.

"I'm finally home," Mia whispered from the backseat. "It hasn't changed at all."

"We are going to be happy here, Mom, I can feel it," Lucas said.

"I hope so, son. I truly do."

Lucas continued down the street that soon became shaded on both sides by huge magnolia trees.

"These houses are enormous," Zoe wondered. "And absolutely gorgeous!"

Stately historic homes lined Ocoee Street. Passing each expertly crafted home, Lucas knew they all had a unique story. His father had instilled in him from an early age an appreciation for building and crafting. He would have loved these old houses.

He sighed, "Yeah, they are and dad would have loved them."

"This is it, Lucas," Mia pointed. "Just pull in the driveway."

The large two-story grey Victorian sat on a cozy corner lot. It looked like a gingerbread house with its intricate lattice trim, green slate roof, round turreted second story window and wraparound porch. Ceiling fans were spinning, lush green ferns were hanging and white wicker furniture with bright yellow cushions looked inviting. A beautiful stained glass window topped the front door.

As soon as he parked the car, a woman ran across the lawn to greet them. It had been a year since he had seen his Aunt Audrey but she hadn't changed at all. Her chestnut hair was shorter than he remembered but there was no mistaking those dancing green eyes and her merry laugh. Dr. Audrey McCant was dressed simply, with an air of urban chic. His aunt was an English professor at Centenary College.

"I thought y'all would never get here," Audrey McCant exclaimed in her thick East Tennessee accent.

Mia was the first to get out and hug her sister. Lucas knew that Audrey had been the constant in his mother's life before she had married Eli. He hoped that she would fill that gap once again.

"When are you going to learn? You can't put me on a schedule like I'm one of your students," Mia laughed.

"Probably never. I don't give up easily, remember," Audrey replied. "Now, Lucas, come on out here and let me see you."

He unfolded his athletic frame from the driver's seat in one fluid movement and wrapped his arms around his aunt's petite frame.

"Hello, gorgeous!"

"Hello, yourself," Audrey laughed. "You haven't changed a smidge, young man—still a charmer." She stepped back from him and looked him up and down. "So tall—and that thick brown hair and those big green eyes—a killer combination! And you still have your freckles. I bet all the girls are crazy for you."

"None of them are as pretty as you, Aunt Audrey," he grinned.

"Oh my, I can see your Daddy all over you. Your smile lights up a room just like his did."

"Yeah, but I'm still your favorite," Zoe planted a kiss on Audrey's cheek.

"Zoe, my little miss, you are all grown up! And who is this beastie?"

"His name is Jack. He followed me home one day from school and we've been inseparable ever since."

"Well, its nice to meet you, Jack." The white German Shepherd lapped at Audrey's hand. "It's been too long, my precious family."

"I know, you're right, but we are here now," Mia squeezed her sister's hand.

For the first time in a very long time, Lucas felt the tight grip on his heart loosen. Maybe the nightmare would finally end for all of them, especially Lily. She was standing to the side, headphones dangling from her ears, looking as if she couldn't care less about seeing her aunt or her new home. He could feel her internal wrestling, no matter the lack of emotion on her face. He had always believed it was just a twin thing, a connection of sorts. But over the last few years, he realized his ability to sense what was unseen was more powerful than he had imagined.

"Hey Lily, you could at least say hello," Lucas urged.

Lily frowned slightly and turned her attention towards her aunt. "Hi, Aunt Audrey."

"Hey, sweet girl," Audrey smiled and put her arm around her niece for a quick hug. "I can't wait for you to see your room, Lily."

"I'm sure it will be great, Aunt Audrey," Lily replied non-committedly.

Mia suggested quickly, "Why don't y'all unpack the car? Audrey is gonna show me around the place." She hooked her arm in her sister's and walked toward the house.

Lucas and Zoe started unloading the sum total of their lives from the back of the SUV. Lily just stood, gazing at the house, making no attempt to help her siblings. When Zoe carried the first box into the house, Lucas cleared his throat. "How bout some help, please? Or you just gonna stand there and stare a hole in the house?"

Lily turned to him and said, "This is the last time, Luc."

"I know you're tired, Lily. We all are. But, I believe Cleveland is gonna stick."

"That's exactly what you said about Savannah and Indianapolis before that!"

"But, we're with family now. We can make this work. You just gotta give it a chance."

"You and I both know it's only a matter of time until mom gets one of her "feelings" and then all bets are off. We'll pack our bags in the middle of the night, leave our friends and run away, just like always. I'm done moving from place to place on her paranoid whim."

"You don't mean that. You have no idea what mom has sacrificed for us. If you did, you wouldn't be so selfish."

"Shut up, Lucas! I don't need you to go all big brother on me!"

"This is not all about you, Lily. It's about family...our family!"

"It doesn't matter. As soon as I can, I'm going to live my own life, somewhere away from her—far away."

"Fine, Lily. Stay angry. Shut out the people who love you. Leave us if you want. But you are fooling yourself if you think you will ever be happy if you do."

Lucas picked up two big suitcases and stalked angrily into the house. He was beginning to think his sister really was lost to him.

CHAPTER 4

Specs

• • •

LILY SHOOK HER HEAD, REFUSING to believe that her brother might be right. For as long as she could remember, she had been angry. Her anger was limitless, deep, and raw. Her father was dead. Her mother was crazy with fear. And her brother, well, he was just a liar, insisting Eli had been killed by some kind of monster out of a fantasy book. But her anger protected her. She would never allow herself to care deeply for anyone again, even her family. Caring meant pain; it meant loss. She knew that she would break, lose herself, if anyone was taken from her again. She bided her time, counting the days until she could walk away from the family who loved her but who could also destroy her if she loved them in return.

She needed to run. As soon as the bags were unpacked, she was going to escape and clear her mind. She bent down to pick up a bag, and when she straightened up, she met a pair of coffee-brown eyes staring at her from behind a pair of horn-rimmed glasses.

"I'm sorry. I didn't mean to scare you."

Lily studied the young man in front of her. He was bigger than Lucas, but his baggy jeans and ill-fitting t-shirt swallowed his wiry frame. He had a nice face but nothing out of the ordinary. Lily fought an automatic reflex to reach out and sweep his shaggy blonde hair from his face. She noticed him shifting awkwardly on his feet as he waited for her to finish sizing him up.

"Umm, no, that's okay, you just startled me. My name is Lily Quinn. And you are?"

"Jude Butler. I live next door. So I guess that makes us neighbors. Dr. McCant told me you would be moving in today. Dad teaches with her at Centenary."

"Yeah, just pulled in from Savannah."

"So would you like some help with your stuff?"

"Sure, that would be great."

When Lily transferred a load of bags to Jude's arms, her running shoes fell to the ground.

"You like to run?"

"Can't get enough of it, it seems. I ran a half-marathon earlier this year. What about you?"

"Nah, never a real race, but I do it to clear my head from time to time."

"Me too, the world sort of slips away."

"Well, if you're up to it, we could take a run in the morning? But, I mean, if you have something else to do I totally understand…"

"Tomorrow morning would be perfect. Come on in, you can meet my crazy family."

When Lily and Jude entered the house, they passed Mia who was propping open the front door for easy entry and exit.

"Mom, this is Jude Butler. He lives next door."

"It's nice to meet you, Mrs. Quinn."

Lily grinned when she noticed Jude's glasses fogging up. The coolness of the interior of the house was in stark contrast to the hot June day outside.

"Nice to meet you too, Jude. Thanks so much for helping us move in."

"No problem—I'm glad to do it."

"Which room, Aunt Audrey?"

Audrey hollered back from the kitchen, "First one on the right, Lily."

Lily tugged on her new friend's arm. "Let's go, neighbor."

She climbed the stairs with Jude following close behind. When Jack bounded down the stairs chasing a tennis ball, Jude tripped. Trying to regain his balance, he bumped into Lucas who was on his way down to get another load.

"Sorry, my bad," Jude said.

"Don't worry about it, man," Lucas waved his hand, continuing down the stairs and out the door.

"Don't mind him," Lily offered.

She and Jude made the right turn down the hallway towards her new room.

"Where do you want this stuff?"

Lily pointed to the far side of the room without answering. She was soaking it all in. The walls were painted a calm shade of azure, like the ocean. The queen-size bed and matching dresser were antique white. The furniture was old and a little worn but warm and inviting. It was perfect. Lily reminded herself to thank Audrey for putting so much effort into making her feel welcome. The warm summer sun was streaming through the windowpanes and glancing off of her long honey-blonde hair, making it glow in the afternoon light. She was so lost in thought she was oblivious to the young man's unguarded expression of admiration.

"This room is perfect."

"Sure, if you like blue?"

"It's my favorite. When I was a little girl, my dad painted my room this very shade of blue."

"Who are you, cutie?"

Lily turned around to see Zoe leaning against the door-frame with Jack by her side.

"Zoe, this is our neighbor Jude Butler. Jude, meet my little sister, Zoe."

"Cool, it's nice to meet you." Zoe said and stuck out her hand for a quick handshake.

When Jack sniffed suspiciously around Jude, Zoe laughed, "Don't worry, Jack is harmless."

"I think he likes me," Jude grinned sheepishly.

"Yeah, he does. Jack doesn't usually take to strange men. He's very protective," Zoe agreed.

"Well, I guess he's a good judge of character," Lily interjected.

"And looks!" Zoe teased.

"Just ignore her. We all do," Lily said wryly. "Come on, there's still lots to unpack."

When all the bags and boxes were empty, everyone collapsed on the couch in the family room.

"Please tell me this is the last time we are going to move," Zoe pleaded.

"Well, at least we had Jude to help. Thank you," Lily said.

"No problem. But I better be getting home. My mom will send out a search party."

"I'll walk you out," Lily offered, following Jude into the foyer.

When she returned, Zoe asked slyly, "So…?"

"You're kidding, right? That's ten levels of crazy!"

"Maybe, sweetie, but he's a really good guy. You know, cute in a nerdy sort of way," Mia teased.

"Yeah, Lily, who knows? Maybe Jude could tutor you in the finer aspects of human anatomy?" Lucas quipped.

"Really? Is that the best you can do?" Lily countered with a laugh. "You are such a pain in the…"

She caught herself smiling. It had been a long time since she and Lucas had teased one another. She was surprised that she missed it. When the front doorbell chimed, her good mood was broken. Mia got up to answer it.

"Hey kids, come here for a minute," Mia beckoned from the foyer, "I want you to meet someone."

Lily was surprised to see Mia warmly embracing an older well-built man. He was comfortably dressed in jeans and a black t-shirt. Deep soulful blue eyes accented his strong face. His short dark grey hair was streaked with white at the temples. Who was this man? And why was he hugging her mother?

Mia announced. "Dr. Nolan Gable, these are my daughters, Lily and Zoe. Of course, you remember Lucas."

Lily was dumbfounded when Lucas embraced the older man. How did he know this Dr. Gable?

"I am pleased to finally meet you girls," Nolan greeted. "Your mother has spoken so highly of you. How was your journey?"

"Long," Lily answered pointedly. "So how do you know my mother? And my brother?"

"Dr. Gable was my history teacher at Centenary College," Mia interjected.

"Did you know my dad, too?" Lily asked.

"Indeed. I knew your father very well. He was one of my favorite students," Nolan answered.

Before Lily could ask him how he knew Lucas, Audrey called from the kitchen, "Dinner's ready. Let's eat."

Everyone followed the aroma of meatballs and marinara into the dining room. Lily noticed the front door was wide open and Lucas was standing on the front porch. He was studying the thick trees across the street. She joined him. It was not quite day but not quite night either. Shadows falling, fireflies flitting to and fro, crickets chirping; it was the gloaming.

"There's something out there," he whispered.

A cold sense of dread slowly crawled along her spine. She shivered despite the warm humidity of the night.

"Luc, it's nothing, let's go inside."

"Something is out there."

"I don't see anything. You're being ridiculous. Come on."

Lucas took her arm and followed her inside. Noting his pallor, she asked, "Are you okay?"

"I don't know. I haven't felt like this in a long time. Since…" Lucas shook his head. "I'm sure its nothing, you're right."

"Yeah, I am. And you should remember that more often."

• • •

They were so close.
She could smell them
in the heavy damp air.
She flexed her hands,
releasing the tension.
It had been too long
since she had tasted
the sweet satisfaction
of a kill. Too many times,
this cursed family
had escaped her.
They were protected
on all sides. But their time
was running out.
She would not be denied,
no matter the cost.
The Master's plan
was unfolding. She knelt
and ran her hand over
the soft grass. "Soon,
children, your blood will run
sticky sweet on the ground
just like your father's did.
I swear it will be so."

CHAPTER 5

Secrets

• • •

DINNER WAS ORGANIZED CHAOS; EVERYONE was talking at once. Going through the motions, as she always did, Lily ate, not even tasting the spicy pasta. She wanted to be alone, away from the family she was growing more distant from with each day. Her family's light banter only irritated her.

"Aunt Audrey, this is fantastic," Zoe complimented. "You gotta teach mom how to make this sauce."

"How about I teach you?" Audrey smiled. "Lucas, you inhaled your food. Would you like some more?"

"Yes, please." He handed his plate over for a refill. When he took a bite, he said, "It's like heaven in my mouth."

"You say that about everything you eat, Luc," Zoe teased.

"I'm not really hungry. It's been a long day. Can I be excused?" Lily asked.

"Wait, Lily. I'm sure Dr. Gable could tell us some great stories about dad, right Dr. Gable?" Lucas suggested.

"Yes, of course," Nolan agreed.

"Okay, sure," Lily said with reluctance. She was conflicted. She wanted to hear stories about her father hoping somehow they would make her feel warm inside again. But, she knew of she allowed herself to remember him, to think about him, it would only tear her shredded heart into tinier pieces.

"The first day I met Eli, he impressed me. He was so eager to learn and full of questions. At least, that is, until he met your mother," Dr. Gable said with a smile. "Isn't that right, Mia?"

"Yes, we were pretty inseparable," Mia mused. "I was just nineteen when we met. Not much older than you are now, Lily."

Mia's blue eyes took on a dreamy quality. Lily was jealous that her mother could remember Eli with such happiness while she only felt pain.

Her mother continued, "He sat by me on the first day Dr. Gable's Ancient World History class. After, we went for coffee and were never apart for even a day after that. He bragged later to Scarlet that when he saw me for the first time he knew I was the one for him."

"Scarlet was your twin sister, right? The one who died back when you were in college?" Zoe asked.

"Yes, baby girl. She would have loved it that Eli and I ended up together. Scarlet loved to tease us about being Barbie and Ken dolls."

"That's really sweet, Mom," Zoe offered. "I bet you and dad were so cute together back then. Don't you think so too, Lily?"

"I guess so," Lily shrugged her shoulders.

"We got married after graduation and started our life in Colorado. Eli was building houses and I was teaching school. It wasn't long before we added the rest of you to the mix. He was the love of my life. I was honored to be his wife," Mia finished wistfully.

Lily listened to her mother reminisce with growing frustration. This was the woman who had left her husband alone in the city morgue. No family to bury him—no one to mourn him. What kind of love was that? Her leg started to move up and down very fast under the table. Lucas, as was his habit, put his hand on her shaking knee to calm her. She jumped—no longer able to control her anger and resentment.

"Aw, isn't that sweet? Too bad your love didn't last long enough to honor my father with a decent funeral!"

"Lily Amanda Quinn, you will not speak to your mother that way, not in my house," Audrey chided.

"Well, it's the truth, isn't it mother? I mean, my goodness, you drug us from our home with no explanation except for the delusions of a ten year old boy who was obviously in shock."

"That's enough, young lady. I know it has been difficult for you, for all of you, but I was just trying to protect our family," Mia responded vehemently.

"Protect us from what exactly? And don't you dare tell me some scary story about demon monsters and things that go bump in the night! I want the truth."

"But it is the truth," Nolan said quietly. "Demons did murder your father. Everything Lucas has told you is the truth. I was there that awful day—don't you remember me?"

Recognition slowly dawned. "You were the park ranger that found me and brought me home. But how can that even be possible?"

"Unlock your mind and your heart. Evil is real, Lily. It hunts us. It's time for you to open your eyes."

"No more!" Slamming her hands on the table. "I'm tired of all these crazy lies. Demons do not exist. There is no evil trying to destroy us. You told us that day my dad was killed by a bear, plain and simple. Remember, I was there too. No matter who you really are or what Lucas may think he saw. It wasn't real."

She ran from the room and bounded up the stairs. She slammed the door and shut out the world.

● ● ●

"You stay," Audrey said to Mia. "I'll go after her."

After Audrey left the room, Zoe asked, "Can somebody please explain what just happened? I don't understand any of this."

"Why don't we all go sit on the porch and talk?" Mia suggested quietly.

"I think that is a wonderful idea, Mia," Nolan agreed.

Zoe followed her mother and Nolan outside and sat on the porch swing. Lucas joined her and squeezed her hand. "It's gonna be okay, Zoe. I promise."

"Honey, you were so young when it all happened, I didn't think you could understand," Mia said.

"Mia, I believe it's time for her to know it all," Nolan suggested.

"Of course, you're right," Mia agreed.

"I know you must be very confused right now, Zoe," Nolan said softly. "I am a stranger to you, but I have known your family for a very long time. Will you let me explain?

"Dr. Gable, I don't know you but my mother trusts you. So I guess I will too. Please, tell me why my dad died?" Zoe asked.

"In order for me to answer your question, I need to ask you one first."

"Okay, what is it?"

"Do you believe everything, good or bad, happens for a reason?"

Zoe didn't hesitate. "Yeah, of course. So you're saying even though my dad's death was an awful thing, it served a purpose?"

"Yes, a great purpose. Good and evil, darkness and light, angels and demons, men and women fighting a battle for their very lives—nothing happens by chance, Zoe. Your father's sacrifice is part of a much larger plan."

"Whose plan?"

"Elohim's plan, Zoe," Lucas said.

"Elohim? Like the Elohim from mom's stories? You mean he's real?"

"Indeed," Nolan replied. "Elohim is the source of all light and life. He is the maker of all things, both natural and supernatural, and He has a plan for all His creation. And that includes your father, Zoe."

"So Elohim's plan for dad was a horrible death? How can that be right?"

"What was intended to harm, Elohim intended for good to accomplish what will be done. I believe your father's death was the catalyst."

"The catalyst for what?"

"The saving of many lives," Nolan answered.

Lucas squeezed her hand. "Zoe, remember the stories mom used to tell us about the great war of the angels?"

"Sure, a very beautiful angel named Abaddon was favored by Elohim. But he was vain and selfish. He wanted to be like Elohim. So he led a rebellion against Him. But Abaddon and his angel army were defeated. So Elohim cast them all out of the heavens. Now, Abaddon and his fallen angels walk the earth trying to destroy everything considered pure and good."

"Yes, exactly. But there is more," Nolan continued. "To combat Abaddon, Elohim appointed twelve men, warriors of His Light. He named His light-bearers the Sorcha. Each possessed a unique gift that could be wielded in man's supernatural fight against Abaddon and his demon-armies. The gifts of the original twelve Sorcha have been passed down throughout the centuries. Each light-bearer is powerful, but when all are united they produce a force that is unstoppable."

"Gifts? You mean like supernatural powers?" Zoe asked.

"Yes, exactly," Lucas responded and squeezed her hand.

Nolan continued, "Abaddon fears the Sorcha above all. He must destroy them before they unite the light within them. His army of demons, the Scáths, are led by Cain, his most trusted warrior. Throughout the centuries, Cain has been relentless and has shown no mercy. Your father met him in the woods that day."

"Dad was a light-bearer?"

"Yes, Zoe, he was, and your mother as well," Nolan answered. "Your family is directly descended from the Sorcha line. Eli's death was the catalyst for the next generation of light-bearers to rise up and fight."

"Mom? Is this true?"

"Yes, baby girl, it is. Your father and I were light-bearers. Nolan taught and trained us both at Centenary. But we were never able to unite with the rest of our generation. Cain made sure of that. He killed so many of us, even my twin sister, Scarlet," Mia explained. "Now Lucas is the first of the twelve in this generation. He has a star-shaped mark behind his left ear. It is a symbol of the Light he carries within."

Zoe immediately pulled her brother's ear back. "It's there. I've never noticed it before. How long have you known all of this, Luc?"

"The day dad died I knew I was different. I could see things that no one else could. I was scared because I didn't understand at first. But, over the past few years, Dr. Gable has helped me to accept my gift and to prepare for what's coming. Do you understand, Zoe?"

"It's a lot to wrap my head around but yeah, I think so. So much of our life since dad died makes more sense now. Mom took us away that night to protect you from Cain. We've been running ever since because you are in danger. I totally get it.

But surely the Scáths will find you? How can Lucas ever be truly safe, Dr. Gable?"

"Right now, Cain is not aware that your brother is a light-bearer. We must do everything we can to keep this knowledge from him. Elohim created an army of warrior angels, the Dìonadain, for that very purpose, Zoe. They shield, protect, and hide the Sorcha. Always watching, ready to defend."

Zoe looked at Dr. Gable, realization dawning. "Are you an angel, Dr. Gable?"

Nolan smiled, "I am."

CHAPTER 6

Sawdust

• • •

LUCAS WALKED DOWN THE STREET, thankful for the darkness and the cool it brought to the sultry night. He stopped dead in his tracks. Before him was a series of grand brick buildings, some old, others new, but all majestic and filled with southern charm. A large sign illuminated the words: Centenary College. He exhaled sharply. His father had likely stood in this same spot years ago as a college student.

He could imagine Eli full of life, ready to conquer the world. He could almost see him strolling through the quad, laughing and holding Mia's hand. Not a care in the world. Had he known the pain that would come? Did he realize the darkness that was already shadowing his path? Would he have tried to run away from it if he knew? Had his father felt alone? He wished so badly that he could talk to Eli, ask him how he had prepared for what lay ahead. He needed his father now more than ever.

He walked over to a fountain sitting in the center of the front campus lawn and sat down on its edge. He dipped his fingers in the water noting its coolness. He propped his elbows on his knees and hung his head. He didn't often allow himself the luxury of mourning his father. He had to be strong for his mother, his sisters. His throat constricted thick with emotion. A tear slid down his cheek unchecked. He closed his eyes and remembered.

He was running across the yard to his father's woodshop. His Saturday chores were done and he couldn't wait to join his dad. When he flung open the door, he breathed in the pungent scent of sawdust. Wood shavings scattered across the floor. Sunlight cast a warm glow over the handcrafted furniture stacked against the walls.

He loved this place! His father was a master craftsman. He had built the family home and almost everything contained within it as a labor of love. On a whim, he had even crafted the cuckoo clock that hung on the wall in his woodshop.

Lucas looked at his father in awe. Eli was standing in the center of the room carving a piece of wood. He was singing as he always did when he was working with his hands—creating his masterpieces of wood. His father's deep voice rumbled, "You Are My Sunshine", one of his favorites. Eli was shaping the wood, using a knife to concave and convex the wood into its perfect shape.

"I finished all my chores. What are you making?"

"Something for you, little man!"

"Is it what you promised? One of my very own?"

"I always keep my promises, Lucas. What do you think?"

Lucas ran his small hand down the neck of the handmade guitar.

"It's perfect, thank you, Dad." He wrapped his arms around Eli's neck.

"Well I could use some help finishing her up. Why don't you hand me that small saw over there?"

He searched for the tool on and around the worktable against the wall. There were so many he wasn't sure which one his father wanted. He finally chose one with a well-worn handle and long blade. Intricate designs were etched into the blade itself.

"Is this it?"

Eli looked at the saw and touched it reverently. "No, but it is a special tool. It's been in our family for generations."

"Why?"

"This saw is a symbol of our family's commitment to our craft. My father passed it to me and one day it will be yours."

"What are all those squiggles on the blade?"

"I asked my dad the very same question. The squiggles are actually words. It's a very old language spoken by a tribe of ancient people called the Celts."

"Like Braveheart?"

Eli laughed. "Yes, just like that but even older. Our ancestors were woodcrafters but also fierce Celtic warriors. The etchings on the blade are the words the warriors would chant before battle. Pretty cool stuff, huh?"

"More than cool. I promise when it's my turn, I'll take real good care of it."

"I know you will, Luc. I'm counting on that."

"I won't let you down, Daddy. I mean it."

"Well now that's a pretty serious statement to make, Luc. When a man gives his word, he must keep it, honor it, no matter what, he is committed to it. Do you understand?"

Lucas nodded his head solemnly. "Yes sir, I do."

Eli looked at him for a long moment—his green eyes gazing intently into Lucas' own—talking his measure. He figured his father was satisfied with what he saw when he grinned and said, "It's done then. Now let's get busy on your guitar."

Profound regret filled his heart. He hadn't kept his word. In the rush to leave his home the day Eli died, he had left the saw behind. He had never forgiven himself for the broken promise. He opened his eyes and noticed the ring of bricks surrounding the fountain where he was seated. The bricks formed an intricate design. They were embossed with letters and an all to familiar symbol—the star-shaped sign of the Sorcha. He wasn't surprised when he saw his father's name, as well as his mother's.

No one in Cleveland, not even the five thousand students who went to school here, had any idea that Centenary College served as the stronghold of the Dìonadain and home to the Sorcha. Nolan had told him long ago that Centenary was the perfect place for each light-bearer to be trained to use their gift. It was secret and safe. His father, mother and aunt had learned here and now so would he. He felt more connected to his father at this moment in time than any since that day in the clearing. He would not let his father down again. He would finish what his father had started. He would become a warrior. He would fulfill his purpose.

"I've always wondered about those names and that strange symbol."

He started at the bottom. Her blood red toes peeped from bronze gladiator sandals. Long tanned legs graced her denim shorts. A thin white blouse skimmed her broad shoulders. Jet-black hair fell in a blunt sweep. Ebony eyes glittered beneath thick lashes. Lucas was glad he was seated because the sight of her was knee weakening. Recovering quickly, he flashed his most charming smile.

"You know this is my first day in town and you are definitely the best thing I've seen all day."

"Well, aren't you a charmer?"

"Enough to get your name?"

She smiled and sat down beside him. "I'm Lysha. And you?"

"Lucas…Lucas Quinn. Are you a student here?"

"Not anymore. I graduated in May, actually, with a degree in Communications. I'm working at a company in town now. I don't think I've seen you around before. I would have remembered you," she teased.

He returned her smile. "Nah, I'm the new guy. I just moved in down the street with my family. Enough about me—tell me about you. Where do you work?"

"Talbot Industries, do you know it?"

"Of course I know it. Multi-billion dollar Internet company built from the ground up by Flynn Talbot. It must be a really cool job?"

"I love it so far. I'm actually working in their non-profit sector trying to raise awareness for their charity projects via social media. I just got back from Southeast Asia."

"Impressive! I've always wanted to travel outside the states. Tell me about it."

"It was beautiful and very exotic. Time moves slowly there—like you're in a dream, you know? It was the most marvelous place."

"I bet it was." He couldn't tear his eyes away from her striking face. This woman made it hard to think straight. Searching for something else to say, he was glad when she absentmindedly touched the unusual necklace clasped around her throat. He had never seen anything like it before. A small silver vial hung in the middle of a silver chain flanked on either side with intricately designed butterflies.

"Did you get that on one of your trips? It's very unusual."

"It is, isn't it? I got it on my first trip actually. The silver butterfly is my lucky charm; it's full of good karma." She turned those fathomless eyes onto him, "Now, it's your turn. How old are you, Lucas?"

"Old enough. Don't break my heart just yet, Lysha. We're just getting started."

"You don't play fair, do you?" Raising her eyebrow, she said, "I believe you just might be trouble for me."

"I hope so," Lucas grinned mischievously. "Would you like to get some coffee with me?"

"I was on my way to meet my brother and some of his friends for dinner. Would you like to come?"

"Best invitation I've had all day. I accept."

"Great! It's just a few blocks down the street."

They chatted as they strolled companionably downtown. Most of the storefronts were closed, so the streets were empty. Passing Courthouse Square, they came to a park. Massive trees, their branches heavy with foliage, surrounded the area. Providing cool shade in the day and shadowy seclusion in the evening, the grand oaks must have been a hundred years old. An outdoor amphitheater anchored one end and at the center stood the giant head of a Native American carved from an oak tree rooted in the ground. The sober Cherokee kept a silent vigil over the deserted space.

"Sleepy town," Lucas remarked.

"It certainly can be, but there's plenty of excitement around if you know where to look. Here we are. You are going to love it!"

CHAPTER 7

Chicken-Salad

• • •

WHEN HE WALKED INTO DELLA'S Diner, he immediately felt like he was in the middle of a really cool yard sale. Old album covers, from Lynyrd Skynyrd to the Bee Gees, decorated one wall while pictures of customers, old and new, lined the opposite one. Intermingled between all the wall décor were athletic jerseys, sports memorabilia, old toys, and other vintage junk. The chairs, tables and even the walls were like a high school yearbook covered with signatures, words of wisdom and funny jokes left by customers.

A dance floor occupied one end of the large room. Country music boomed from the jukebox in the corner. T-shirt clad servers were weaving in and out through the packed space delivering fried pickles, chicken-salad sandwiches and sweet tea to the customers. It was loud and it was friendly. Everyone seemed to know everyone else. Lucas loved everything about the quirky place.

He followed Lysha to a large built-in gazebo with a private booth at the back of the diner. The occupants looked like they owned the place and everyone in it. He watched her plant a kiss on the cheek of a guy who had to be related to her.

"Hey, handsome. I've brought someone for you to meet. Lucas Quinn, this is my brother, Aiden Talbot," Lysha introduced.

"Talbot?" Lucas looked at Lysha. She winked slyly. He realized there was much more to the lovely Lysha. "As in Flynn Talbot?"

"Guilty as charged. My sister does like her secrets...surprises too, for that matter," Aiden replied. "Have a seat, Quinn. I heard you were moving into town today. You know, small town, word travels fast."

Aiden smiled slightly at him. Although he looked deceptively relaxed, Lucas sensed Aiden's tightly leashed energy. This guy was wound up. Interesting. He knew without a doubt that Aiden Talbot was definitely the leader of the group sitting around the table. No surprise there—his father was Flynn Talbot.

Lysha's cell rang. "I need to take this," she said to Aiden. "It's dad."

Before she walked away, she bent and whispered in Lucas's ear, "See you later."

"Most definitely," he answered. He, along with every other male, watched her exit the diner.

"Welcome to Cleveland, Lucas! I'm Reese Pooley."

The slow cadence of her voice oozed sweetness. Thick brunette hair fell straight past her shoulders. Eyes the color of molasses complemented her oval face. Reese was the quintessential southern belle.

"Now for the rest of them. This is Grayson Ramsey Lee III. Gray's family was among the first to settle in Cleveland—old southern money and a pedigree to match. Don't let his smile and surfer boy good looks fool you—Gray is as cold as ice. Aren't you, darlin?

"Can't hold a candle to you princess," Gray smirked.

"Here's the life of every party, Marshall Cooper—never a dull moment with this one!"

"I aim to please," Marshall joked.

When Reese reached out and ruffled Marshall's curly brown hair, Lucas caught the longing expression in his brown eyes. It only lasted a split second and then it was gone replaced by an impish grin. Marshall definitely had a thing for the southern belle but was trying to hide it.

Reese continued, "This is the one and only Jenna Mabry—my pretty little partner in crime."

Jenna winked flirtatiously at him tossing her blonde fringed bangs back form her heart-shaped face. Then she scooted closer to him in the booth. She smelled like strawberries.

"It's very nice to meet you, Lucas," Jenna said sweetly.

"Believe me, the pleasure is all mine," Lucas returned with his most winsome smile.

"And last but certainly not least, Daryl Stuart—looks like a bulldog but harmless as a fly," Reese finished. "And that's us."

Lucas thought Daryl looked more like a Mack truck—big, burly and rough. Aiden's friends were definitely an interesting crew.

"Well, y'all, what will it be tonight?"

Lucas looked up at the rusty sounding voice. Della was dressed head to toe in the orange that most Tennesseans favored. Her platinum-blond hair was pinned in the back with a jeweled banana clip. But her bangs were something to behold. They made Della at least an inch taller. Everything about her was loud but lovely just the same. Her friendly eyes crinkled when she smiled. It was easy to understand why everyone felt at home at Della's.

"I think we'll go light tonight, Miss Della. Sweet tea all-around, two orders of wings, some fried pickles, a couple of baskets of fries, and throw in a chicken-salad sandwich for my new friend here, Lucas Quinn." Looking at Lucas, Aiden continued, "You haven't lived 'til you've tried Della's homemade chicken salad."

Della nudged Aiden's shoulder, "That's my boy. Now, Lucas, you listen to Aiden. He won't steer you wrong."

"Yes, ma'am, I'll do that."

After the drama at home earlier, Lucas was happy to put reality to the side. A hot woman, plus some cool new friends, and melt-in-your-mouth food were a great recipe for forgetting who he was for awhile. Enjoying his extraordinary stroke of good luck, Lucas ignored his cell vibrating in his pocket more than once.

He asked, "So what do guys do for fun in this town?"

"Well, as you can imagine, the possibilities are just endless," Marshall drawled sarcastically.

"Besides eating at Della's and catching a movie every now and then with these clowns, there's not much going on until school starts back," Reese added.

"So says the party girl! If I remember correctly, you enjoyed getting pretty wasted last night," Gray interjected.

"Shut up, Gray. I was just a little buzzed. Ain't that right, Aiden?"

"Whatever you say, sweetheart. So where you going to school, Lucas?"

"My sister and I start at Centenary in the fall."

"Cool. I'll be a sophomore this year. Centenary can be brutal, man. But it does grow on you," Aiden remarked.

Marshall added with a wink, "Too many rules equal no fun. But we find a way, don't we?"

"You got it," Gray agreed. "But I think the new guy might not be a rule-breaker?"

"Ignore them, Lucas I always do." Reese winked flirtatiously, tossing her hair over her shoulder when she scooted closer to him. "Why don't you come with us to the river tomorrow? It's gonna be a scorcher and the water will feel real nice."

"Reese, give the man a chance. He just got here," Daryl interrupted. "He may have something else to do."

Before he could think twice, he said quickly, "I got nothing else to do. Count me in."

Daryl continued. "Great, but seriously dude, our town may be small but we've got a drag-race track that's open every Friday and Saturday night. The most beautiful lake you've ever seen just up the road. You can wakeboard on crystal blue water for miles. We got the mountains for climbing, hiking and camping. But, bar none, the best thing we have going for us is the Ocoee River—wicked class 4 rapids."

"Solid, I'd love to try it sometime," Lucas returned.

Conversation stopped when Della served up their order steaming hot from the kitchen. When Lucas took the first bite of his chicken-salad sandwich, everyone around the table paused to watch, including Della.

"So?" they asked in unison.

"Wow, it's really good," Lucas said honestly with a mouthful of chicken-salad.

As the group enjoyed their dinner, Lucas noticed a black and royal blue basketball jersey hanging on the wall above the booth. Talbot and number 5 were emblazoned on the back.

Marshall noticed his interest, "Yeah, that's Aiden's jersey. He was the man in high school, you know, captain of the team and basket at the buzzer to win the state finals. It's the same at Centenary."

When Reese got up from the table and pulled Aiden with her to the dance floor, Marshall remarked, "That guy is gold, man. Everyone who knows him wants to be him."

Lucas asked, "So I guess they're a thing?"

"Yeah, those two have pretty much been joined at the hip this past year," Gray answered.

"Reese doesn't even go to the bathroom without his permission. He definitely wears the pants, know what I mean?" Marshall added.

"Psh, you guys don't even go to the bathroom without running it by Aiden first. Lap dogs!" Jenna scoffed. Turning, she asked sweetly, "You want to dance with me, Lucas?"

"Sure, why not?"

He followed Jenna to the dance floor. She was easy to look at and made him laugh. He had never really had time to pursue girls. Now two beautiful women had crossed his path in the very same evening. How much luckier could he get? Maybe this move to Cleveland was going to be much better than he had ever dreamed. As they swayed to the country music, he noticed his vibrating phone in his pocket. It had to be his mom. She was probably worried. It was getting late and most of the customers had already left the diner.

An immediate change in the atmosphere made him shiver. Two guys strolled in the diner and sat at the bar. Each wore a baseball cap with the Centenary crest emblazoned on them. Lucas felt the tension in Aiden from across the room.

"Let's go," Aiden announced. "It's late. Miss Della needs her beauty sleep. Don't ya, darlin'?"

Although it happened within the blink of an eye, he sensed a current of electricity pass between Aiden and the two men when they passed by them on the way to the door.

"Bye, Della! I really enjoyed it," Lucas said, following the others out.

"You come back soon, honey!"

CHAPTER 8

Differences

● ● ●

"Who were those guys?" Lucas questioned.

"A couple of jerks!" Gray said dismissively.

"The boys had a run-in with them at school this past semester," Jenna whispered.

Aiden interrupted. "Forget it, okay?"

A midnight-black Bentley pulled up to the curb in front of them. A well-built young man exited the driver's side door. He was a study in contradiction—intimidating in stature but graceful in movement. His ink-black skin was stark in contrast to his white linen suit. His kinky hair and piercings in both his nose and ears were set off by his strangely colored amber eyes. Everything about this guy was disconcerting.

"He freaks me out, no lie," Jenna whispered nervously. "They call him Mr. K."

"What does the K stand for?" Lucas whispered back.

"Kayanja. I'm pretty sure it's African. He's Lysha and Aiden's brother. Mr. Talbot adopted him from somewhere in Zimbabwe before Aiden was born. I guess he thought Lysha needed a brother but then Aiden came along. Anyway, Mr. Talbot never goes anywhere without Kayanja."

Mr. K opened the passenger door and out stepped none other than Flynn Talbot. Not only was Talbot richer than Midas, owning companies and land that stretched across the globe, but he was also the chief executive of the most lucrative Internet conglomerate in the world. Lucas had read all about Talbot Industries when he was researching a paper last year for a school assignment. Now here the man was in flesh and blood.

Dressed in a well-fitted dark suit and red silk tie, Flynn Talbot was indeed larger than life. He was lean and well muscled like his son. His dark wavy hair was swept back from a striking angular face. He had a strong countenance—one that exuded power and control. Flynn Talbot radiated a raw energy that drew people to him. Lucas had to admit he was a little awed. He felt a little pang of jealously when Aiden and his father shared a quick embrace. He wondered how he and Eli would have greeted one another as father and grown son.

"Who's your new friend, Aiden?" Flynn Talbot politely inquired.

"Dad, this is Lucas Quinn. He just moved into town today."

Extending his hand Lucas said, "Hello, Mr. Talbot. It's very nice to meet you, sir." He felt the restrained strength in Flynn's hand.

"Welcome to our little city, Lucas. It seems you have already made a good impression on my son as well as my Lysha," Flynn gestured toward the backseat of the car.

Lysha waved her hand and winked slyly at him. He knew right then he was hooked.

Tearing his gaze from the sultry Lysha, he replied, "Yes, sir, everyone has been really great. I researched Talbot Industries last year for a school project. Your company is doing life-changing things for people all over the world."

"Kind words, Lucas." Flynn said with a hint of amusement. "Serving others has always been of value to me. You will find Cleveland has much to offer a young man such as yourself. Drop by one day; I would be happy to give you a personal tour of the offices."

"Thank you Mr. Talbot. I will definitely take you up on that offer."

"Aiden, see you at home soon?"

"Yes, sir. I'll take Lucas home and be along."

As Mr. Talbot's Bentley sped off, Lucas acknowledged for the second time his good luck today.

"So what's the plan for tomorrow?" Daryl asked.

"Let's meet at your house at nine. Then we'll swing by and get everyone else." Aiden responded. "You better be ready Marshall, or you can walk to the Blue Hole."

"You know I'm not coherent before noon. I'll just meet you there," Marshall complained.

"Will I be seeing you later?" Reese asked grabbing Aiden's arm.

"What do you think?" Aiden kissed her pink lips. "Come on Quinn, I'll give you a ride home."

Lucas followed Aiden to his car parked down the street. When they stopped beside a sleek black BMW M6 convertible, Lucas whistled in admiration.

"Sweet ride, yeah?" Aiden asked with a grin. "It was a Christmas present from my dad."

Aiden climbed in behind the wheel and Lucas settled in the plush leather passenger seat. When Aiden pushed the ignition button and the engine roared to life, he looked at Lucas and shrugged nonchalantly, "I like speed."

"Who doesn't?" Lucas countered.

They arrived at Audrey's house very quickly, too soon for Lucas. He would have liked to cruise in Aiden's car a bit longer.

"I'll pick you up in the morning?" Aiden asked.

"Sure. Thanks for the ride home."

"No problem, dude," Aiden before speeding into the night.

Lucas sighed—back to reality. He knew his mother would be waiting up for him. He had a lot of explaining to do. He was always so careful not to worry her; always following the rules. Now, he guessed he would get to experience what Lily did all those nights she stayed out too late. Behind the front door was a reckoning with his mother he didn't relish, especially after the fun he had had tonight.

"Oh well, I might as well get it over with," he said to himself.

He was careful to be quiet when he opened the front door.

"Where have you been, young man? I've been worried sick," Mia scolded. She was sitting on the bottom step of the staircase in the foyer of the house.

"I know I'm late. I'm sorry, mom. I went for a walk and met this really pretty girl and her brother and then one thing led to another. Time just got away from me, ya know?"

"You do have a cell phone, right?" Mia asked. "One call or text to let me know that you were okay, that's all you had to do. I've been crazy imagining the worst."

"I know, I know. It won't happen again, I promise." He joined his mom on the stairs.

"Lucas, you know better, you can't take a risk like that, even if we are protected here. It's too dangerous right now."

"I do understand, mom. It's just been so long since I've been able to live a normal life. For a few hours tonight, I was just a regular guy. And it felt good."

"I know our crazy life hasn't been easy, Luc. You've had more than your fair share of heartache and change. But you know as well as anyone the danger we are in. Will you promise me you will be careful?"

"Yes, ma'am. I promise." He embraced Mia and placed a light kiss on her forehead. He loved this woman with his whole heart. He hated to disappoint her.

"One more thing, will you talk to Lily? She's shut up in her room and refuses to talk to any of us."

"I'll do what I can."

Lucas went to his sister's bedroom praying for the right words. Her light was still on so she was awake. He tapped lightly on the door. "Lily, it's me. Can we talk?"

"Go away. I'm not in the mood."

"Please, let me help. I...," he was interrupted when she flung open the door.

"Save it! I'm not the one who needs help. You are! You're so delusional you don't even see it."

"I know it's difficult for you to accept but what Dr. Gable said tonight is true—all of it."

"Believe what you want...I don't care anymore. The truth is this...dad was killed by some crazed animal, a bear, not a bunch of blood-thirsty demons. For the life of me, I can't figure out why you've created this crazy fantasy. And the worst part is, you've convinced Mom and Zoe that your delusions are real! You need help, Lucas—you all do. Tonight I realized just how much."

"I'm not crazy, Lily. If you would just let yourself remember that day, you would see that I'm not lying to you."

"I'm done. I've lost eight years of my life running from the so-called demons and darkness you see everywhere you look. You need to grow up, Lucas. Your little boy nightmares are not real!"

"I know you, Lily, better than anyone else. You're pushing me away because you're afraid you could be wrong about all this. But most of all, you're angry with mom because she believes me and not you."

Lily's dark blue eyes welled with tears. "I didn't even get to say goodbye to Dad. Mom didn't have the decency to stay in Colorado long enough for us to even have a funeral. I'll never forgive her for that."

"She did what she had to, what was best for all of us."

"Ever the faithful Lucas!"

"If you keep frowning at me, Lily, you're gonna have permanent wrinkles on your face," Lucas teased trying to lighten the mood.

"Ugh! Stop trying to be funny. I just have one question for you. If there is an Elohim, who cares about us so much and has the power to protect us from anything, then why did he let Dad die? Can you answer that? No? Well I can. It's because there is no Elohim or God or whatever you want to call him, at least not one who truly cares. Why would so many bad things happen if what you believed was true?"

"Lily, please…"

"Good night, Lucas. Just leave me alone."

He sagged against the doorframe, his hand on the closed door. His heavy heart ached for his sister.

CHAPTER 9

Guardians

• • •

NOLAN KNELT IN THE SHADOW of the magnolia tree, contemplating the enormity of the task before him. Elohim had charged him, as commander of the Dìonadain, with the training of all His angel warriors as well as the guardianship of the Sorcha. For thousands of years, he and his brothers had fought many battles to secure the Sorcha and their powerful gifts of light. So many had died. He prayed he and his brothers would succeed this time.

"Elohim, strengthen the Dìonadain for what lies ahead. Whatever is required, whatever the cost, guide us, quick and sure, to the others."

Rising, he spoke into the deep shadows. "What news, Asher?"

The dark figure of a man emerged soundlessly from the gloom. He was tall like Nolan but powerfully built with long dark hair and deep-set hooded hazel eyes. Asher was Nolan's most trusted warrior; he had fought by his side for over a millennia. Asher's days defending the Knights Templar during the Crusades had prepared him well.

He spoke quietly into darkness, "Lucas met the Talbot siblings. He has plans with Aiden and his friends at the lake tomorrow."

"Send Tov and Kiefer to guard him," Nolan replied. "Even though the Scáths are more cautious here because of our great number, we must be alert. Cain will be vigilant."

"Agreed. When Cain does sense the uniting is close, they will become more bold."

"We have no margin for error, Asher. The light-bearers must be found and protected. We must do what we must."

"Understood. The Council is waiting, sir. A messenger has arrived from Spain."

"And so it begins."

Nolan and Asher flew across the starless sky to a small marble mausoleum adjacent to the old Centenary chapel. The tomb inside was a sober reminder to the Dìonadain of the urgency of their mission. The crypt was the final resting place of little seven-year-old Nina Craigmiles. She had been tragically killed when the horse and buggy in which she was riding was hit by an oncoming train. Nina's death had proved a fatal blow to the ability of the Sorcha to unite more than a hundred years ago.

Her father built the mausoleum and entombed her in a glass coffin so he could always look upon her dear face. The day after Nina was laid to rest, blood-red stains appeared on the white stones of her crypt. For years, people had tried to remove them but they would always return. No one had ever solved the mystery of the stains, so most considered the place to be haunted. Nina's ghost and the mystery of the mausoleum provided the perfect place for the Dìonadain council to meet.

Nolan and Asher slipped easily through the mausoleum's great iron door. He released a spring lever hidden underneath the great marble sarcophagus. It slid away, revealing a set of marble stairs. Through a series of dark tunnels, the Dìonadain moved effortlessly. The glowing light from their spectral bodies illuminated the path. A natural rock archway signaled the entrance into the chamber itself. In the center of the chamber stood a great stone table—four ornately carved stone chairs sat around it. Suspended above the table was an iridescent globe. It rotated slowly marking the exact movements of the earth. Around the walls, like sentries, stood one hundred Dìonadain, radiant in their battle armor of purest gold. Their glorious topaz wings, full and thick, were folded behind them.

Although the ground beneath Centenary College served as the home of the Dìonadain, many of the order were stationed throughout the world—all charged with different responsibilities depending on their role. Watchers observed the movements of the Scáths keeping tabs on their location and activity. Messengers were appointed to search for the Sorcha and relay all communication coming to and from the Dìonadain council. Warriors fought the Scáths and defended the Sorcha in battle. Guardians protected the Sorcha at all cost, even fighting along side them if needed. Once the Dìonadain were assigned a light-bearer to protect or a task to complete, the angel would not leave their post or shirk their duty regardless of the peril.

Whether in angel or human form, the Dìonadain were a mighty force to be reckoned with.

Nolan joined the other three members of the Dìonadain council. Because he was the Chief of Guardians and Commander of the Dìonadain, Nolan was also the leader of the council. He respectfully regarded the others around the table—each one fiercely beautiful and brilliant to behold. Othiel, Chief of Watchers, studied the globe intently—his legendary patience and analytical mind made him an exceptional observer of everything around him. Hila, Chief of Messengers, stared at Nolan ready to begin. Her long angular face was drawn and tense. The massive Andreas, Chief of Warriors, rubbed his thick red beard thoughtfully. Nolan knew his brother's mind, never at rest, was surely weaving strategies of defense in preparation for what was to come.

"Let the messenger come forward and speak," Nolan commanded. He spoke in a melodic language not known to man. His words sounded like a haunting melisma sung in an ancient cathedral.

The Dìonadain messenger was incredibly lovely yet frighteningly intimidating in her manner and physique. The only softness about her was thick sable hair tied loosely behind her neck and earnest grey eyes. "We have located a light-bearer in Algeciras, Spain," Agatha announced.

"Yes, the globe shows an emerging. You are certain you have the right one, Agatha?" Hila asked sharply.

"Of course, she is sure, Hila, or she wouldn't be here. Doubt does not become you," Andreas stated.

"And the mark?" Othiel asked quietly.

"It is visible," Agatha confirmed. "I have seen it myself."

"We must be swift—timing is critical," Hila implored.

"I concur," Andreas offered. "We would be foolish to underestimate the Scáths.

"Agreed," Othiel offered. "Their network of informants will have already relayed the same information to Cain."

"Yes sir, the Scáths are en route," Agatha reported.

"Very well, we are in agreement," Nolan announced. "Asher, the task is yours. Bring the light-bearer to us. We must pray we are not too late."

CHAPTER 10
Whales

• • •

ALGECIRAS, SPAIN

Alvaro Diaz pulled a pillow over his head to block the blaring horn. He moaned, "Benicio, it's too early."

Hanging out late with friends in town last night may not have been the best idea considering the pounding in his head. He wished he hadn't told his seventeen-year-old brother Benicio he would take him to see the whales this morning. But a promise was a promise! Alvaro would have done anything for the boy who was his constant shadow.

He rolled out of bed. His head was throbbing. Squinting at his blurry reflection in the mirror, he ran a hand through his thick brown hair. This morning, he looked much older than his twenty-two years.

"Oh, well," he muttered as he swallowed two aspirin. Leaning out the window he shouted, "I'm coming!"

"Vamos, Alvaro," Benicio waved impatiently.

Alvaro loped across the yard stuffing a banana into his mouth. He hopped up into the cab of the dilapidated truck and cranked the engine.

"I think it's too early even for the whales today."

"Oh no, they are waiting on us!" Benicio smiled. "You should get more sleep, brother."

"I'll sleep when I'm dead," Alvaro laughed.

The Diaz brothers were fishermen, spending most days casting and pulling in nets from the tuna rich waters of the Strait of Gibraltar. Because the Strait was so rich in food, it was a migration route and natural habitat for several different species of whales. Today, Alvaro and Benicio would join the many tourists who traveled by boat from the port of Algeciras out into the bay to watch the mammoth giants of the sea.

As he drove through the city to the docks, the sounds and smells around him reminded him again how much he hated his job. He didn't want to end up like his father, tired, weathered, old before his time with no more ambition in life than to bring in the next catch. He had bigger dreams. He wanted people to know him when he walked down the street.

Parking the truck at the pier, he said, "Alright, little brother. I'm your captain for the morning. Let's go see some whales."

Alvaro followed Benicio to the boat. He often wondered how two completely different people could have come from the same parents. Benicio was quiet and unassuming, never asking for anything for himself. Alvaro knew when Benicio wasn't helping his father with the nets or his mother with the vegetable garden; he was helping neighborhood families with odd jobs or tutoring younger kids in school. Benicio was everything Alvaro was not. He smiled ruefully. He knew Benicio thought he had hung the moon—it was displaced hero worship to be sure—but Alvaro was thankful for it today.

Working together, it didn't take the Diaz brothers long to ready the boat for departure. The early morning sun was already hot. Alvaro pulled a hat on as he maneuvered the boat out into the smooth waters of the bay.

Benicio pointed to a passing boat, "Whale watchers!"

Gone was his brother's meek and reserved nature, and in its place was a young man full of energy and curiosity. Alvaro dropped anchor a few yards from one of the larger safari boats and settled back in his seat. Pulling his hat low, he watched Benicio scan the water for the whales he loved so much. Smiling to himself, he took joy in the small role he played this morning in making his brother happy.

"Look, Alvaro, there he is."

A large Orca whale emerged about sixty meters off the portside. As the magnificent whale left the depths of the bay, a tall geyser of water erupted from his blowhole. He rolled over in the water and dove quickly out of sight only to rocket out of the water a few meters further away. Benicio cheered with delight. After a few minutes, lulled by the warm sun and rhythmic rocking of the boat, Alvaro closed his eyes and drifted off.

Suddenly, a loud boom startled him.

"What was that?"

Clouds of black smoke billowed from a safari boat just three hundred yards away. Flames engulfed her stern. People were jumping from the boat in a panic. Alvaro didn't hesitate. He transmitted a distress call, weighed anchor, and fired the engine.

Benicio choked out, "Closer, Alvaro. They are swimming the wrong way."

He made out a small group of people thrashing in the water. Unable to see in the thick smoke, they were actually swimming back towards the sinking boat they needed to avoid.

Benicio yelled, "Aqui!" *"Here!"*

The frantic people showed no sign of hearing his brother. "They can't hear you, Beni. Go to the front of the boat and be ready to pull them in. I'm going to use the loudspeaker."

"Deténganse! Se están alejando! Aqui, aqui!" *"Stop! You are moving away. Here, here!"*

The desperate people turned towards his voice but the confusion on their faces confirmed his worst fear. They didn't understand Spanish. Alvaro wiped his arm across his face to clear the soot marring his vision. "I don't know how to make them understand. Think of something, Beni."

When his brother didn't respond, he turned to find Beni staring intently across the churning water. He yelled, "Beni, snap out of it. I need you to help me."

Benicio turned slowly toward his brother, his face pale but confident. "Say exactly what I tell you, okay? Use the loudspeaker and repeat after me," his brother commanded.

Alvaro was puzzled, Benicio never acted this confidently, but he nodded his head in agreement anyway.

Benicio said, "Hier! Schwimmen zu mir." *"Here! Swim this way."*

"What does that even mean?"

"Trust me, Alvaro. Just say it."

Benicio repeated the German command again for Alvaro.

He had no idea how in the world Benicio knew German but he bellowed the phrase into the loudspeaker. Immediately, three of the people in the water responded and swam towards the boat.

"Again, Alvaro."

He repeated the command until they were close enough for Benicio to pull them from the water.

"Now, say it this way."

Alvaro awkwardly repeated the same phrase in Russian and then again in Korean at Benicio's direction. Recognizing their native tongue, the people in the water responded, swimming to their rescue. Once all five were safe on the boat, Alvaro tried to steer away. It was difficult work. The churning water around the sinking ship created a forceful whirlpool. When the engine sputtered and died, Alvaro was scared.

"We're not gonna make it, Benicio!"

Benicio rushed below to try to restart the engine.

"Try it now," Benicio shouted.

Alvaro cranked the engine and it roared to life. Whatever his brother had done below, it had worked. Alvaro sped away from the danger zone and headed back to port. Rescue boats, sirens blaring, were moving out towards the wreck now. When Alvaro docked the boat, a flood of anxious people and a news crew crowded around. When they realized the six tourists pulled from the water were from different countries and spoke no Spanish, interpreters were found so their stories could be told. Soon, everyone knew the rescue was in fact due to Alvaro's ability to communicate with the survivors in their own languages. Alvaro opened his mouth to correct this faulty assumption but was stopped short when Benicio announced proudly, "My brother, Alvaro, is a hero."

Immediately, he was surrounded. The crowd was cheering and congratulating him on his bravery. Only in his wildest dreams had he ever imagined a moment like this. Alvaro looked at his little brother. He gestured to Benicio to join him but his little brother just shook his head slightly and stepped back from the crowd.

"Alvaro, how did you know what to say to the people? How many languages do you know?" the reporter asked.

"I don't know any language except Spanish. The words just came to me, like someone was whispering them into my ear. I can't explain it. I'm just glad I could help."

"It's a miracle. Three cheers for Alvaro!"

Alvaro laughed as the crowd hoisted him on their shoulders and carried him into the city for a celebration.

• • •

She smiled as the perfectly wicked
plan evolved her mind. It would be almost
too easy. Men are such stupid creatures,
slaves to their lustful bodies and minds.
Too easily are they manipulated by wicked
women who use their sensuality to ensnare.
Their pretended innocence and desire
will lead them astray. Men are weak-minded
and selfish beyond measure. One only had to feed
their pathetic egos, to compliment their form
or their deed—make them believe that you
wanted them, needed them, desired them
and they become slaves to your whim.
They are too shallow and blinded
by their own desire to realize the truth:
that you are lying, using, and ultimately destroying
them, all for your own pleasure or gain.
The player is so easily played.
She would take her time with this one.
Savor the chase, the seduction.
It would be delicious and sweet.
Death would not come quickly,
she would make sure of it.

CHAPTER 11

Mix-up

• • •

AS THE DAY PROGRESSED, STORIES of the miraculous rescue at sea filtered across the world's television stations and Internet sites. Alvaro's ability to understand and speak languages he had never heard before was touted an unbelievable miracle. The world celebrated with Alvaro but none more than the city of Algeciras.

Joaquin Diaz boasted of his son's deeds to all that would listen. Anna Diaz cried tears of joy thankful her son had saved not only the people in the water but her sweet Benicio as well. People who had never noticed Alvaro before were now seeing him for the first time. Benicio enjoyed his brother's fame and fortune from the sidelines throughout the day. Alvaro was happier than Benicio had ever seen him.

As he watched the townspeople lift their voices to cheer for Alvaro, a gnawing in the pit of his stomach plagued him. He was scared. Throughout the day, he had replayed the rescue over and over again in his mind and he still could not explain what had happened to him.

Why did he understand what the people were saying? How was he able to speak the correct words? How was any of it possible? It didn't make any sense at all. He rubbed his throbbing temples.

He heard one of his brother's friends. "Let's get the real party started. Everyone is going to La Ballena."

"Alvaro, can I go with you? I am seventeen, you know," Benicio urged.

His brother smiled broadly. "Of course, you can. You're my good luck charm."

In the main room of the bar, La Ballena, loud cheers greeted them. Music was playing and people were dancing. Smoke filled the air, making everything hazy. Benicio sat at a small table in the corner and quietly watched his brother celebrate with his friends.

"You must be proud, eh?" Tomas, the proprietor, said. "You're brother saved the day."

"He's a hero," Benicio agreed. He looked longingly at the plate of steaming paella Tomas held in his hand.

"Hungry?" Tomas laughed setting the plate in front of him. "Enjoy, it's on the house."

He dug into the paella. He hadn't realized he was so hungry. The warm spicy food filled his empty stomach. Slowly, his nerves calmed. He pushed the empty plate away, satisfied and happy. Alvaro was across the room surrounded by old and new friends, laughing and boasting about his deeds. Thinking he would just rest a bit until Alvaro was ready to go home, he laid his head on the table.

Just before he gave in to sleep, he noticed Alvaro dancing with a dark-haired woman in a red skirt. "He always gets the pretty ones."

When he opened his eyes again, the bar was quiet. How long had he been asleep? He scratched the tingling itch behind his ear. The bar was almost empty—he must have slept for quite awhile. He looked around the room but didn't see Alvaro.

"He just left, Benicio. And I don't think he wants any company if you know what I mean?" Tomas snickered.

Benicio left the bar to walk home. Passing a narrow street, he noticed Alvaro and the pretty woman from the bar going into a tiny hotel. He wasn't surprised. His brother had always been popular with the ladies. He went around the side of the building and sank down against the wall in the alley to wait. It was almost dawn. Not too much longer he hoped. He must have dozed off because he jumped when he heard the front door of the building slam open.

Peering around the corner, he saw the pretty woman walk out. She was talking on her cell. He gasped when he saw the knotted rope bracelet around her wrist. It belonged to his brother. He had given it to him for his birthday. When a silver car with tinted windows pulled up to the curb, the woman got in and sped away. Something wasn't right. Where was Alvaro? He left the alley and went into the building to find him.

The hotel lobby was small, dingy and dimly lit. There was no one at the front desk. The place looked deserted.

"Hello, is anyone here?" He rang the bell at the front desk a few times. The shrill sound echoed in the silent lobby. He thought it strange but climbed the stairs to the upper level anyway.

He called out, "Alvaro, are you here?"

Down a long hallway with several doors, he tried each one but all the rooms were empty.

"Alvaro, stop playing around. Where are you?"

When he reached the last door, he burst through and his brother's name froze on his lips. Alvaro was lying facedown across a dirty mattress in the center of the room.

He bent to his brother and whispered brokenly, "Alvaro, no." He turned his brother's body over and inhaled sharply.

Vacant eyes stared back at him. His brother's face was torn and ragged, deep bloodless gashes from his temple down into his neck. Dark purple bruises mottled his chest and his forearms. His brother's neck was distended and twisted at an awkward angle. Benicio lay over Alvaro's body and wept. He grabbed his brother's cold hand and squeezed tightly, "Please, Alvaro, don't leave me."

His body was shaking—he couldn't breathe. His heart was literally beating out of his chest. Hundreds of questions flashed through his mind. Had his brother suffered great pain? Did the woman kill his brother? Why would she want Alvaro dead? What would he tell his parents? How would he ever smile again now that his brother was gone? What should he do now? He needed to get help but he didn't want to leave Alvaro. He was terrified—afraid to move.

When he heard a car door slam, his panic ceased, replaced with a great sense of urgency. He crawled to the window and peered out the grimy glass. It was the silver car again. She had returned—the woman in the red skirt. She stood on the street flanked by two sizeable men dressed in black. He moved away from the window—his back against the wall. He knew beyond a shadow of a doubt he needed to get away. He had to think—to move—or he would end up like his brother. He went back to Alvaro and kissed his cold cheeks in farewell.

"I'll come back for you," he promised.

He could hear the voices of men below. They were in the hotel. Sprinting across the hall, he opened a door and ran up the stairs to the roof. Maybe he could jump to the next building. He prayed that he was right and hurled himself into the air. He cleared the distance with no trouble.

Back over his shoulder, he saw a man burst through the door. Flattening himself immediately to the roof, he hoped the man would not see him. He held his breath while watching the man scan the surrounding rooftops. When the man turned his head, he jumped up to run.

Too late, he realized his mistake. The man had only been waiting on him to move. Dumbfounded, he watched the man shape-shift into a fearsome black bird with cold blue eyes. As the creature spread its wings to take flight, he ran. From the roof, down the stairs, and onto the narrow street, he fled. All thoughts vanished from his mind, save one. He had to escape.

As Benicio zigzagged through the market streets of Algeciras, the black bird exploded into a dozen screeching feathered creatures all barreling towards him. He ran faster into the crowded market. Weaving in and out of booths filled with ripe fruit, smelly fish, and colorful baskets, he skidded to a stop when a small child riding a bicycle crossed his path. Barely keeping his balance, he turned, veering to the left down a smaller alley. Still the birds followed. He jumped a cart full of oranges and ducked under a green and white awning hoping to lose his pursuers. Unfortunately, he knocked over a cart full of fruit and the angry shouts of the vendor drew the birds closer.

He had to move faster. They were gaining on him. His lungs were bursting. Rounding a corner, he found himself under the shadow of a church bell tower. He changed direction, darting quickly into the cool darkness of the sanctuary. The church was empty at this early morning hour. Seeing no one that could help him, he ran down the aisle toward one of the confessional booths that lined the west side. He jerked open one of the stalls and shut himself inside.

He sat still, afraid to move, trying without much success to control his heavy breathing. If they found him, there was nowhere else for him to run. He clasped his hands in prayer.

"Please help me…"

The wooden panel inside the confessional booth slid open, revealing a small window covered with tiny metal mesh. Benicio was startled but hopeful.

"My son, do not be afraid," a soothing voice said from the shadows on the other side of the window.

"Padre, I need your help. I'm in big trouble. They killed my brother and now they're chasing me."

"You are safe here, my son."

"You don't understand, padre. Something is out there. I don't know…I can't explain it. At first I thought it was a man but then…he started flying like a bird. I know it doesn't make sense but you have to believe me…please."

"I do believe you, Benicio. Now, listen to me and do exactly as I tell you. Can you do that?"

He wondered how the padre had known his name but pushed this thought immediately from his mind. It didn't matter. For the first time this morning, he thought he might be safe.

"Yes sir, I can."

"Good. There is a small latch on the wall behind your seat. I want you to unhook it and open the panel. I will meet you on the other side. Do it now."

Counting his blessings that he had thought to run into the church, he found the latch and slid the back panel of the confessional booth aside. The kindest and warmest eyes he had ever seen greeted him.

"Do not be afraid, Benicio," the man said softly but with great authority.

He wasn't afraid. He knew he should have been wary of this strange man but he wasn't. He couldn't tear his eyes away from the man's gentle ones. They were like unfathomable pools of peace.

"My name is Asher. I have been sent here to help you. Will you trust me?"

"I don't know why I should but I do trust you."

He felt an incredible sense of peace as he followed Asher through a series of hidden pathways that were revealed behind the sliding confessional door. The longer they walked the more confident he became, which was unusual for him. Asher opened the door at the end of the passage. Benicio followed him outside into an empty alley. Then right before his eyes, the padre was transformed into a hulking golden warrior with spectacular wings that waved gently in the air. The sound was like ocean waves rolling in at tide.

Benicio stepped back in awe. He gasped. He was struggling to accept the incredible and undeniable truth standing right before his eyes despite the clouds of doubt swirling within his mind. He was sure Asher could see his uncertainty.

"It's a lot to take in all at once. But, we don't have much time. They are almost upon us. I need you to be bold."

He swallowed hard. He didn't understand what was happening but he knew he didn't have another option. He squared his shoulders and said, "Tell me what to do."

Asher wrapped a strong arm around him. "Hold on," he whispered.

CHAPTER 12

Waffles

• • •

STANDING ON THE FRONT STEPS of her new home, Lily pulled her hair back into a ponytail, enjoying the coolness of the morning on her skin. She couldn't wait to run and clear her head. She had tossed and turned all night. Anxious to get going, Lily crossed the yard.

The Butler house was a charming two-story Tudor-style brick structure that looked like it belonged in some quaint English. She lifted the brass doorknocker and gave it a loud rap. A buxom woman, with a friendly smile and a flaming red updo, dressed in an emerald green housecoat opened the door.

"You must be Lily. Aren't you pretty as a peach? I'm Pearl Butler. Jude said you would be comin'."

"Thank you. It's nice to meet you, Mrs. Butler." She shook Mrs. Butler's well-manicured hand.

"Come on in, honey, and have some breakfast. Homer is fixing his famous homemade buttermilk biscuits and sausage gravy."

"Can't mom," Jude interrupted from behind her. "Lily and I are going for a run."

"Well, alright, you two have fun. Come back soon, pretty girl. You're welcome any time."

"Thanks, Mrs. Butler, I will."

Lily followed Jude to the end of the street to the entrance to a shaded running trail.

"How far is the trail?"

"About six miles, give or take," he replied. "You ready?"

"Let's just see if you can keep up."

Lily set a breakneck pace for the first three miles. The creek that ran beside the path bubbled and swirled in the early morning light. Birds sang in the low-hanging trees and the sounds of the waking city echoed all around them. Despite Lily's challenge, Jude kept pace with her easily.

"Need a break?" Jude asked.

Wiping the sweat from her brow, she checked her watch, calculating her pulse and elapsed time. She felt good. She was finally relaxing a bit. She looked at Jude. He looked as cool as a cucumber. He wasn't even breathing hard. In his deep blue eyes, Lily saw something she couldn't quite put her finger on.

"No way! Let's keep going." Lily laughed. "Running helps me put things in perspective...it's like my own little therapy session."

"What could you possibly need therapy for?"

"Aunt Audrey says everyone needs a little counseling," she shot back.

"Well maybe," Lucas agreed. "Look, I know we just met but I get the feeling that something is going on with you, Lily. Could I help?"

"I doubt it. Let's keep things simple."

"What if I don't like simple?"

She searched his face for some sign of insincerity. But all she saw was genuine concern. She felt drawn to him. She slowed her pace to a walk and exhaled slowly. "Okay, here goes…I watched my dad die—I was only ten years old. Nothing has ever been the same since that day."

"I can't even imagine how hard it must be for you. I know you must miss him."

"Every day. After Daddy died, I just sort of shut down. But when I run, I feel like I get a little closer to the girl I was before. Crazy, right?"

"No, not crazy at all. You are much stronger than you think, Lily Quinn."

She squeezed Jude's hand in thanks. No one had ever come this close before. She didn't understand why she felt so comfortable with him, but she did. At that moment, the world fell away. Lily wasn't aware of anything but Jude. Facing one another, hands joined, looking into his eyes, there was only him. She was startled when he stepped back suddenly. The moment was gone as quickly as it had come.

"It's getting really hot out here," Jude pushed his glasses up higher on his nose. "Maybe we should head back?"

"Sure, okay."

They didn't say much as they ran back home. Lily felt awkward all of a sudden. She had really let her guard down with Jude and she wasn't sure if she regretted it or was excited about it. Rounding the corner of her street, Jude stumbled and fell hard to the pavement.

"Are you alright?"

His face winced in pain, his hand on his knee.

"Yeah, sorry. I'm such a klutz."

Lily laughed. "Poor baby. You want to come in for some breakfast?"

"You don't have to ask me twice."

With a slight limp, Jude followed Lily into the house and back towards the kitchen. Classic southern rock was blaring from the iPod dock in the kitchen.

"Hey, Lily, just in time for bacon and waffles."

"Set an extra plate, Aunt Audrey. Jude and I just finished the most amazing run and we're famished."

"Perfect! There's always room for one more at my table," Audrey said from behind the stove where she was dancing and frying bacon.

Lily and Jude joined Zoe at the big farmhouse table and dove into the warm waffles oozing with maple syrup. Jack was lapping up the scraps of bacon Zoe was dropping under the table for him.

"Zoe, where's Luc this morning?" Lily asked.

"Don't think he's up yet. You know how he loves his beauty sleep," she answered.

Audrey joined them at the table with a steaming mug of coffee. She opened the morning paper to the crossword puzzle inside. "Hey, seven-letter word for an eighties hair band?"

"Bon Jovi," Zoe and Lily answered in unison.

Audrey laughed. "That's my girls—I have trained you well."

"She has a thing for rock bands," Lily whispered to Jude.

"My mom does too. Can you imagine them back then?"

"I try not to."

"Well I better get going," Jude said. "My mom is planting her garden today and she gave me strict orders to be home and help. Thanks for the run this morning, Lily. I had fun."

"I'll text you, later, okay?" Lily asked.

"Sounds good. Thanks for breakfast, Dr. McCant." Jude waved on his way out of the kitchen.

"Any time, Jude," she answered to the empty space Jude had vacated so quickly.

"When that guy is ready to leave, he doesn't waste any time, does he?" Lucas said when he walked into the kitchen. "Where's mom?"

"In her happy place," Zoe answered.

"Back porch swing and a boring romance novel, got it," he said, heading to the porch.

"Lucas, tell mom I'll be back in a bit. I've got a date with Jack and his leash. The boy is getting fat. See ya, Lily."

"Bye, Zoe," she answered absently, watching her mother and brother through the window. They were talking with their heads very close together. The familiar pangs of jealously filled her heart. Her mother had always loved Lucas best.

CHAPTER 13

Kamikaze

• • •

Zoe walked Jack down the shady street. She was still reeling from the events of last night. She knew it was the truth, even though her common sense disagreed. She guessed she had always known deep down in her soul.

"Good morning, young lady," a female voice called from a flower bed close-by. "You must be one of Audrey's nieces?"

"Yes, ma'am. I'm Zoe, actually, and this is Jack."

The woman stood less than five feet tall. Her close-cropped dark hair was speckled with grey and her merry eyes sparkled. Her wide brimmed straw hat flopped around her face as she walked over to Zoe.

"Well it's a pleasure. I'm Dorothea Martin and I've lived on this street going on thirty years now. I was tickled pink when Audrey bought the old Sweezy place. She's poured herself into remodeling that house. So what do you think of our little town?"

"It's great but very different from where I used to live."

"It will grow on you. I was born and raised here. Know most everyone too. Not much goes on without me getting wind of it, to be sure."

"I can't imagine. I don't remember much before my parents passed away and the Quinns adopted me. We've never been one place for too long."

"Adopted? Well, I've always said it doesn't matter where you get your start, if love finds you then that's all that matters. Love is a powerful thing, ya know?"

"Yes, ma'am, I do know."

"Zoe, would you do an old woman a favor?"

"Sure, Mrs. Martin, what can I do for you?"

"Well, my two boys are grown and moved away. Since Mr. Martin and I retired, we just sit around twiddling our thumbs waiting to be blessed with some grandchildren. Unfortunately, my boys are not in any hurry to settle down. So when Dr. Gable—he's that nice professor who works with your aunt at Centenary College—asked us if we would like to sponsor an exchange student from abroad, we jumped at the idea. Imagine—a young person in the house again."

"I know Dr. Gable. I met him last night."

"Well, that's just wonderful. Anyway, Dr. Gable called us last night. He needed to place a student right away. Of course, we said yes! Dr. Gable brought him by late last night. Poor thing, I don't know if he needed food or sleep more. But he got both. He's up now and I'm sure he would love to meet you. He's just your age."

"Sure, I'd be happy to meet him."

"I knew I could count on you, Zoe. Wait here just a minute."

Mrs. Martin went into her house and returned with a young man in tow.

"Zoe Quinn, this is Benicio Diaz. All the way from Spain, can you believe it?"

Zoe smiled at the young man with brown skin and jet-black hair. He grinned back shyly. They were just the same height. He did look tired but there was also a hint of sadness around his eyes. She figured he must miss his family and home so far away. Her heart went out to him.

Zoe bent down and ruffled her dog's neck. "I was just taking Jack for a walk around the neighborhood. Would you like to come?"

"Yes, I would like that. Is that okay, Mrs. Martin?"

"Well of course, my boy! You two have fun," Mrs. Martin waved enthusiastically and returned to her pink geraniums.

"Mrs. Martin seems really nice," Zoe remarked as she and Benicio walked down the tree-lined street.

"Yes, she is—and her husband too. I don't think they were expecting me so soon. My coming here was sort-of, how do you say? A last-minute thing?"

Zoe laughed. "Well, you could say, last-minute totally defines my life lately. Do you mind if I call you Beni?"

"Beni is good. I like it. It's very American."

"You know we have a lot in common. My family just moved here yesterday to live with my Aunt Audrey. I bet it's hard to be away from your family?"

"It hasn't really sunk in yet."

They stopped when Jack barked at something down the street.

"Hey, it's a snow cone truck. I'd recognize that annoying music anywhere. I haven't had one in forever. It can be your first All-American dessert. Come on, my treat!"

Zoe waved at the snow cone truck. The driver slowed to a stop. Zoe and Beni walked around the back of the truck. They were soon joined by a couple of little boys from the neighborhood on their bikes. They all gathered around the big chest of shaved ice and a colorful array of big plastic bottles with dispensers for the different syrup flavors that were set up in the flatbed.

"What'll it be, boys?"

"I'll have cherry, please," the freckle-faced boy answered. "And my friend Noah wants blueberry."

"Can't the boy tell me himself what he wants," the snow-cone man barked.

"Nah, he can't talk, mister. So I take care of it for him."

Zoe couldn't help but smile at the two boys. They couldn't have been more than eight years old, but the bond between the two was unmistakable. They walked away with their cones already dripping in the hot summer heat. Zoe watched them ride down the street on their bikes.

"How 'bout you, girly?" the man smiled. He took off his baseball cap and wiped the perspiration from his forehead. "I got ten different flavors or you can be real brave and try a 'kamikaze.'"

Jack growled.

"Be quiet, Jack," Zoe commanded. "Sorry, mister, I don't know why he's so upset."

"Two grape snow cones, please," Beni said quickly.

"Sure, coming right up."

While he was making the treats, he asked, "Is it just you two? Or you got some friends around?"

"No, just us," Zoe replied.

He handed them their cones. "It's a hot one today. Those cones will melt before you know it. I'd be happy to give you a ride back to your house?"

Zoe instinctively retreated a few steps back when the man moved closer. Beni stepped in front of her and took Jack's leash from her hand. The dog was barking riotously.

"We will walk, thank you," Beni insisted. "How much?"

"No charge for the girly there—you neither, boy. Consider it a gift."

"Thanks." Beni took her arm and headed back towards the sidewalk.

"Let's walk fast. He gives me the creeps," Zoe said.

"I'm trying, but your dog is not cooperating."

Beni tried to pull Jack without much luck.

"Here, give me the leash."

Zoe was nervous. The whole situation was getting stranger and scarier by the minute. The snow-cone man was still standing by his truck watching them. She knew they needed to find some other people real fast. Her mother's warnings about strangers were ringing in her ears. When she heard the truck engine roar to life and the silly music play, she felt herself relax just a little. But then she noticed the truck was following them slowly down the street.

"I've got a bad feeling about this," Beni said urgently.

Jack's barking intensified as if he was agreeing with Beni. When Jack jerked against his leash, Zoe was caught off guard. She lost her hold and Jack tore off across the street toward the snow cone truck. When she turned, she screamed in horror. The little boy named Noah was crossing the street on his bike. Out of nowhere, a car sped towards him. Tires squealed when the driver slammed on brakes. It was too late. At impact, Noah was catapulted into the air. He landed with a thud on the hot asphalt street. Zoe ran quickly to him. Beni, who had managed to catch Jack, followed behind.

The driver got out of her car quickly and ran over as well. Shock and remorse played across her features. "Oh no! I didn't see him. I'm so sorry, so sorry."

Zoe fell to her knees beside the boy. Noah's contorted body was motionless as he labored to breath. Zoe started to shake all over, her face white with disbelief.

"You're gonna be okay, little man, just hang on," Zoe reached out a trembling hand and stroked his brow. Tears slid unchecked down her cheeks. She was faintly aware of the woman's voice calling 911. Beni, his face pale and drawn, was kneeling on the other side of Noah. Jack whimpered and nudged the boy's feet with his nose. Zoe felt a tug on her arm.

"I don't want him to die; he's my best friend," the freckle-faced boy sobbed. "Please help him."

"He's not gonna die. Don't you give up, Noah. We need you to stay with us." Weeping, she laid her head down on Noah's chest and prayed. "Please Elohim, let this sweet little boy be okay. Help me to help him."

She was startled when her hands grew very warm. Her palms tingled. Then her fingers burned as if a bee had stung her. She felt the force of the heat within her hands flow into Noah's broken body. Instantly, the boy began to moan and twitch.

"What's happening to him?" Beni asked urgently.

Zoe looked up in painful confusion. "I'm not sure, but I can't move my hands."

It was like a magnet was holding them to the boy's chest. The searing heat coursing through her hands was becoming almost unbearable. Suddenly, the heat diminished and her hands cooled. Noah's body was still, his breathing even and peaceful. She lifted her hands and stared at them in wonder. No burns, none at all.

Noah's eyes fluttered open and he slowly sat up. He rubbed his head and then reached out his hand to the dog sitting at his feet. Jack immediately nuzzled up to him and licked his face. Noah laughed happily.

"This is impossible," Zoe whispered.

"Apparently not," Beni replied with a slight smile. "Here comes the ambulance now."

Zoe stood up. She walked over to Beni, reached for his hand and squeezed, communicating without words her joy as well as her wonder at what had just happened to her and to Noah.

"Thank you for making Noah all better," the freckle-faced boy sniffled. He buried his face in Zoe's shirt and hugged her tightly. He let go abruptly and said, "Noah wants a hug too."

Zoe turned to the little boy who had been broken and bruised minutes ago. He was standing, smiling and holding out his arms for a hug. It was the best hug Zoe had ever had!

The paramedics arrived. One talked with Beni about the details of the accident while the other examined Noah. Zoe held Noah's hand for encouragement.

"You are one lucky boy. Only a few minor scrapes and bruises," the paramedic announced.

Zoe ruffled Noah's blond hair, "See there little man. You're gonna be ok."

Noah and his friend were only too happy to ride in the ambulance to the hospital where their parents would be waiting. Zoe waved goodbye to the boys until the ambulance turned the corner, disappearing from sight. Walking back over to Beni, she noticed the skin behind her ear was burning slightly. She touched the skin gingerly.

"Where is the lady who was driving the car?" Zoe asked.

Beni shrugged his shoulders. "I have no idea. She called 911, but she must have driven away after that. I was so focused on you and Noah that I didn't notice."

Zoe stiffened when she heard a familiar voice behind her.

"My goodness," the snow cone man whistled. "I ain't never seen nothing quite like it. I could've sworn that boy was a goner."

"Yeah, we were lucky," Zoe spoke abruptly. She forced herself to not look at the man. He was inching closer to them.

"I don't know if I'd call what just happened luck, girly. But I'm guessing you two will be wanting that ride now."

"I think not," another male voice commanded.

It was one of the paramedics who had treated Noah. He must have stayed behind at the scene of the accident. Zoe could barely contain her relief. The snow-cone man raised his head and studied the man across the street. She noticed the slight flaring of his nostrils and the look of disgust that passed across his face. The paramedic's statuesque height, broad shoulders, incredibly muscular arms, square jawline and short spiky hair created an imposing figure. Why hadn't she noticed that about him before? She glanced nervously back and forth between the men. Apparently, the snow-cone man saw something in the paramedic's ocean-blue eyes he didn't like.

"Hey, just trying to help. No harm done."

The trio watched intently as the snow-cone man hopped into his truck. The silly melody hung in the air long after he disappeared from sight.

"Are you two alright?" the paramedic asked. "My name is David Tov, by the way."

"I think so, just a little freaked out. I'm glad you were here!" she replied. "Who was that creepy guy?"

"I believe he was someone who intended you and Beni harm," Tov explained.

"Wait, how do you know our names?" Zoe asked taking a step back.

"It's okay, Zoe," Beni encouraged. "I think he's actually one of the good guys."

Beni grinned. Her friend didn't appear surprised at all that this stranger knew their names.

"Beni's right," Tov smiled. "Don't be afraid, Zoe. I am a friend of Dr. Gable's. Do you understand?"

Her realization of this man's true identity slowly dawned. "Oh my gosh, you're an angel?"

"Yes, your guardian angel," Tov stressed. "I am here to protect you."

Tov placed his hand on her shoulder. Instantly, her confusion and anxiety dissipated.

"Mine? But why do I need my very own angel?"

"I think you know, Zoe," Tov assured with a gentle smile.

She touched the tingling skin behind her ear again. Her mind was spinning with conflicting images and emotions. She was only sixteen but somehow she knew the direction of her life had just shifted in an unsuspected and incredible way.

"Why don't you tell me about the accident?" Tov suggested.

"Noah was crossing the street on his bike. Out of nowhere, this car came barreling down the street and hit him. I ran to him. He was barely breathing—so little and helpless. I could only imagine the pain he must have been feeling. I wanted to help him, so I put my hands on his chest and I prayed. My hands tingled and burned. I'm not sure what happened next, but the heat coming from my hands went into his body. And then he opened his eyes and smiled at me. It was unbelievable."

Tov took Zoe's hands in his. "We find it difficult to believe in the impossible because it doesn't make sense to us or we are afraid. But what happened to you just now was real. You asked Elohim for Noah's healing. The light within you, Elohim's light, made that little boy whole again. He has gifted you, Zoe, with the power of healing."

For the first time in her life, Zoe was at a loss for words.

"The snow-cone man knew it too, didn't he? That's why he tried to get us in his truck? He was a demon, wasn't he? Just like the ones who chased me?" Beni asked.

"Yes, you are both dangerous to him and those like him," Tov assured.

"Beni and I are like Lucas, aren't we? Part of the twelve?" she asked in awe.

"Indeed, Zoe. Come—we have much to talk about."

CHAPTER 14

Butterflies

• • •

A CAR ENGINE RUMBLED OUTSIDE Lily's window. Lucas must be home from the river. She needed to talk with him about last night. She pulled the curtain from the window and saw a black sports car.

Down the stairs and out the back door she went. Unobserved, she watched her brother and a young man, who could only be described as gorgeous, shooting basketball at the far end of the driveway. He captured Lily's attention immediately. His wavy black hair was cut short. Although clean-shaven, a grain of whiskers lying just beneath his tanned skin darkened his square jaw. Moving with the ease of an athlete, he was tall, lean and well-built. She felt her stomach flutter. She was startled when Lucas yelled, "What's up, Lily?"

"Hey, nothing really. Where have you been?"

She deliberately kept her gaze on her brother, ignoring the stranger that made her heart beat a little faster. She didn't like that feeling and was quick to try to shut it down.

"Swimming." Lucas smiled and then made a short jump shot.

"Appreciate the invitation," she walked down the steps from the porch and made her way across the lawn.

"Lily, this is Aiden Talbot. We met last night in town," Lucas passed the ball to Aiden. "Heads up!"

Aiden caught the pass but then dropped the ball abruptly in the grass and looked at her. He offered his hand. "Hello, Lily, it's a pleasure to meet you."

"Yeah, you too." Lily moistened her lips nervously trying to appear more confident than she felt. But when Aiden covered her hand with his, all bets were off. His simple touch was like a spark of electricity. It startled her and she dropped her hand quickly.

"Quinn, you didn't tell me you had such a pretty sister," Aiden chided.

When her brother noticed Aiden was staring at her intently, Lucas said, "Maybe there's a reason I didn't tell you."

An awkward silence followed. Lily looked down at her flip-flops and missed the glance the young men exchanged.

"Well, Aiden, thanks for the swim today. I'll catch up with you tomorrow," Lucas said abruptly.

"Sure, no problem. Glad you could hang out." Turning back to Lily, he added, "Next time you'll have to come too, darlin'."

She smiled noncommittally.

Lily felt the flutter again in her stomach, only stronger this time, when Aiden winked goodbye. As soon as his friend drove away, Lucas demanded, "What the heck was that?"

"What? It was nothing." Lily shrugged her shoulders. "What's your problem?"

"Be careful, Lily. He's older than you and has a rep with the ladies. Don't encourage him."

"Are you kidding me? It doesn't matter anyway; I'm not interested." She spun around and stalked back toward the house.

"Hey, I'm not finished talking to you."

"Well, I'm finished with you."

Just then Audrey walked onto the porch. "What's going on, you two?"

"Nothing, Lucas is just being Lucas…a regular pain in the butt."

"Well, that's why we love him, isn't it, sweetheart?"

Lily answered with an exasperated shrug.

"You two won't ever stop, will you?"

"Wouldn't be as much fun, would it?" Lucas flashed a quick grin.

"I guess not," Audrey agreed good-naturedly hooking her arms with Lucas and Lily. "I've got something to show you both."

Lily walked with her aunt and brother across the lawn away from the house.

"You know, Aunt Audrey, I think I'm gonna like living here," Lucas continued.

"I hope you both will. Cleveland is a special town. I've always thought there was a little bit of magic here."

When Lily rolled her eyes at her aunt's comment, Lucas teased, "I'm not so sure Lily is sold on this place yet."

"Give her time. We'll win her over," Audrey winked. "Maybe I can convince her with this."

Audrey stopped in front of the small garage at the back of her property. Lily had no idea what was behind the garage door but she was definitely curious. When Audrey lifted the creaky door, Lily sucked in her breath, "Are you kidding me?"

"You both know your dad was like my big brother. After you were born, he gave me something to keep for you, something he wanted you both to have when you got old enough. I think the time has finally arrived."

Lucas whistled appreciatively. "This is the best surprise, ever, Aunt Audrey."

Lily ran her hand gently across the hood of a vintage 1972 metallic blue Ford Mustang. Keystone chain wheels gleamed in the afternoon sunlight streaming through the small windows on either side of the garage. Lucas didn't waste any time. He opened the driver's side door and plopped behind the wheel on the cream leather seat.

"This was Dad's?" he asked.

"It was a piece of junk when he bought it. But Eli knew what he was doing. He spent a ton of hours restoring this beauty," Audrey explained. She handed the keys to Lucas.

"Want to take her for a ride, Lily?"

"You don't have to ask me twice," she replied hopping in the passenger seat. She looked at Lucas with a devilish grin. "Don't get too comfortable in that seat, Luc."

"I know, I know," he laughed. "You never did like to share!"

For a moment, Lily forgot she was supposed to be mad at her brother. Driving out onto the street, music blaring on the radio and the summer wind in her hair, she was truly happy. It felt good.

● ● ●

She watched hundreds of live streaming images
from across the globe on screens lining the walls
of the circular room. Any reference to unexplained events,
miraculous happenings, or people performing impossible tasks
would be investigated.

At the center of the room was a single leather chair
on a raised dais. Only one creature called it his:
her master, Cain, Abaddon's chosen one,
the legendary commander of the Scáths.
Throughout the centuries, Cain had used any means
available to track his prey, hunt them down and kill them.
He had been chosen for his extraordinary intellect and lethal skill.
Well-versed in all realms of warfare, Cain believed himself
invincible.

She knew Abaddon would never allow the light-bearers to unite
and join their great powers. If they did, they would unlock the
secret of destruction for the Scàths.
Abaddon had been very clear about his desire.
He would rule the world and enslave Elohim's creation

to his dark will. He would not rest until the Light was extinguished.

She sensed that the battle over the Twelve in this generation would be unlike any other before. So far, the Dìonadain had been one step ahead of her at every turn. Despite careful planning and quick action on her part, the angels had secured three of the twelve.
Cain was displeased with her.

"By your leave, Master, another light-bearer has been located. My team is ready and awaiting your orders. I will not fail you this time."

"See that you don't! I will not have another slip through our fingers like the boy in Spain. I believe that I will come with you this time to oversee. Make the arrangements."

CHAPTER 15

Headache

• • •

Tyrese Rafferty closed the door to the small apartment he shared with his grandmother in one of the many low-income housing projects dotting the south side of Atlanta. Leaning his dark slender frame against the door, he shook his head. The pounding pain was his constant companion. He had stayed out late again, not because he wanted to but because he had no other choice.

Unfortunately, in his short twenty years, Rafe had been forced to do many things he didn't want to do. Right now, all he wanted was the quiet darkness of his room. He needed to rest, even for just a little, in preparation for the job tomorrow.

Six months ago, he had scored a job for a man he knew only as the "Banker." His Boss's latest scam would require him to hack into the computer mainframes of a slew of local bank ATM machines. The PIN numbers he would steal would give the Banker access to multiple accounts with substantial amounts of money. He was the key to a large fortune for the Banker. The Banker was Rafe's answer to a better life.

"Where have you been, young man?"

He turned to his seventy-two-year-old grandmother with a heavy heart. He knew his late nights, unexplained disappearances for days at a time, and need for secrecy was causing his grandmother a lot of grief lately. It couldn't be helped. Nana was sick—very sick. He had been forced to offer his special skill set to some very unsavory characters to earn the money to pay for her health care. He didn't like disappointing the woman who had taken him in, raised him, and loved him when his parents had deserted him. But he had no other choice.

When he was three, his father had left the house one night after fighting with his mom and had never come back. After that, his mother had sunk into a deep depression, eventually turning to drugs to ease her pain. She had overdosed when he was only seven. His grandmother was the only decent person he had ever had in this world.

"Nana Rose, you should be in bed," he said, crouching beside her old ratty recliner.

"Not until you tell me where you've been, Tyrese. And don't lie to me, 'cause I saw you, from my bedroom window, talking to that boy Darius."

"You worry too much, Nana. I was talking to Darius yesterday, but it was just about a part-time job. We need the money—you know it's tough for us right now."

"What kind of job?"

"Darius knows I'm pretty good with numbers, so he told me the community center was looking for a tutor to help the kids get ready for their GED."

"I'm sorry, Rafe. I know you're a good boy. I just want you to have a better life than the one your momma and daddy gave you. You're special and need more than a sick old woman to take care of and a minimum-wage job."

He smiled slightly, "I've got everything I need right here, Nana. The money I'm making at the computer store will get us out of this place soon. You just need to concentrate on getting better, you hear me?"

He would not sacrifice this woman for anything, no matter the cost to himself. He needed her more than she had ever needed him. He lifted her small frame easily into his arms and carried her to her bed. He pulled the yellow crocheted blanket over her. He leaned over and kissed her wrinkled brow.

"Goodnight, Nana Rose. I love you."

Nana reached both hands up to hold his face close to hers.

"I love you, too, my sweet boy. There is so much good inside you, don't you ever forget it!"

"No, ma'am, I won't."

"And Tyrese?"

"Yes ma'am."

"I like that new haircut, my sweet boy. You look just like Grandpa Sam did when I married him," she said softly.

He rubbed his hand over his new low fade haircut, carefully avoiding the tender place behind his ear. The barber must have nicked him. He smiled. "Night, Nana."

He left Nana's room and went across the hall into his own. He laid down, willing the throbbing pain in his head to stop. He had to be at his best tomorrow. There were no second chances if he failed. Just one more job and he could make a new start for them both. He closed his eyes and fell into a troubled sleep.

He awoke groggily to the sound of his cell phone. He looked at the number and answered immediately.

"You ready?"

"Pick me up at the corner in ten," he answered.

He rose quickly and dressed. When he looked, Nana Rose was sleeping peacefully. Throwing his backpack over his shoulder, he left the apartment and met Darius at the corner. He was silent during the twenty-minute ride to the Ritz Carlton Hotel located in the center of Buckhead. Darius valeted the car and he followed him into the hotel. Well-dressed men and women were milling about the beautiful lobby looking like they had just stepped out of a magazine. He was definitely out of place. It was surreal to think just minutes ago he was riding down the street in one of the toughest and poorest neighborhoods in Atlanta and now here he was in the lap of luxury. He took a deep breath and the fragrant flowers adorning every corner of the lobby filled his nostrils. Nana loved flowers. One day, he would be able to bring her to a place like this. He hoped today would be the day.

They rode up to the twentieth floor where the Banker kept a suite of rooms. Two men in dark suits searched him and then opened the door for him to enter. Although he had never seen the Banker before, he knew the man reclining on the gold upholstered couch could be no one else. His black hair was slicked back from his head and curled around his neck. He wore a navy pinstripe suit with a crisp white shirt. Lights from the crystal chandelier suspended from the ceiling glinted on his expensive gold cufflinks. The smile he offered Rafe never reached his hard eyes.

"Sit down, Mr. Rafferty," the Banker motioned to a chair across from him. "You are prepared for today?"

"I'm ready," he answered with a bravado he didn't quite feel. He was nervous. There was so much riding on his success. "And I want the $25,000 you promised me before I open my computer."

"You do what I have asked and then you will get your money."

"Money first or no deal," he replied quietly.

"Give the young man his money," a voice commanded from the far side of the room.

He hadn't noticed the other man standing at the window. He never turned from the glass so all Rafe could see was his shoulder-length auburn hair and his grey suit.

The stranger continued softly, "You are wasting my time."

"As you wish."

The Banker nodded his head slightly. A woman, dressed in black leather, carried a small duffle bag across the room and put it on the dining table. Her long braid swung slightly when she turned and joined the strange man at the window.

"It's all there, count it if you want, but do it quickly. It's almost time."

Rafe unzipped the bag and tried to keep his face impassive. Inside the bag was more money than he had ever seen in his life. He closed it and tossed it over his shoulder. His head was pounding again. He rubbed his left temple. He needed to get this job done and never look back.

"Good luck, Mr. Rafferty," the man at the window said softly.

A chill slid down his spine. However dangerous the Banker was, somehow he knew the man at the window was much worse. He realized his fear of the Banker had been misplaced. He and his boss were just pawns in the mysterious stranger's game. No matter—he had his money. He followed Darius out of the suite, his mind focused on the job ahead.

● ● ●

"Do not challenge me again in front of my men.
You wouldn't be here right now if I hadn't told you
about this kid," the Banker commanded.
Too late, the Banker realized his mistake.
In the whisper of a second, Cain was across the room.
Her master towered above the pitiful human.
He shrunk back against the velvet couch.
She marveled at his eyes, frightened,
yet surprised as well. What must it feel like?
To be so utterly powerless and pitiful?

What a fool! Her lip curled with contempt.
"You forget your place," Cain admonished.
"Please I meant no disrespect. It won't
happen again," he pleaded.
"No, it surely will not. Finish it."

She understood her Master's command.
Blue flames darted from her hands and squeezed
the Banker's neck. The Banker struggled in vain.
It took only a moment to take his worthless life.
His lifeless body slumped over on the couch.

She followed her Master from the room,
the dead man behind her already forgotten.

"He is the one. I am sure of it. Move quickly.
The Dìonadain will be close," Cain spat.

"Yes, Master," she replied as the elevator closed
behind him. Speaking into her cell phone,
she commanded, "Take him now."

CHAPTER 16

Storms

• • •

RAFE FINISHED THE LAST SEQUENCE of commands and tapped into the computer mainframe at the bank. He had complete access. With a few keystrokes, small sums of money were being transferred from multiple accounts at multiple branches into an untraceable account he had set up for the Banker. He had done it. Freedom waited for him outside this dark room. He pulled off his headphones, his favorite jazz music still playing, closed his laptop and reached for the black duffle bag by his feet. He stopped cold when he felt the cold barrel of a 9mm pressed to the back of his head.

"Where do you think you're going?" Darius taunted.

"I did the job, man. Just let me walk away."

His eyes darted to the only exit. Too far—he would never make it. He had to figure out another way.

"Can't do that, Rafe. I gotta do my job. On your knees."

Desperate situations called for equally desperate measures. He had no weapon but himself. He slammed his entire body weight back into Darius knocking them both to the concrete floor. Darius dropped the gun in the scuffle. Rafe had been in his fair share of fights. Agility and quickness were his assets. He pulled Darius underneath him and pinned him with his strong legs. He grabbed his collar with one hand and pummeled his face with the other. He stopped, his fist midair, when a shot was fired.

"Hold it right there! You're under arrest!"

Rafe looked up from Darius's bloody face at the four large men surrounding him with guns drawn. Obviously, he hadn't heard them kick in the door. He sat back on his heels. The men weren't dressed in uniform so that could only mean one thing: undercover cops. He shook his head in exasperation. The cops had probably been on to him for days. He should have been more careful. Now everything he had planned for Nana was ruined.

"On your knees, both of you, hands behind your head, " the biggest of the four commanded.

Rafe knew this guy was obviously in charge. He towered over the rest—his muscles had muscles! The guy was totally ripped! His long black hair was parted down the middle and hung straight past his shoulders. His brown skin, dark eyes and sharp nose gave away his Cherokee descent.

"We got it. This computer has all the access codes, sir," one cop announced.

Rafe watched miserably as one cop picked up his computer and another grabbed the duffle bag with his and Nana Rose's future inside.

"Which one of you is the computer genius?" the cop in charge demanded.

"I don't know nothing," Darius cried.

He looked pointedly at Rafe and asked, "You going to deny it too?"

Rafe knew it wouldn't take long for the cops to figure out it was his computer. He made up his mind quickly. The best thing he could do was to tell the truth and maybe they would give him a break.

"No, sir, it's mine."

"Looks like we got our man. Get the 'techie' outta here," the cop in charge ordered the two men closest to Rafe. Then he turned to the cop beside Darius and said, "You stay behind with this one."

Outside, Rafe was a little surprised to see only one car in the deserted parking lot. He ducked into the back of the car and cringed when the cop in charge sat beside him. Things could always be worse, he thought. At least he wasn't lying in a pool of his own blood, dead from a gunshot to the head. Looking out the window, already trying to figure out his best plan of action when he arrived at the station, he watched two officers exit the building. His computer and duffle bag were dumped in the trunk—then they both got in the front seat of the car.

"Hey, where's Darius? They aren't just going let him go, are they?"

"They're coming," the cop sitting beside him said with a faint smile.

"Who's coming?" he asked, confused.

The cop driving the car revved the engine and kicked it into gear, peeling out into the street. Rafe struggled to remain upright. A crack of white-hot lightening lit the darkening sky. Two sleek silver cars appeared from a side street and gave chase. He ducked his head when gunshots were fired.

"What's going on? Who chases a cop car?" he yelled to no one in particular.

The men in the car with him didn't bother to answer. What was wrong with these guys? They showed no signs of being anxious about the cars chasing them or the guns shooting at them. Leaving the deserted streets around the warehouse, the car sped out onto the busy downtown streets of Atlanta. Up ahead was a stoplight.

"Turn green, turn green," he begged. The driver accelerated through the red light. Cars swerved and slammed into one another. Still they raced on.

Rafe squeezed his eyes shut and prayed for the first time in his life. "Okay, big guy, if you're really up there, I promise I won't steal anymore. Just get me outta this, please," he prayed.

He opened his eyes and looked at the cop beside him. He looked like he was having the time of his life. When an oncoming car swerved to miss them and hit one of the silver cars pursuing them instead, the officer smirked, "One down, one to go. Our odds are definitely getting better."

Before Rafe could respond, three motorcycles roared from a side street to join the chase. The officer driving the car swerved dangerously but somehow kept the car on the road.

"We're gonna die," Rafe wailed.

"Not today," the cop grinned.

When the cop touched his shoulder, he felt a soothing calmness flow through him. He had been scared out of his wits a moment ago, but somehow he wasn't anymore. He felt better than he had in a long while.

"Bring it on!" Rafe roared with laughter.

The cop car veered off the street and sped down the sidewalk. People were running and screaming trying to avoid the car barreling toward them. When the car swerved back to the street, the last silver pursuit car followed and was broadsided by a *Cocs-Cola* truck. But they weren't out of the woods yet. The three motorcycles were closing in.

"Hey chief, you guys better get me outta this alive," Rafe urged. The man beside him actually laughed.

He was surprised when one rider lost control of his bike, crossed the median, and slid under an oncoming car. Another suddenly stopped dead in the middle of the road and its rider flipped head over heels over the handle bars. The last rider, smaller than the other two, gave up the chase and sped down another street, disappearing from sight.

"It's over. They gave up," Rafe exclaimed. He couldn't decide if he was surprised or relieved?

"For now," the cop beside him said, nodding.

The car slowed and turned onto a quiet residential street. When the car stopped, Rafe took a deep breath. The chase was over. Reality returned. He had broken the law and he had been caught. The question was, by whom? He was certain these guys were not ordinary cops. A rap on the window startled him.

The cop beside him opened the door and helped him from the car. As soon as he was standing, Rafe demanded, "I have rights, chief. I want to know what's really going on. 'Cause I think it's pretty obvious you're not just undercover cops? Are you FBI? CIA?"

He replied easily, "Something like that."

"What do you want with me? I'm no one special. It's the Banker you want. Maybe we could work a deal."

"It's you we want, Mr. Rafferty."

All bets were off! He wasn't going anywhere with these men. He took off running full speed, hoping the element of surprise would give him a head start. He was caught almost immediately within a steely embrace.

"You have nothing to fear," his captor whispered in his ear.

The overwhelming calm welled up within him again. He relaxed. The cop loosened his grip.

"Close your eyes, Rafe," he requested softly.

He felt the cop rest his hands lightly on either side of his face. The last few minutes replayed across his mind just like watching a movie on the screen. He saw himself in the back seat of the patrol car. But this time he saw what he had not seen before. Outside the racing car, he saw what looked like medieval warriors of old. Light radiated from their bodies and they catapulted through the air in an explosion of colors. They wore lightweight armor the color of rich gold. Their breast-plates glowed warmly just like their bodies. He looked at the cop sitting next to him and realized he too was filling the space with warm golden light.

Bright silver lights shot by the window. The lights transformed into men whose skin and armor pulsed with cold silver light. Frozen blue eyes, like shards of glass, shown through the slits in their glittering masks. They were terrifyingly beautiful. Intense blue flames shot from their hands, burning anything they touched. He knew what he was seeing was real but like nothing he had ever dreamed.

The golden warriors formed an impregnable shield around the car. Their dazzling swords and shields cracked with lightening when deflecting the blue flames of the silver sentinels. It was an intricate dance of hand-to-hand combat, a clash of massive proportions. Swooping from their perch atop the car, they overturned empty parked cars, placing obstacles in the paths of the three motorcycle riders in pursuit.

He opened his eyes dumbfounded. He couldn't explain what he had seen but he knew beyond a shadow of doubt it had been real.

"I'll come with you but not without Nana Rose."

"We thought you might feel that way. We've taken your grandmother somewhere safe."

"You know my name, but I don't know yours, chief."

"You can call me Kiefer."

CHAPTER 17

Unicorn

• • •

MIA MARVELED AT HER GOOD fortune. Arriving in Cleveland with her family two weeks ago, she was broke and unemployed. But this morning while walking downtown, she had noticed an advertisement for a job opening in the window of a magnificent historic home that served as the main office for the Cleveland Historical Society. Cleveland was established in 1837 and named for Colonel Benjamin Cleveland, a commander in the American Revolutionary War. The small town had a rich and vibrant past. On impulse, she had applied. She guessed her degree in history made up for a lack of experience in event planning because the director, Gemma Bradley, had hired her on the spot. She was now the Director of Events.

The rest of the morning had been a whirlwind of activity. The historical society was planning a fundraising gala at the Museum Center at Five Points, and her first project would be to coordinate the event. Her predecessor had suddenly quit and the gala was only a few weeks away. Mrs. Bradley was afraid the event would be a total bust without an immediate makeover.

An afternoon planning meeting had been scheduled at Talbot Industries, a major donor for the museum, to discuss the details of the charity event.

She walked into the spacious two-story lobby, eager to begin. Alternating between the glass windows that surrounded the lobby were large video screens showing images from the charity endeavors of Talbot Industries. Medical supplies to South America, orphanages in Rwanda, houses built in New Orleans after Katrina—all were larger than life on the screens. She marveled at the sheer enormity of good works Flynn Talbot conducted around the world. She was so focused on making a good first impression in the meeting she didn't notice the man standing by the elevators on the left side of the lobby. Nor did she notice his admiring gaze when he entered the elevator and disappeared. She walked over to the receptionist's desk and introduced herself.

"Good afternoon, I'm Mia Quinn from the Historical Society."

"Oh yes, Mrs. Quinn, we have been expecting you," the receptionist replied.

When her phone buzzed, the receptionist murmured, "Excuse me, please." She focused her attention on the voice at the other end of the line. "Yes, sir. Mrs. Quinn is scheduled to meet with Ms. Yamada. Yes, sir, I'll make the change." Looking back at Mia, she said, "Mrs. Quinn, take the elevator to the tenth floor. Ms. Yamada will meet you."

In the elevator, she prayed her first meeting on the job would be a success. At the tenth floor, the doors slid open. A striking woman with short perfectly-coiffed black hair, dressed in a well-tailored black power suit, greeted her. She felt under-dressed in her white summer skirt and matching petal pink twinset. She wished she had taken the time to straighten her naturally curly blonde hair.

"Good afternoon, Mrs. Quinn. Welcome to Talbot Industries. I am Kimiko Yamada, Mr. Talbot's assistant."

"It's a pleasure, Ms. Yamada."

"Gemma called to let me know you would be taking over the last minute details for the event. Our meeting is down the hall. Right this way."

She followed the sophisticated woman down the hall. For the first time, she thought she might be in a little over her head. The hardwood floors gleamed a deep cherry. Bronzed light fixtures adorned the rich cream walls. Beautiful paintings of rich and startling color adorned the walls.

"These pieces are remarkable," she mused.

"Yes, quite so. Mr. Talbot's collection of modern art is extensive. Klimt, Chagall, Kandinsky—he has an eye for the unusual."

She had never been impressed with money or the things it could buy. But history and its natural companion art did get her attention. Her twin sister Scarlet had been an accomplished artist before her death. She and Audrey had spent many happy Saturdays traipsing through art museums with their bohemian sister. The exquisite paintings made her feel as if Scarlet were close.

Her reminiscing was interrupted when Ms. Yamada opened the heavy double doors at the end of the hall. The richly decorated room possessed an old world charm with its antique furniture and plush Aubosson rug. A crystal chandelier was suspended over a circular table in the center of the room. Around the table were four hand-carved chairs in the shapes of mythical animals: a gryphon, unicorn, phoenix, and dragon. The tapestry-covered walls only enhanced the medieval atmosphere of the room. Floor to ceiling windows at one end of the room provided a panoramic view of the town below as well as the rolling ridges and mountains in the distance. Over the fireplace a family portrait hung—a proud father and his two smiling children.

"Good afternoon, Mrs. Quinn. I'm Lysha Talbot. It's so very nice to meet you. Lucas speaks so highly of you."

Mia was struck by the young woman's exotic beauty. "I didn't realize you knew my son."

"Yes, we met a few weeks ago. Please have a seat. May I offer you something to drink?"

"No, thank you," Mia replied. She chose the unicorn chair. Lysha and Ms. Yamada joined her.

"Why don't we begin with the preliminaries? My father will join us when he can. Mrs. Quinn, what are your ideas for the gala?" Lysha asked politely.

"Because the money raised at the event will fund the museum's new 'Artisans of Glass' exhibit, I would like to suggest a Venetian masquerade ball for the gala theme. Period costumes and masks, Italian finger food and desserts, candlelight, classical music, and of course, dancing would create the perfect atmosphere to celebrate the new exhibit."

Ms. Yamada replied, "Isn't that a bit extravagant for an event like this? Not to mention the gala is scheduled in less than three weeks."

"On the contrary, Yamada, a masquerade is a perfect idea."

The deep baritone voice could only belong to Flynn Talbot. His face was a series of chiseled planes like an ancient marble statue on display in the Louvre; his thick wavy hair only added to the effect. His indigo eyes were flecked with grey. The crisp white open-collar shirt he wore with his navy suit fit his 6'2" powerful frame like a glove.

"Mr. Talbot, I'm Mia Quinn. It's a pleasure to meet you."

When her hand touched his, she felt a charge of electricity. He flashed a dazzling smile. "Please, it's Flynn. May I call you, Mia?"

"Of course."

He sat down and said, "Please continue with your proposal, Mia."

Somewhat flustered by her reaction to the man across from her, Mia fought to focus on the event plan for the gala. She soon forgot the other two women in the room. Flynn was focused entirely on her throughout her presentation. When she finished, he nodded his head in approval.

"How much money will you require, Mia?" Flynn asked.

She slid a copy of the proposed budget across the table to the man who unnerved her more by the second. "It's a large sum. But considering the time crunch, and leaving room for the unexpected, I believe it's a fair estimate."

Flynn gave the budget sheet a cursory glance. "Agreed. Yamada, please release the funds for the society to move ahead with the project."

Mia exhaled a breath she didn't know she had been holding. It had been almost too easy.

Flynn laughed. "Mia, money should never be an obstacle when pursuing something for the greater good; we are blessed here at Talbot Industries and we give back unconditionally."

"Thank you so much. The society is committed to doing everything possible to make it a grand event."

"I have no doubt you will succeed," He lifted her hand to his mouth for the barest whisper of a kiss. "It was lovely to have met you, Mia."

He dropped her hand and left the room; the magic of the moment faded away.

"I'll see you out, Mrs. Quinn," Lysha offered.

Mia collected her bag and followed Lysha from the room still a little flustered from her encounter with Flynn Talbot.

Lysha must have noticed her dazed demeanor because she asked, "Are you alright, Mrs. Quinn?"

"Oh yes, I'm sorry. I guess I'm just a little out of sorts."

Lysha smiled, "My father often has that effect on people."

Mia tried to hide her embarrassment. Obviously, Lysha recognized her attraction to Flynn. Changing the subject, Mia remarked, "I look forward to working with you on the plans for the gala, Lysha."

"Why don't we have lunch tomorrow?" Lysha suggested. "We have a lot to do and it would be lovely to get to know you better, Mia. I can call you Mia?"

"Of course, my dear. I would love to have lunch."

"Perfect! It's a date then. Goodbye, Mia," Lysha smiled.

The elevator doors slid open and Mia walked inside. Alone in the small space, she remarked, "Wow, just wow." On her drive home, she replayed the meeting in her mind. She was ecstatic about the outcome but unsettled by her response to Flynn Talbot. She entered the house deep in thought.

"What are you doing just standing there?" Audrey asked abruptly.

Her sister's voice startled Mia back to the here and now. Audrey was sitting in the living room reading a book with Jack snoring loudly at her feet. Vivaldi's *Four Seasons* played softly in the background.

"You would not believe my day," Mia said.

She joined her sister on the couch and put her head in Audrey's lap. She sighed with a mixture of exhaustion and wonder.

"Wow, this is about more than just your new job. Out with it."

"Alright, first off, I do love my job. Mrs. Bradley didn't waste any time giving me an incredible assignment." Mia paused for effect, enjoying the anticipation on her sister's face. "The museum gala, can you believe it?"

"Oh my goodness, what an opportunity! But I know you're still holding out on me. Spit it out."

"Okay, okay. It all happened when I went to Talbot Industries today. They are sponsoring the gala. No big deal, just a planning meeting. I wasn't expecting..."

"Expecting what?"

"Him." She sat up nervously.

"Him? Who are you talking about?"

"Flynn Talbot."

"The Flynn Talbot? Oh, do tell."

"I was presenting my proposal and he just walked into the room. He is so handsome and charming but he also has this energy about him. I didn't think I was going to make it through my presentation because I was so out of sorts. When he looked at me, I felt like I was the only one in the room. And when he touched my hand..."

"Go on..."

"I don't know. I haven't felt like this in a long time. Crazy, right?"

"No, honey, you're not crazy. You're a woman responding naturally. Flynn Talbot is a very attractive man. No one would fault you for moving on with your life. You and I both know Eli would have wanted you to be happy."

"My head understands, but my heart is a different thing all together. I'm afraid, Audrey. Maybe the relationship I had with Eli was a once in a lifetime kind of love."

"I know it must be scary to think about moving on with your life and find love with someone again. It will definitely be different but it can still be good." Audrey squeezed her hand. "You deserve happiness, Mia. Just think about it, okay?"

"I will I promise. Where are the kids, by the way?"

"Zoe went to the Martin's house for dinner with Beni. And Lily went to the movies with Jude. Those two are becoming good friends."

"I know. Truthfully, I'm thankful she has found someone like him to hang out with. Lily is usually drawn to the wrong crowd."

"I couldn't agree more."

"What about Luc?"

"He left a couple of hours ago to visit a friend," Audrey said with a wink.

"A friend? Did he mention who this friend was?"

"Yep, he sure did."

Her sister was grinning ear to ear. "Seriously, Audrey, just tell me who he is with," Mia urged impatiently

"Hmm, I think he said Aiden Talbot. Isn't it a small world?"

"Too small if you ask me," Mia laughed.

"On a serious note, Nolan came by earlier. Another light-bearer has arrived. They found him in Atlanta. I met him and let's just say he's got lots of personality. His name is Rafe."

"Another one? So soon? Maybe the uniting will happen this time. Maybe our fight is almost over."

Audrey's reply confirmed her unspoken fear. "I'm afraid, dearest sister, the fight has just begun."

CHAPTER 18

Knights

• • •

Lucas drove his car through the ornamental iron gates at the entrance to Magnolia Park, the Talbot estate. The stately residence sat at the end of a long driveway lined with majestic magnolia trees. The beautiful Smoky Mountains rose in the distance. Although he and Aiden had been hanging out for a couple of weeks, this was his first visit to his friend's home. His love of architecture was more than satisfied as he took in the details of the house.

Typical of antebellum homes of the South, an expansive porch with a large balcony resting on gleaming white neo-classical Greek columns greeted guests. He could just imagine men in Confederate grey uniforms flirting with pretty girls in hoop skirts. Tall French windows with wooden plantation shutters accented the smooth white exterior of the house. After parking his car, he made his way to the oversized mahogany front door and rang the bell. Aiden opened the door.

"Hey Luc, it's about time you made it to my place. Come on in."

The warm cream-colored walls were topped with richly carved crown molding. An extravagant sparkling crystal chandelier was suspended from the high ceiling. A grand staircase leading to the floors above anchored the opulent Italian marble floor.

"Incredible house, man," Lucas remarked.

Lucas tagged along behind Aiden towards the back of the extravagant house. When they passed a dark paneled room set with a roaring fire, he stopped dead in his tracks. Broadswords, longbows, spears, maces, and battleaxes, all ancient and showing use, lined the room from ceiling to floor. Gleaming suits of battle armor stood guard on either side of the fireplace. Faded tapestries depicting knights waging battle against foe and dragon hung along one wall. Intricate miniature models of castles were displayed in glass cases in the center of the room. Lucas felt like he had just walked on the set of a *Lord of the Rings* movie.

"Fantastic, right? This is my dad's collection of weapons and artifacts from all-around the world. When I was a kid, I would play for hours in this room."

"Of course you did—who wouldn't love this? I mean look at this sword."

Lucas picked up a wicked sickle-shaped blade from its resting place on a table. It was a khopesh, an early sword, popular in ancient Egypt between the first and third millennia B.C. The hilt of the sword was smooth ivory; the bronze blade lay heavy in Lucas's grip.

"Ramses III carried a blade like that, thousands of years ago," Aiden said.

"Wicked cool! I could live in this room for the rest of my life and be happy."

Aiden laughed, "No doubt!"

"Your dad must have been collecting this stuff for years?"

"Yeah, he acquired a lot of his collection at different auctions around the world. But, his most prized possessions are the ones he found himself."

"Seriously?" Lucas asked.

"Not many people know this but dad majored in archeology. After college, and before he started Talbot, he spent a few years working at the British Museum in London."

"I would never have guessed that."

"I think he likes keeping at least one part of himself a secret."

"When I was researching him and Talbot Industries for a paper, I wondered. But, I figured he majored in international business or maybe computer science."

"Everyone thinks the same thing as you. Dad doesn't bother to correct them. He lets people assume what they want. He's never really cared much for what other people say or think about him."

"Why should he? Your dad had made Talbot a household name. He's successful and respected. But, it must be hard to be in the spotlight all the time? Everyone knowing who you are and watching what you do?"

Aiden shrugged his shoulders. "I don't know. Maybe. I've never known anything else."

Lucas wondered around the room in awe. He had never seen anything like it. He was in heaven. His eye was caught by a worn copy of *Morte D'Arthur* lying on the table in the center of the room.

"The absolute best book ever written."

"Agreed. I wanted to be like Galahad, the pure-hearted warrior," Aiden smiled.

"A lot to live up to," Lucas mused.

"Yeah maybe," Aiden agreed. "You hungry? I've got some leftover pizza from last night."

"You read my mind. Lead the way," he answered.

Lucas followed Aiden to the home's state of the art kitchen. Bobby Flay would have been jealous of this elaborate set-up. "The Talbots don't do anything half-way, do they?"

Aiden smirked, "What would be the fun in that?"

"Touche," Lucas returned.

Pizza and sodas in hand, they settled in Aiden's game room. High ceilings and hardwood floors created a space ready for play. A large billiard table stood in the center of the room. A huge plasma screen was mounted on the wall perfect for playing the latest in video games. Oversized leather chairs fronted the screen. A basketball goal was located at the opposite end of the room with an indoor court floor ready for some one-on-one. Large black-and-white framed family photos of the Talbots visiting vacation spots around the world covered the walls.

"Dude, how have you not shown me this room before now?"

"Sorry, man. I just had to be sure about you. My father taught us to be guarded about sharing too much with people before we knew we could trust them. Not everyone is like you, you know."

"What do you mean?"

"Some people just want to get close to us because of what they think they can get. Money is great but it makes it difficult to know who your real friends are. Even Gray and Marshall, I sometimes wonder what they're really after."

"Well, if they're anything like me, they're after your Beemer," Lucas laughed. "Seriously, I've never had money and I don't think I ever will. I like to keep it simple. Money complicates things."

"Sounds like my dad...except the money part," he chuckled. "No ties, no burdens, no problems! Kind of like his philosophy of women. There's been a revolving door of girlfriends for as long as I can remember. If it gets too complicated, he walks."

"Has he always been that way? What about your mom?"

"No, she was special. After Lysha's mother left him, he met my mom. Thought it was his second chance at love, ya know? She was the love of his life. But then she got real sick. I don't think he's ever gotten over losing her."

"If she was anything like my mom, I understand why it's hard for him to move on."

Aiden smiled sadly. "Every day, my memories of her fade— except her long dark hair. I remember how soft it was. I loved to twirl it in my fingers."

Aiden paused—his eyes had a faraway look Lucas could relate to. He figured he looked just the same when he was reminiscing about Eli.

"I'm scared one day I won't remember her at all," Aiden said quietly.

"It's the same with me. My memories of my dad are getting cloudier. It's like I lose him a little bit more every day," Lucas said. "Some days I don't think about it much but then other days…"

"I know exactly what you mean. Sometimes I close my eyes and imagine my mom's still with me. But then I open them and it's the real world again. Weird?"

"Not weird at all, man."

"What about your sister Lily? Do ya'll ever talk about your dad?"

"No, Lily doesn't talk to anyone about dad or anything else for that matter."

"Pretty private person, huh?"

"Hmm, not private, just closed-off, I guess. She really shut down after dad died. Honestly, I'm kinda worried about her."

"That's tough, man. But, everyone handles death in his or her own way. Can I help? She seems like a great girl."

"She is," Lucas agreed. "Lily is really special—she doesn't know it, but she is. I hope being here in Cleveland with family and going to Centenary in the fall will help her to finally heal. I miss the old Lily—the girl she was before dad died."

"Well, if there is anything I can ever do for you or your family, I hope you'll ask."

"Thanks for listening, man. I feel like you've got my back."

"Well, let's just see if you feel the same way after I kick your butt at *Call of Duty*," Aiden challenged with a smile.

CHAPTER 19

Patrol

• • •

MOSUL, IRAQ

"Please, Elohim, don't let them find me," Daniel Barzani whispered.

Even though he had grown accustomed over the last twenty-two years to the unending civil and religious unrest in his city, he still feared it. Mosul, the third largest city in Iraq, was a microcosm of Iraq's most explosive and unresolved conflicts. His life, as well as his family's, was in constant peril. Just last week, many Kurdish civilians in the city had been arrested on false pretenses and their property had been seized. This time his family had been spared, but Daniel wondered how long their good fortune would last.

Daniel had experienced considerable pain and persecution in his life. Where it would have hardened or broken many, it had only strengthened Daniel's resolve and commitment to living a life of peace and forgiveness. Crouching low, he peered around the corner of what had once been his school. It now lay in ruin, an eerie shell looming in the rising Iraqi sun. He had been on his way home from the market with bread for his family's breakfast when the men had started to follow him.

There were four of them, all lean and hungry, their hearts and minds fueled by anger and resentment for a war they didn't cause and a life they didn't choose. They needed someone to hate. They needed to make someone else feel worse than they did. He was the perfect target, a Kurd. He was different, believing in a foreign God and supporting the American cause for peace and freedom. The Kurds had been singled out for their beliefs as well as their loyalty to the American soldiers. Many of his friends had left home for work or school one day and had never returned. So he waited. He had learned to be patient during years of hiding, ducking his head, remaining silent, avoiding certain areas, and making himself invisible.

"Filthy Kurd, you can't hide from us," a man's voice boasted from about hundred yards away.

He remained still but his heart was racing.

"Gotcha!"

Strong arms clamped down on his shoulders and hauled him from his hiding place. Disoriented, caught by surprise, he tried to scramble away from the angry men. The largest of the four held him from behind while two others delivered gut-wrenching blows.

"Nowhere you can hide, Kurd. Where's your God now? Or your dirty American friends?"

The leader grabbed his shirtfront and slammed his wiry frame into what was left of a concrete wall. His nose and mouth were bleeding. His stomach was knotted and clenched. He fought to stand up straight.

"I have no quarrel with you. Please, let me go."

The leader spat contemptuously in his face, "Today, you will see your God."

He slumped against the wall in excruciating pain when the leader drove his fist into his left side. His breath was ragged. He prayed for a way out. When the leader turned his back on him, he saw an opportunity. Throwing his body at the leader, he knocked him to the ground. He was able to land a couple of quick body punches before the other three pulled him off. His courageous attempt to fight back only fueled the savagery in the men. They threw him to the ground. He was tough-- hardened by twenty-two years of survival and cruelty but a boot kick to the gut was excruciating all the same.

Rifle shots rent the air. The men fell back. A U.S. Army foot patrol stood thirty yards away. The gang scattered, leaving him bleeding and broken on the dusty ground. The patrol leader knelt to check him for broken bones. Despite his aching body, he had to admit he was a little star struck. He had always greatly admired the American soldiers. They were strong and courageous, always protecting and helping those who were persecuted or too weak to help themselves. He had seen soldiers in the city but he had never been this close to one before. The black-skinned patrol leader was a big man with a friendly face and serious eyes.

"Nothing broken, but I'm not gonna lie—you are going to feel awful tomorrow. You got guts, man. Four against one... not the best odds."

With the soldier's help, he stood. After wiping the blood trickling from his mouth, he flashed the soldier a crooked grin.

"I am in your debt."

"I'm glad we came along when we did. Get on back home, now."

Daniel nodded his head. "Thank you for helping me."

The soldier said to his troops, "Okay, we're finished here. Let's move out."

He watched the patrol leave the schoolyard as quickly and quietly as they had entered. He raised his head to the heavens and whispered, "Thank you, Elohim, for sending them just when I needed them."

He took the soldier's advice and raced home through the winding streets. He climbed the stairs to his family's small apartment. He hoped his mother wouldn't be too frightened when she saw him. She always imagined the worst. He opened the door and was met by a chorus of concerned cries.

"Daniel, my son, what's happened to you?"

His mother rushed to him, fear written all over her face. She ran her hands lightly over his bruised face.

"I'm fine, mother. I'm a little battered but I'll heal. I was cornered by some men but the American soldiers helped me."

His father laid his hand against his son's angular face. "We must give thanks to Elohim for your rescue and safe return to us."

"Yes, Father." He smiled. "Let me change. We must not be late for church."

"Are you sure, my son?"

"Yes, I've felt all morning as if I would burst if I couldn't get to church. I need to pray. I want to be in Elohim's presence, now more than ever."

His father smiled. "My son, all your life you have spent more time in the church than anywhere else. When you are not home, I always know where to find you. There is safety in Elohim's house, a sanctuary for our prayers. Yes, we must all go."

The Barzani family made their way to the dilapidated stone building that was their place of worship. His father was right. He had always been at peace here, spending countless hours talking with the church elders, exploring the scriptures, praying for his family, his people, his country. Lately, he had been burdened to pray more and more. He knew not for what specifically. Often, he had no words, running through his prayer list long before the desire to pray had left him. In those times, he had just been still, focusing on Elohim and nothing else at all.

He joined the congregation as they lifted their voices in song. He looked around the small space, marking everyone, each person important to him and his life. When the pastor began reading the scripture, the back doors of the church slammed open.

Everyone turned around, startled by the loud noise; horror dawned on their faces when their greatest fear was realized. Standing at the back of the church, a man with crazed eyes, a black vest affixed to his chest and his finger on a trigger, screamed, "You are all doomed!"

CHAPTER 20

Shrapnel

• • •

"You blasphemous Kurds will pay for your allegiance to the Americans," the crazed martyr spat.

Daniel knew without a doubt the man was serious. He could see the stony resolve in the suicide bomber's dark sunken eyes. He would lose everyone he loved most in the world in a blast of dagger-sharp pieces of glass and metal, rocks, pointed nails, and screws. Being the closet person to the man, he had to do something, anything.

"Please, sir, you don't have to do this," Daniel insisted. "Think about your family."

"What family? I have nothing since the Americans came. Their bombs killed my wife and my son. They took my family from me."

"I'm sorry you lost your family. I truly am. But my family is here with me. Please don't make me lose mine."

"My life was spared so I could deliver judgment upon you on this day. I know it now. My body will be the instrument of your death."

"Please, there are women and children here…"

"They are no better than you," he spat. "No more talk. Everyone stand against the wall!"

He had failed. He stood beside his mother and father and held their hands. His church family—men, women, and children, old and young, stood along the four walls of the small room. Many were crying while others prayed.

"Silence! Your noise is making my head hurt," the bomber shouted. "Turn around and face the wall."

Daniel looked at his father. His faith was strengthened seeing the unwavering courage in his father's eyes. He knew what he must do. Instead of turning to face the wall along with everyone else, he laid facedown on the hard stone floor. Prostrate, he stretched out his arms and started to pray aloud.

"You there, what are you doing? Get up!" the bomber commanded.

His prayers became louder. He was driven towards a singular purpose: an appeal to Elohim, begging for protection and deliverance, a symphony of heart, mind and spirit. Words no longer mattered; his soul was reaching toward heaven. He no longer knew what was going on around him, nor did he care, so vast was his desire to connect with Elohim on behalf of his people. All-around him, men, women, and children joined him, lifting their voices in a chorus of prayer. When their prayers turned into a haunting melody, the bomber grabbed his ears in agony.

"Stop, stop," the bomber begged.

Daniel's body dripped with sweat. But he would keep praying until he could pray no more.

The floor started to shake and a current of electric shock passed through him.

The bomber screamed. "You will not stop me!"

An explosion of hot air enveloped him and then he heard a very loud boom. When he opened his eyes, debris was floating in the air. Nothing remained of the bomber, his body torn apart by the explosion. Dumbfounded, Daniel looked around the church. Every person standing against the wall was still there, alive and breathing. Shrapnel, pieces of glass, nails, and metal were lodged in the wall, clearly outlining the shapes of everyone who had stood against it. No one's flesh had been pierced. No one had been injured. It was if something or someone had stood in front of all them, blocking the bomb's destructive force. He raised his hands and proclaimed, "We have been saved."

"It's a miracle," the people around him cried.

He tried to stand but was unable. His body was incredibly weak, numb from energy spent by his zealous prayers. His father reached down to help him.

"My son, your great faith and prayers moved the heart of Elohim."

"Father, I don't understand. But I believe I have just witnessed a true miracle."

"Indeed, we all have. You must mark this day. You must never forget His provision for His people."

"Yes Father, I will remember," he promised.

"More will come when they discover the bomb failed. Let us seek sanctuary with the American soldiers."

With the help of his father, he and his mother left the church. Winding through the crowded and panicked streets of Mosul, they traveled south into the desert. On a sloping hillside outside of the city, next to a junkyard of destroyed Iraqi army tanks, he and his parent entered Iraq's oldest Christian monastery, St. Elijah's. The fortress-like complex of buildings was now located within the perimeter of the U.S. Army Forward Operating Base, Marez.

The soldiers welcomed them to stay outside the perimeter of the base in tents designed to be a safe haven for refugees from the perils of the city. After settling his parents in a tent, Daniel wandered towards the ruins of the monastery. He had recovered his physical strength but still felt an unexplainable weakness in his spirit. He had never felt such an unquenchable thirst for communion with Elohim as he did now. He had spent countless hours in the church before, studying and praying, but never with the intensity he had experienced this morning. And how was it possible no one had been hurt? The bomber's body had been obliterated. He knew Elohim was all-powerful but he had never witnessed the magnitude of His authority before.

Passing the monastery, he marked the slow descent of the sun, marveling at the richness of the orb's setting glow. Hot colors faded into peaceful hues, signaling the approach of cool darkness. With the sky awash in shades of pink, orange, and purple, he wept. His soul cried out in praise but also despair. They had been saved, but the bomber had lost his life. What kind of agony leads a man to such destruction? His heart was heavy because he knew the bomber had had another choice.

He didn't have to let the grief overwhelm him, filling him with anger and bitterness. He didn't have to strike out at others to assuage his aching soul. He didn't have to choose death; he could have chosen life.

Daniel wiped tears from his face and rubbed behind his ear. Some debris from the bomb must have scratched him. He would get his mother to look at it when he returned to camp. He climbed a small outcropping of rocks. He needed some time before he went back to his parents. He wasn't ready yet to talk about what had happened in the church and he knew they would be full of questions. He just wanted to sit for a bit and gaze at the stars. But someone else had already claimed the best spot. It was the American soldier who had helped him this morning. Daniel thought the soldier looked less intimidating than before, just sitting there perched on the rock.

"I'm sorry sir, I didn't know anyone else was up here."

"Plenty of room for one more."

The soldier grinned in recognition. His white teeth flashed against his dark face.

"Hey, I know you, from the school this morning, right? You look pretty good considering the pounding you got."

"I wouldn't have lasted long, sir, if you hadn't come along when you did. Thank you. My name is Daniel."

"Glad I was there, Daniel. What brings you to Marez?"

"I'm not sure I even know where to begin."

"I've always been a sucker for a good story. And I've got nothing but time. Start wherever you like."

"After you saw me this morning, my family and I went to church. But then a man burst through the doors with a bomb strapped to his chest."

"What happened?"

"He made everyone stand in a circle facing the walls of the church. I felt so helpless. I didn't know what to do."

The soldier squeezed Daniel's shoulder. "I'm sorry. It must have been really tough."

"I've never been so scared. But I wasn't afraid for myself. All I could think about was my family. I didn't want them to die."

"So what did you do?"

He looked earnestly into the sergeant's dark eyes and said simply, "I prayed."

"You did what?"

"I laid down on the floor and I prayed. I didn't even know what words to pray. I just focused on Elohim and the faces of my family. I started to shake and sweat, my arms were aching and my head was pounding, but I kept praying. Soon, everyone was praying and singing. The bomber didn't like it. He shouted at us to stop. But we didn't."

"Unbelievable. Then what happened?"

"I don't know. He screamed then the bomb exploded. It was so strange. No one was hurt but the bomber was gone. We were protected somehow. My father said it was a miracle."

The soldier whistled in amazement. "Well, I guess it was a miracle for sure. You said you felt it in your gut, didn't you? I always follow mine, hasn't failed me yet."

"Yes, but how were we all protected? How did the explosion miss us? Not a scratch on one person. It was like someone was standing in front of us against that wall."

"It must have been His angels, Daniel. My grandma used to tell me stories about our guardian angels. She said they were mighty soldiers that protected us from evil. It makes sense, doesn't it? The angels deflected the debris from the bomb. They shielded you from harm."

"Yes, I believe that you are right."

"You have a gift, young man. Age and circumstance make no difference to Elohim. He will use whomever He chooses when He chooses. He chose you today. And I believe He has chosen you for what is to come."

"I don't know about that. I am just a simple man."

"You are much more, Daniel."

"I'm not sure I understand."

"You will soon enough. I'd like to talk with your family. Will you take me to them? And by the way, you can call me Ira."

CHAPTER 21

Twelve

• • •

LUCAS AND THE OTHERS FOLLOWED Nolan into the old church. Behind the heavy iron doors, the interior of the church was cool. The last rays of the setting sun shone through the colorful stained glass windows, casting prisms of color on the stone floor. Wooden pews flanked the long center aisle of the sanctuary.

They walked the entire length and stopped at a plain wooden door behind the large pipe organ. Lucas marveled at Nolan when he extended his hand in a slight movement towards the iron lock and it clicked open.

"Wow, this place is beautiful," Zoe sighed.

"It reminds me of my church back home," Beni added.

"Not me—I think it's downright creepy," Rafe whispered. "It looks like a church in one of those horror movies about vampires and witches."

Lucas laughed under his breath. He couldn't have agreed more. But he was learning things were not always what they seemed to be. When Nolan turned around, the look in his eyes quieted any further chatter. Down a set of circular steps, he led them further through a series of torch-lit tunnels. The deeper Lucas traveled, the more alert his senses became. He felt like he was entering another world entirely when they stopped at a large natural archway in the rock. The Dìonadain warrior known as Ira was waiting there with another young man. He was dressed in jeans and a grey ARMY t-shirt.

"Light-bearers, I want you to meet Daniel Barzani. He has traveled a great distance from Iraq to come to us. His extraordinary faith marks him as the Believer," Nolan announced.

Daniel bowed in greeting. "I am thankful to join you in service to Elohim, my brothers and sister."

Lucas embraced Daniel. "Same here, Daniel. Welcome."

"Hi Daniel, I'm Zoe. This is Beni and Rafe. We are so happy to meet you."

Never one to be shy, she blurted out, "What happened to your arm?"

"Zoe, shut up!" Lucas warned.

"No, it's okay, Lucas," Daniel said. "It's nothing really—just an old wound."

"Well, it looks like something to me. Come on, man. How did you burn your arm?" Rafe insisted.

"Don't pressure him, Rafe. He obviously doesn't want to talk about it," Lucas said.

"Well, if I have to trust this guy and work with him, I don't want any secrets," Rafe retorted.

Lucas wasn't sure why Rafe was being a jerk, but something about Daniel had obviously gotten under his friend's skin.

Daniel looked at Rafe long and hard. "I got too close to a shell blast."

"Satisfied?" Lucas asked Rafe.

"Yeah, I guess so," he muttered.

"Are you finished with this useless banter?" Nolan asked. "We have significant matters at hand."

Lucas and the others followed Nolan into the darkened chamber behind the stone archway.

"The Hall of the Sorcha. Only those chosen by Elohim may enter this chamber. Within, you will learn about the power of his Light within you," Nolan announced.

Lucas stepped through the archway and a bright light shining from a large silver orb suspended from the stone ceiling illuminated the chamber. Huge stone columns covered in ancient script surrounded the long rectangular space. Between each column stood a life-size marble statue. At the foot of each statue was a seat carved into the base of the statue itself.

"The chiseled likenesses you see before you are the first light-bearers, your ancestors," Nolan spoke reverently. "Here is the Leader of the twelve. A strategic mind and courageous spirit for battle were his gifts from Elohim. The Perceiver with his sensory gift can discern the two worlds, seeing what is not visible to the human eye. Lucas bears this gift."

Lucas looked into the eyes of the Perceiver. He marveled thinking he had this power inside of him. He was humbled he had been chosen to carry this great gift.

"Communicating and understanding languages, no matter their origin, is the gift of the Speaker. Just like you Benicio,"

Nolan continued. "Strength beyond measure is the gift of the mighty Warrior. Here is the Crafter, who can fashion any substance into a weapon used to fight evil."

"My father was the Crafter," Zoe said.

Lucas could see the great respect shining in his sister's eyes. He remembered watching his father create a shield out of the snow. He had been astonished that day, not understanding the great gift his father wielded.

"Yes, he was," Nolan affirmed. "The ability to heal all living things from physical, emotional or psychological sickness or injury is the gift of the Healer—your gift, my dear Zoe. And you, Rafe, just like the Knower who stands here, have the ability to harness the illuminating power of knowledge and use it to solve any mystery."

"What about the others, Nolan? What are their gifts?" Lucas asked.

"The Wielder can accomplish the fantastic, even the miraculous, in the name of Elohim to alter the course of nature. The Psalter has an extraordinary gift of music. His voice instills fear within the enemy and banishes the evil spirits seeking to plague and destroy the Light. The interpretation of visions and prophetic dreams is the gift of the Dreamer. Here stands the Believer. The Believer's unshakeable faith connects the twelve and moves the heart of Elohim. Daniel bears this gift. And finally, the Exiler, the one who wrestles with demons and casts them from the human bodies they inhabit and control. Take your seats, light-bearers. In order for you to unite your gifts to defeat the Prince of

Darkness, you need to understand the history of your quest," Nolan commanded.

Lucas shivered as a swirling mist filled the room. Within the thick vapor, images took shape. Nolan was creating a vision they could all see. He and the others saw a small cluster of rough-hewn buildings surrounded by a wooden fort stood atop a grassy moor. A steady rain was falling from the darkening sky. A man was standing at the door of one of the ancient dwellings.

Standing in the small village he called home, Simon looked across the windswept moor. It was late and all was quiet. His clan slept peacefully unaware of the supernatural struggle going on around them. Because he was the leader of his people, their welfare was his own. He had led them here across the ocean to a place where they could begin anew. Marriages, births and deaths, the cycle of life, were shared here on the tor.

Closing the door of his dwelling place, Simon sat heavily in his chair. There was still much to do, much to record, and he felt as if his time was running out. He had been plagued of late with an increasing sense of dread. People in the neighboring villages were acting strangely towards his clan, whispering amongst themselves about witchcraft and sorcery. When he and his family had first come to this island in the north, the people welcomed them eager to hear the Word of Elohim. But attitudes had shifted dramatically.

Simon believed evil had taken root in the hearts and minds of many in the villages nearby. Those who committed their lives to Elohim were no longer safe. Even though he and his people were protected within their fortified encampment, he still felt he was being watched. Simon knew the task he had been charged with long ago must be completed if the future of the Sorcha was to be secured. Before the light entered his life, Simon had been a warrior, a zealot, a man who fought for the freedom of his people and their cause. He was no stranger to battle. He knew this was the very reason Elohim had given him this task.

He ran a weathered hand through his thick dark beard speckled with grey. He had not eaten much over the last few weeks and the effects of his sparse diet had only accentuated his long hooked nose and angular jaw line. He looked at the bowl of soup and hunk of brown bread Marhe prepared for him hours ago. He smiled wistfully. His wife worried about him but would never speak it aloud. It was just her way.

Picking up his quill, he wrote on the parchment scroll before him. His brothers had all been charged with specific tasks; his was to record and protect this sacred testament. Once his book was finished, he knew the Scáths would never give up until they destroyed the scroll and the powerful words it contained. This text would usher in the destruction of evil itself. So far, he had lived undetected, but he knew that Abaddon's demons would find him soon. Maybe they already had.

He labored on, the light from the oil lamp burning brightly in the night. Just before dawn, he put down his quill and rolled up the scroll, binding it with a thin strip of leather. He sat back and exhaled deeply. "It is finished, Elohim."

A hard rap at the door startled him. He crossed the dirt floor quickly and opened it to find his most trusted companion, his beloved son.

"Amhlaid, what is it?"

Simon saw the urgency on the young man's craggy face. Amhlaid looked just like him in his younger days except for his reddish-blond hair.

"We must go, Father. They are out for blood this time," Amhlaid insisted. "I have been watching the people in the neighboring village—someone has stirred their hatred against us. They are screaming sorcery and death for you."

Bowing his head, he said gravely. "I will not leave my people, my son."

"Please, Father, there's still time for us to flee," Amhlaid begged earnestly. "You and mother must come with me. The gates will never hold against the crowd marching upon us now."

Walking back into the room, Simon untied the binding and unrolled the scroll he had just completed on the rough-hewn table. The pages glowed warmly in the lamplight.

Amhlaid gasped. "You have finished."

Simon pulled one of the pages from the rest and then bound the scroll again. He tied the single page he had removed with a worn piece of leather and offered it to Amhlaid.

"Keep it safe, no matter the cost, even if it means your own life," Simon said with conviction. "It is the key to understanding what I have written. The twelve will find you when it is time. Go now, quickly, my dearest son."

Amhlaid took the scroll without question. Simon had prepared him as best he could for what was surely to come. He kissed his son's forehead in blessing. He watched Amhlaid until he disappeared into the thick dawn mist.

He knew the key to the book would be safe parted from the whole. He sat before the dying embers of the fire and waited.

"And so it begins," he whispered resolutely.

When the mob came, their bloodlust was palpable. They drug him from his home and forced him to watch as they cruelly slaughtered his whole village—every man, woman and child. His people's screams rent the air and their blood soaked the wet ground. They saved Marhe for last. His eyes never left hers, willing her to be brave. He cried out in anguish when they slit her throat. A sudden blow to his head turned his world black.

When he came to, his hands were bound behind his back. His head throbbed. He could only open one eye, the other swollen shut. The metal taste of blood in his mouth made him queasy. He surveyed the crude space he was in. It was small and dank. Rain fell through the hole above him. He looked up—the sky was grey and ominous. He could hear people arguing and shouting. He bowed his head asking Elohim for strength and resolve. He knew his time had come. He grieved the loss of his family—his wife—but he knew he would be with them soon. His mission on Earth was complete. The scroll was written and its true message would remain a secret. Amhlaid had the key and only the light would reveal it. The path was now paved—the door open—the Sorcha would awaken and evil would be bound. At least he could face the terrible death he knew would be his with hope for the future.

The ground where he was kneeling trembled. He wasn't shocked to see a winged man with flaming blue eyes appear in the corner of the small space. Although his face was covered with a silver mask, Simon had no doubt to his identity. It was his

Dionadain guardian, Cain. He had betrayed him and his broth-
erhood of angels. Cain was clutching the scroll Simon had written
in his hand. He must have taken it from Simon's home before it
burned to the ground. Simon breathed a sigh of relief knowing the
contents of his scroll would be protected. Cain was unaware of the
key.

When Cain approached him, Simon roared, "Woe to you and
your kind—you who have devised such wickedness. When the
morning dawns, you will be destroyed."

A triumphant smile spread across the fallen angel's face, "You
are going to die Simon. And I, well, I will live on. Know that the
work you and your brothers of light began will be for naught. The
darkness will not suffer the light."

Before he could respond, rough hands pulled him up from the
hole. He landed in the mud surrounded by a mob of feral faces
singularly focused on his doom.

The images faded and the room was returned to normal.
Lucas was burning with a hundred questions.

"What happened to Simon? Where is the key now?" he
asked.

"Only when the twelve unite will you have the ability to
discover the answers you seek, Lucas," Nolan answered.

"But how will we find the others?" Zoe asked.

"The task of finding the others rests with the Dìonadain.
You must focus now on mastering your gifts. Learn to use the
power of the light within you. Prepare yourselves for what is
coming. Simon knew the extraordinary knowledge contained
within the scroll would help future light-bearers defeat the

march of darkness across the earth. So he protected it by separating the key to understanding the words in the scroll from the scroll itself. The immeasurable power within Simon's book cannot be understood without that key."

"Cain was the winged man that took Simon's scroll, wasn't he?" Beni asked.

"It was Cain, I'll never forget his face," Lucas said bitterly.

"Yes, Cain was Simon's protector—my brother. Tempted by greed and the promise of great power from Abaddon, himself, he betrayed Simon. But the part of the scroll he took is incomplete. He cannot read it without the key."

"That's why he hunts the Sorcha, right?" Rafe asked. "He's desperate to prevent us from uniting so the key will be lost forever."

Nolan nodded, "Yes, exactly."

"Nolan, once we are all together, do you believe we can find it? Can we really beat the Scáths?" Lucas asked.

"Darkness can't withstand the light," Daniel said reverently.

"Daniel is right. Even the smallest fraction of light illuminates the darkest of nights. You must believe this as well," Nolan answered.

CHAPTER 22

3:26 am

• • •

LILY WOKE UP IN A cold sweat. She grabbed her cellphone from the nightstand. 3:26 am. She called him anyway.

"Lily, it's late," Jude said in a sleepy voice. "What's wrong? Another dream?"

"Yes and it was awful. I can't go back to sleep."

"Okay, calm down. Was it the same as before?"

"Yeah, I was walking down a long hallway. I think it was a museum. There were paintings all over the walls. A woman's voice kept calling to me."

"What did she say?"

"I don't know. I can't remember and it's driving me crazy. But, she sounded terrified. I tried to find her. Then she screamed, the pictures turned crimson red. They exploded. I was covered in blood. When I realize it's me screaming, I wake up. I'm so scared Jude."

"It was just a dream, Lily. Look around. You're safe in your room."

"I know. But this is the third time I've had the same dream. I'm really scared. Do you think it means something?"

"Maybe. I don't know. Are you going to be at church this morning?"

"You know I am. I don't really have a choice."

"Okay, try to get a little sleep and we can try to figure it out later."

"Thanks, Jude."

"For what?"

"Being my best friend."

"Always. See you soon."

She closed her eyes and fell into a dreamless sleep. When her alarm went off a few hours later, she moaned. It was Sunday and the last place she wanted to be was in church. Mia insisted they all go to church as a family. Ugh! She resented being told what she should or should not think or do. She was eighteen for crying out loud. It was her life—she could decide for herself. She got up dreading the next few hours. At least, she would see Jude. She pulled a blue sundress from her closet and slipped in on. It was already 9:30 am so no time for makeup. She ran a brush quickly through her hair and stopped by the bathroom to brush her teeth. She put on some lip gloss and ran down the stairs to join her family.

She was the last one out of the car, wanting to delay the agony of congregational hymns, prayer, and the pastor's message for as long as possible.

"Let's go, Lily. Out of the car. I don't want us to be late," Mia urged, hurrying to the front doors of the church.

"Right behind you, mother dear. I just need some coffee first. I slept terrible last night."

"Lily, I know what you're trying to do, young lady."

"I'll meet you inside, mom, I promise. If I don't get some caffeine, I'll just sleep through the sermon. You want me to pay attention, right?"

"Fifteen minutes and you better be in the pew beside me," Mia warned and walked away.

"Seriously, Lily, it's just one hour out of your day. You know you just might learn something! Besides, it's important to mom," Lucas pleaded. "And it was to dad, too."

Lily swore under her breath, watching her brother's back as he walked away from her. She was here, wasn't she? She was going to church. She wished her family would get off her back. She crossed the street and went into a quaint coffee shop. After placing her order for a latte, she noticed Aiden Talbot at a small table in the corner. Her heart skipped a beat. He was talking and laughing with an absolutely stunning dark-haired young woman. Lucas had told her that Aiden was dating a Barbie lookalike, Reese Pooley. So who was this girl? And why did it matter so much to her anyway? Obviously, her brother had been right. This guy was a player. Besides, she looked nothing like Reese and she couldn't hold a candle to the woman he was with now, no matter how hard she might try.

She felt her face flush when Aiden looked up and caught her staring at him. A slow smile spread across his gorgeous face.

"Mornin', Lily."

She waved quickly, too embarrassed to even open her mouth. She made a beeline for the door and crossed the street to the church.

"Ugh, I forgot my coffee," she said under her breath.

She joined her family on a pew toward the back of the packed sanctuary. The congregation was already singing the opening hymn.

"I was about to come and drag you out of the coffee shop," Lucas threatened.

"Hush, I made it, didn't I? Just like I said I would."

"Please be seated," Pastor Hugh Bennett requested from the pulpit. "This morning, I would like to take a few minutes to recognize a very special family. Mr. Talbot, would you and your precious children join me on the stage?"

"You have got to be kidding me...the Talbots?" Lily questioned.

"Rich people go to church too, Lily," Lucas replied sarcastically.

"Shh, you two," Mia admonished.

She cringed when she recognized the young woman from the coffee shop following Aiden and his father up to the stage. How stupid was she? Of course she was his sister. Why hadn't she seen the resemblance before?

"What are you grinning about?" Lucas asked.

"Nothing, just happy to be in church, that's all," she answered sweetly.

The Talbots were certainly a stunning trio! Stylishly dressed and coiffed, they carried themselves like a royal family. Aiden was absolutely gorgeous in his linen suit and tie. She could no longer deny she was interested in Aiden Talbot.

Pastor Bennett placed his hand on Flynn's shoulder. "The Talbots have been members of our congregation here at

St. John's for many years. Today, I want to publicly thank Flynn for his extraordinary contribution to this church and its ministry. He has humbly offered to donate a piece of land right here in the heart of downtown, as well as the funds needed for construction to develop a state-of-the-art recreational center. Their generous gift will allow us to serve families in our community in more diverse and effective ways."

The congregation stood, joining Pastor Bennett in a burst of applause to show their gratitude for the gift so freely given by the Talbots.

"Thank you, Pastor Bennett. We have been blessed beyond measure and are so thankful to be able to pass along those blessings to our church family. I am proud to be a part of this wonderful church and thankful my children have grown in faith as a part of this congregation. One of the greatest gifts our Creator has given us is family. So I hope this wonderful new space will provide you and your families with many opportunities to laugh and play together."

After Flynn's speech, Pastor Bennett delivered his message. Before the final amen, Lily was out the door. She needed to find Jude. He was waiting for her under a large oak tree in the churchyard.

"Hey, you feeling any better?" he asked.

"I guess so. I don't know. It really doesn't matter." Her pulse quickened ever so slightly when she noticed Aiden approaching.

"Well it mattered enough to call me at three o'clock this morning. I thought you wanted to talk about your dream?"

"Not now, Jude," she urged. She had all but forgotten about the terror of last night.

"Sweet Lily, you look lovely, this mornin'," Aiden drawled.

"Hello, Aiden," she managed. Her voice sounded a bit higher than usual to her ears. "Um, this is my friend Jude Butler."

Aiden smiled. "Hey man, I've seen you around but I don't think we've been formally introduced."

Jude shook Aiden's hand but remained silent. Lily understood her friend's response. Aiden was a bit intimidating to say the least.

"I had no idea your family attended this church," she ventured trying to break the awkward moment.

"Yeah, I grew up here. Pastor Bennett really helped us when my mom died."

"Oh, I'm sorry. I didn't realize."

"No worries. It was a long time ago. Mom passed away from cancer when I was just three."

An uncomfortable silence followed. She couldn't think of anything else to say. She avoided looking at Aiden because she was so nervous. She was thankful when Jude spoke up.

"What your dad is doing for the community is really cool, Aiden."

"I think so too. A rec center will give a lot of kids in this town somewhere to go to have fun and to stay out of trouble. My dad didn't have the easiest childhood. So, he cares about giving kids opportunities he didn't get growing up. I respect him for that."

"He's lucky to have you for a son," she said softly. She had spoken from her heart. Unfortunately, she didn't mean to say it out loud. So stupid! But when she met his eyes, she realized that Aiden had been surprised by her comment. He was the one blushing now!

"I'll take that as a compliment, Lily. See you soon."

It wasn't a question but a statement. Lily wasn't sure what to think about that. She watched him walk away, totally caught in the moment. She felt like she had boarded a fast-moving train and wasn't entirely sure she wanted to get off. He was a player, she knew it, and Lucas had even told her so. He was probably just being nice to her. But the way he had just looked at her made her wonder. Either way, she was most definitely in a world of trouble!

CHAPTER 23

Rapids

• • •

AFTER CHURCH, EVERYONE HEADED TO the river for whitewater rafting. This was to be the first family outing for the Quinns since moving to Cleveland a few weeks ago. Lily had begged Mia until she finally agreed. Her mother didn't like to venture out much, choosing instead to keep her and her siblings cooped up at home. But the new job and Aunt Audrey's contagious high spirits must be loosening her up a little. Lily was beyond excited. She had invited Jude to join them.

She had heard all about the Class 3 and 4 Ocoee River rapids from Jude. In 1996, the Ocoee served as the whitewater venue for the summer Olympics. The challenging five-mile rollercoaster ride was not for the faint of heart. It was a mecca for first time rafters and kayakers as well as those who were more experienced, affectionately known as river rats.

"Be careful, girls. Rafting can be dangerous," Mia warned Lily and her sister. "You too, Lucas."

"Relax, mom, I got it all under control," Lucas grinned. "I'll take care of the girls."

Lily laughed for the first time in a long time—she was actually having fun with her family.

"Love you, mom," Lily hugged Mia unexpectedly. She could tell her mother was surprised by her unsolicited show of affection. Mia kissed her cheek before Lily let her go.

"Be fearless," Audrey called cheerily, earning a frown from her overprotective sister. "We'll have dinner ready when you get back." Then she turned to her sister, "Mia, let them have their fun. They aren't kids anymore."

"I know. It's just nerve-wracking to think of them out there on those crazy rapids."

"I guess you've forgotten the parasailing fiasco when we were their age?"

"Enough said," Mia agreed with a smirk.

"Details, please," Lily urged.

"Not on your life," Mia laughed. "Now go…"

"Wait up, guys," Lily called, following after Lucas, Zoe, and Jude.

When they walked into the rafting office to join check-in, Lily was surprised to see Aiden and his friends at the front desk.

"Aiden, I didn't know y'all would be here today," Lucas said.

"Last minute decision! You should join us, Quinn. It would be a blast to go down together," Aiden answered.

"Perfect, let's do it," Lucas agreed.

Lily didn't miss the look of displeasure on Reese's face. Obviously she didn't want to share Aiden or her friends with anyone today.

"You ain't lived 'til you've ridden the Ocoee, man," Marshall hooted good-naturedly, rapping Lucas on the back.

"Yeah," Gray agreed. "I came close to meetin' my maker the first time I braved these rapids."

He turned to Lucas, using his paddle to joust with him in fun.

"How comforting," Jude whispered to Lily.

"Yeah, it's a real adrenaline rush—nothing like it in the world, and I've been a lot of places," Aiden agreed. "You're gonna love it, Lily."

"Yeah, Lily, just like riding a rollercoaster. Whoo hoo!" Marshall spun around, singing while everyone laughed.

"Stop it, Marshall. You're scaring sweet Lily," Reese said disdainfully. Putting her arm around Lily's shoulders, she continued, "The Ocoee should always be taken seriously, you know. Accidents can happen, in fact, people have been hurt pretty badly in the past when the rapids have knocked them out of the boat."

"Some have even died," Gray added innocently.

"That's why I'm here to make sure that doesn't happen," a dark-haired hippie girl said matter-of-factly.

Even though she only stood about 5'3", it was obvious by her demeanor she was in charge. "Alright, everyone. Let's get to it! I'm Ali and I'll be taking you down the river."

Ali reviewed safety procedures and gave everyone a quick lesson in paddling. After grabbing gear, everyone boarded the bus for the short drive up Highway 64 to load-in.

Lily wasn't sure if she was more nervous about navigating the rapids or sitting in the same boat as Aiden Talbot for the hour-long trip. She felt better when Jude whispered, "The bus trip was too short."

When the bus parked in the lot next to the load-in point, Lily donned her life-jacket and helmut, then picked up her paddle. She joined the others around the raft. The noise was crazy. Guides were yelling instructions, rafters were laughing and shouting, and the water was roaring. It was their turn. She and the others picked up the raft and carried it to the edge of the swift river. Ali was at the back, shouting for them to take their places. Lucas and Marshall sat in the back with Ali. Reese, Gray, Zoe, and Jude were in the middle. And as luck would have it, Lily was in the front with Aiden.

Lucas must have noticed her nervousness because he hollered, "Relax, Lily. Let's have some fun!"

"Here we go!" Ali yelled and steered the raft out into the foaming water.

The raft hit the ledge of the first rapid and jumped into the air then splashed back down hard into the water.

Ali yelled, "Paddle!"

The raft was sucked into the rapid by the hydraulics created by the water hitting the riverbed rocks. Successfully navigating the first rapid, everyone cheered. Lily looked at Aiden and laughed. He flashed a wide grin and winked.

Reese warned coldly, "Don't get too confident—it was only the first one."

"Take it easy, Reese," Aiden ordered.

"Hold on, Lily," Jude urged from behind her. "Hook your feet under the seat in front of you."

"He's right—see that big rock up ahead? It's called Teeter Totter and he's pretty tricky. We need to paddle hard. Right after Teeter Totter is Double Suck. He's a real beast. If we get sucked into the whirlpool there, it will be very hard to get out."

"Bring it on!" Marshall stood raising his paddle in the air.

"Sit down, hot shot," Ali commanded.

Marshall fell back in his seat laughing.

"Remember, Lily, just keep paddling. We'll be fine, I promise," Aiden said.

"We won't be if your friend up there doesn't stop rocking the boat," Jude countered from behind. He reached up and squeezed her shoulder. "I got you, Lily."

"Would you both stop treating me like I'm helpless?" Lily retorted. "I got this."

"If you boys are done?" Ali said. "We need to get down this river—now paddle!"

The raft dove over the first ledge. The water roared in Lily's ears. She dug in her paddle and focused on listening to Ali's commands over the roaring rapids. She screamed when the raft spun and hit Teeter Totter broadside. The force of the impact against the monstrous rock flipped the front end of the raft into the air. She lost her paddle and toppled into the swirling whirlpool.

CHAPTER 24

Rainbow

• • •

LILY FOUGHT TO GET HER head above the churning water. When she broke the surface, she gasped for air but got a mouthful of river water instead. The force of the water sucked her back under. She was spinning head over heels, caught in a vortex just like the spin cycle in a washing machine. She knew she was in trouble. She fought against the current but with no success. It was hard to get her bearings in the water. She started to panic. Her head broke the surface again and she saw the raft in front of her for just a moment before she went back under.

The quick puff of air she managed to gulp wasn't enough to fill her lungs. Her body, battered against the rocks that lay beneath the surface, was screaming in pain. She fought again to escape the sucking force of the water but failed. Her foot was caught in a small crevice between two rocks. Her chest ached. She couldn't hold her breath for much longer.

She wasn't going to make it! She wondered if this was how her father had felt before he died. Her chest ached from the pressure. She knew she was going to die. She was going to open her mouth and feel the cold water rush in and fill her lungs. She was suddenly filled with an overwhelming sense of regret. She would never see her family again. She would never be able to tell her mother how much she loved her. Or tell Lucas how sorry she was for being so terrible to him. And Zoe? She would never see her little sister grow up. In that moment, her disbelief, her anger, her pride all melted away.

"Please Elohim, if you are real, if you really do care, please, save me, give me another chance!"

Her eyes widened as a warm light glowed faintly in the distance. This was it. She remembered hearing stories about going into the light when a person died. But as the light drew closer, she realized it was a man. He was surrounded by an aura of sparkling light. His giant wings waved in the water, propelling him towards her. She knew she must be dead now because he couldn't be real. He looked like the angels her mother had told her bedtime stories about, only larger and more breathtaking. As soon as the rainbow of light around the man touched her, she felt calm. She no longer fought to breathe. It was as if she needed no air. She felt the man dislodge her foot.

When the man lifted his head, she received the biggest shock of her life. Time stopped. The beautiful powerful man whose body pulsed with warm golden light was her best friend. Her rescuer was Jude. She had no idea what was happening to her. Jude wrapped his arms around her and swam swiftly under the water away from the rocks and churning water. She closed her eyes, giving in to the great peace that flooded her.

A sharp slap on her back brought her back to reality. She gulped precious air into her lungs. When hands lifted her to a sitting position, she began to cough and sputter.

"Lily? Are you okay?"

She looked at Jude who knelt beside her on the bank of the river. He was soaked to the skin, hair plastered to his head, and his glasses were askew. He was just as he always was. How? She reached out her hand to his face and whispered, "It was you?"

He solemnly nodded his head. He covered her hand with his and stared fiercely into her eyes. "I will never let anything happen to you."

Before she could demand an explanation from him, the rest of group pulled up in the raft. "There she is!" Aiden shouted. Aiden and Lucas jumped out of the raft and raced towards her and Jude.

"Lily, are you alright?" Lucas questioned. "You scared me to death!"

Lucas ran his hands over her legs and arms. "Nothing broken?"

"I'm good. I thought I was going to die," she said.

"Don't say that, Lily!" Lucas urged. He hugged her tightly. He must have been almost as scared as she had been.

She looked up at her savior, "Jude, you saved me."

Jude shrugged his shoulders lightly. He seemed to be uncomfortable with all the attention.

"Crazy guy dove in before we could stop him. I thought we had lost both of you," Lucas said.

"I'm just lucky I got to her in time," Jude offered shyly.

"Yeah, real lucky." Aiden bent down and lifted Lily easily into his arms. "Let's get you somewhere where you'll be safe."

Aiden carried her to the raft. Ali had the first aid kit ready, and Zoe helped her quickly wrap her bruised and swollen ankle. Jude loped awkwardly back to the raft and sat down in the back.

"You seriously had me worried, sis," Lucas said, putting his arm around her and pulling her close. "Don't ever do that again."

"I'm okay, Luc, really. Just a little banged up."

Back at camp, Aiden carried Lily to a chair. Mia enveloped her daughter in a fierce hug after hearing about her daughter's dangerous plunge into the river. "Are you sure you're okay, honey?"

"I'm fine, mom. Just super tired and sore all over. I don't think I'll be going rafting again anytime soon."

"You got that right, honey—not for a good long while. After we eat and cleanup, we need to head back and get you to bed. I bet you feel awful."

"That's an understatement," she returned ruefully.

Audrey brought Lily a steaming cup of hot chocolate. "Drink this, Lily. You're shivering."

She took a sip of the dark liquid thankful for its heat.

"Where's Jude?" Lily asked, anxiously searching the group.

"Right here," Jude spoke up from behind her. He pushed his glasses up on his face and frowned. He looked like he would rather be anywhere but where he was at that moment.

"Man, I still don't understand how you did it. That rapid was wicked," Gray mused.

"Yeah, you are either the craziest or bravest guy out here," Marshall pondered.

"Really brave," Reese agreed sweetly. "Lily is lucky to have such an amazing guy looking out for her."

"Yeah, he's a real hero," Aiden said without much feeling.

"Jude, what you did, it took real guts. Thank you for saving my sister," Lucas said sincerely.

"Well, as much as I would love to hang out and hear more, we better be going," Reese announced.

"Don't rush off! We have enough food for everyone," Mia invited.

"Thanks, Mrs. Quinn, but we're supposed to be at a party," Reese answered.

Marshall and Gray followed Reese to the car. "Coming, Aiden?" Reese prodded insistently.

Aiden replied, "Go ahead. I think I'll take Mrs. Quinn up on her offer. Lucas will give me a ride home later, yeah?"

"Sure, no problem. Come on, you can help me get the grill going."

Lily watched Reese's face change. For a split second, her beautiful countenance twisted. Obviously, she didn't like what was happening. But just as quickly as it had appeared, it was gone, replaced by a chilly smile.

"Alright, then. Y'all enjoy."

Reese turned on her heel and stalked up the slight hill to the Marshall's jeep. When Aiden's friends drove away, Lily exhaled a breath she hadn't known she was holding. She settled back in her camp chair and closed her eyes. She was a bundle of nerves and emotions. She replayed the events of the day over and over again in her mind. She couldn't believe it but the truth was right there in front of her. Whatever or whoever Jude was, he was not what she had thought him to be. So many questions and no answers didn't help her pounding head.

"Here you go, Lily. I made your hamburger just the way you like it, extra ketchup and pickles," Zoe served a plate to her sister.

"Thanks, Zoe."

Zoe leaned down and gave her a peck on the cheek. "Don't you ever scare me like that again, got it?"

"Don't worry, I'm done with water sports for awhile."

"Hey Zoe, your burger is ready," Lucas shouted.

"You better be," Zoe returned before walking away.

"Mind if I sit with you, Lily?" Aiden asked quietly.

She nodded her pounding head. "Sure." She was too overwrought to be nervous around him.

"What a day. You must feel awful?"

She laughed. "Ha, like I've been through the heavy duty cycle on my mom's washing machine."

"No doubt. You were really lucky."

"I know I was," she said. "I'm just glad Jude was there."

"We all are, Lily," Lucas said as he bent down to give her a quick hug. "No more rafting for you, at least until next week," he teased.

"Not a chance! I've had my fill of the river for awhile." Lily smiled.

When Lucas walked back toward the grill, Aiden mused, "You've got something special."

"What do you mean?"

"Your family is very close. Don't take for them granted, Lily. My family doesn't spend a lot of time together. Dad is always traveling. Lysha goes with him most of the time since she works at Talbot." He paused for a moment. His sadness was clear when he made his next statement. "I didn't realize how much I miss my family until now."

She was surprised at Aiden's transparency. Without thinking, she reached over and squeezed his hand. She felt an immediate connection with him, a hum of electricity crackling just below the surface. He didn't move but kept her hand enveloped in his for a moment. When he finally let go, he didn't look at her but whispered, "Thank you."

They sat in silence, both lost in their thoughts. Lily stared into the night sky with a hint of a smile on her face.

"What are you smiling at?"

"Hmmm, the stars. It's so clear tonight, you can see millions of them."

"Yeah, they're really beautiful."

"You know, they remind me of my dad. When I was little, he would take Lucas and me out onto the roof of our house. We would spread out a blanket and lay there side by side, looking up at the stars."

"You miss him?"

"More than I can even say. But especially so on starry nights like this one," Lily said softly.

"Then I wish many more starry nights for you, Lily."

Lily looked into Aiden's face. He was looking back at her with genuine care. She realized she liked that look very much.

● ● ●

She was eager to begin. She had much to prove.
Legions of Scáths had been arriving day and night
from all over the world, summoned by her master, Cain,
to bear witness to his most prized creation: her.
The world of the Scáths was simple, really.
Follow commands, don't ask questions,
and never make a mistake.
A Scáth existed only to destroy.

But she was no lowly Scáth. Cain had become dissatisfied
with the Scáths. So her master had forged a new evil,
stronger, smarter, and infinitely more wicked than a Scáth.
He had stolen a female member from the last generation
of Sorcha to bear him children. These children,
born of this unholy union, were known as Mescáths:
one part Sorcha and one part Scáth. Embodying
both good and evil, she was a Mescáth,
a fascinating and lethal assassin, a combination
of extremes within one being. Her power was magnified
because of the small amount of Light dwelling within her.

This was her power, her perfection. Tonight, legions of Scáths
would witness her brilliance and power. When she was victorious,
Cain would make her second in command of his legion armies.
She already felt a sense of triumph welling within.

Standing in the darkness, she watched the demon horde
settle in concentric circles around the battle floor.
Crimson hair swirled around their chiseled faces.
They focused fiery blue eyes on Cain where he sat
on the dias far above the crowd. When Cain's eyes flamed,
their thundering chants began. On the battle floor, Rao,
the most fearsome warrior in the Scáth army, appeared.
She felt a rush of adrenaline like none before.
She knew the face shrouded in silver was taut and smooth
like marble. The tattoos adorning Rao's body gleamed
an unearthly blue-green. They writhed like snakes all over
his mighty body. But she wasn't afraid.

The Scáths' chant grew more intense.
They were calling for her: Keket, the mighty Mescáth.
Never before had the demons witnessed what she was
about to show them. Leaving the shadows,
in a burst of hot blue flame, she appeared in the center
of the arena. She knew Rao would make the same mistake
so many other male creatures did. He would underestimate her
deadly skill because of her great beauty.
Her thick braided hair hung down her back.
Her tall, supple body was encased in black leather.

She bowed low to Cain and then turned her cold eyes
on her opponent. She circled Rao, waiting
until the demon chant reached a fever pitch.

"Silence," Cain boomed.

The chanting stopped. She waited for her master's signal.
When Cain lowered his hand, electricity crackled through the air,
filling the space with sharp white lightening. She catapulted
in the air and landed behind the great Scáth warrior.
Fiery blue darts shot from her hands, striking Rao
squarely in the chest. Her opponent spun around like a wild
tornado.
The dark shadows oozing from the warrior as he whirled blinded
her.
But she was too quick and dodged his darts with a complex series
of acrobatics.

"Is that the best you have, Scáth?"

Roaring toward her, Rao knocked her into the air
and then clapped his hands together, sending a powerful
blue surge toward her. The power of Rao's flames suspended her
in midair while twisting around her like a vice. She felt the air
choked from her body. She heard the taunts from the crowd
as she struggled to break Rao's powerful embrace. Her eyes burned
intensely and then faded to nothingness. Laughing, Rao
released his cold flame, dropping her to the ground.

*He saluted his brothers around the arena,
acknowledging their chants of victory.
When the Scáth warrior knelt before Cain, the crowd hushed.*

"Scáth scum!"

*She laughed triumphantly when Rao jerked his head around
to see her crouched behind him. He couldn't deflect her short
intense bursts of flames. The mighty commander fell to the ground,
screaming in agony, his body burning. She advanced toward him,
slowly increasing the power of her deadly darts.
Rao's form dissipated in a cloud of blue smoke.*

*Silence filled the chamber. The Scáths ringing the battlefield
now looked upon the warrior who was half woman and half demon
with a mixture of fear and loathing. The day of the Mescáth had
dawned.
As she approached her commander's perch, Cain stood. She sunk
low
and bowed before him. Cain embraced her and whispered, "My
wicked daughter,
so beautiful, cunning, and strong. Today, you have earned your
greatest desire."
Turning to the demon crowd below him, he announced in a commanding voice,
"Your new commander, Keket!"*

A roar filled the arena. She had done it! Her destiny lay before her.
She, Keket, would bring the final destruction of the Sorcha.
Her lust for blood, her powerful greed, would never be satiated.
After all, she was her father's daughter.
And now, she would make him a prince.

CHAPTER 25

Clearing

• • •

LILY WOKE UP SLOWLY. A steady rain drummed on the roof. Still drowsy, she burrowed under her blanket. She winced when pain shot up her leg. Memories of yesterday came flooding back.

She sat straight up in bed with one thought: Jude. As if on cue, he walked into her room carrying a lunch tray.

"Hey, your mom asked me to bring this up and check on you," he said shyly.

"I hurt all over."

"You got knocked around pretty good yesterday. I'm thankful you're here and on the mend. It could have been a whole lot worse."

"No secrets, Jude. I have to know. What happened in the water? Who are you really?"

Jude sat down beside her and looked calmly into her eyes. "Open your heart, Lily. Promise me you'll listen?"

"I'll listen."

"I've known you all your life, Lily. From the moment you came into the world, I have been watching over you, protecting you. I am your guardian."

"Like a guardian angel? You're saying you aren't human?"

"Yes and yes. Most people have no idea we exist. We live outside your awareness. But can show ourselves as human if needed."

Lily reached up to touch Jude's face. "But you look the same."

"My very own angel," she wondered. "But why are you pretending to be a regular guy when clearly you aren't?"

"We thought it best I take human form for a time. I needed to gain your trust so that I could help you come to terms with the truth you have been avoiding."

"We?"

"The Dìonadain Council, the elders of my order, directs my movements as well as those of the rest of my brothers. We often take human form to carry out the plans of the Council. But we are careful not to draw undue attention to ourselves in the form we choose. Even though we walk and live among you, most people never notice us. We look like everyone else, act like everyone else; we blend in. I must admit I have enjoyed experiencing the world from a more human perspective, especially eating the food."

She bowed her head, her eyes welling with tears. "You saved my life...so why didn't you save my father's too?"

"I'm your guardian, Lily, not your father's. What happened to Eli was out of my control."

"Then why didn't his guardian save him? If the Dìonadain are so strong and mighty, why didn't they save my father?"

Jude stared into the stormy depths of Lily's eyes. "That question is not mine to answer. Elohim's plan is beyond our comprehension, but I can tell you that there are no mistakes."

Lily laid her head back on her pillows and looked at the raindrops sliding down her bedroom window. Tears rolled unchecked down her cheeks.

"Lucas was telling the truth, wasn't he?"

"Yes," Jude answered quietly, "he was."

Lily watched a range of emotions play across Jude's face. He was wrestling with something inside his head. She was sure of it. She knew he had made a decision when he took his glasses off and tossed them on the desk. "Come with me?"

"Of course," Lily answered without hesitation. "But where are we going?"

"You'll understand when we get there."

He lifted her from the bed and carried her outside to a bench in the back yard. The rain had tapered off to a light mist.

"Forgive me, Lily," he whispered cryptically as he took on his full glowing Dìonadain form.

She gasped at his transformation. Under the raging waters of the Ocoee, he had amazed her, but it had all happened so quickly she had not had the chance to study him. His towering form was intimidating in its perfection. His wavy hair framed his flawless countenance. He wore his great strength and beauty like a mantle. His incredible wings, so large they touched the ground, shimmered when he moved. He was the fairest of all creatures.

Before she could think about the mystery of his words, he swooped her up in his strong arms. His wings began to wave very slowly. The sound they made was like low rumbling thunder. They hovered in the air.

"So much for my fear of heights!" she exclaimed grabbing him tightly around the neck. "You won't let me fall, will you?"

Jude looked deeply into her eyes and promised. "You aren't going to fall, Lily. You're going to fly."

And then they were flying high above the clouds. She had always wondered what clouds felt like. She reached out her hand—her fingers dancing through their whispery softness. Lily should have been frightened out of her wits, hurtling through the sky, but she wasn't. She was amazed at her sense of calm. She was actually enjoying the freedom and rush of it all. Before she knew it, Jude was setting her gently down on the ground.

"That was fantastic," Lily laughed. "I could get used to that."

She turned around slowly within his embrace. Her heart stopped. Her eyes took in what her mind struggled to admit. She was standing in the exact spot where she had seen her father for the very last time. Jude waved his hand and the green grass and sunny sky changed. Now, the clearing looked just the same as it had six years ago. On the ground was a layer of newly fallen snow. The sky was grey and overcast. The wind whistled gently through the pine trees encircling the clearing.

"No, I can't be here. I want to go back home, Jude."

"I can't do that, Lily."

"You have to. I'm asking you to. You promised to protect me. So take me away from this place."

"You need to remember, Lily—all of it."

"I can't," she sobbed into his chest. "It hurts too much."

"Trust me." He gently stroked her hair. "You need to be free from the past."

She knew in her heart he was right. For too long, she had been carrying the burden of what happened in the clearing. She had willed a part of herself to die that day. She had been living one day to the next with no real joy or peace since.

Taking a deep breath, Lily warned, "If you leave me, I'll never forgive you."

"That's my girl. Now take me back. What can you remember?"

Leaving the shelter of his arms, she sat on a gnarled stump and allowed her mind to drift back.

"It was early. Daddy loved to walk early in the morning. Lucas and I went with him. We were having so much fun. It was snowing and we made snow angels. I remember my stomach growling because I was so hungry. Dad must have been too because he wanted to head back to the house for breakfast. He called to Lucas but he…"

"Go on, what happened to Lucas?"

She grabbed his hand and pleaded, "I can't do this, please…"

"You must, Lily. I know this is difficult. I can feel your fear, your pain. But you must remember."

She breathed deeply and pressed on into her memories. "Lucas was so still, like he was frozen. He stood just there." She pointed to the spot, remembering the glazed look of terror in her brother's eyes.

Jude crouched down beside her and put his hand over hers.

"I tried to push him, pull him—Dad did too, but we couldn't make him budge. I started crying. I knew something was wrong. Daddy was yelling at Luc but it didn't matter. But then," she paused. She stood up abruptly and turned around slowly in a circle, peering at the dark trees. Memories she had locked deep in her mind flooded her.

"What is it, Lily? What did you see?"

"I saw them standing all around us. They were so very beautiful. I was drawn to them somehow. I knew my father didn't like them because he pushed me behind him. One of them, the leader I think, spoke to my father. When his eyes burned hot blue and he hit Daddy, I realized I had been wrong. These people weren't beautiful at all. They were ugly."

Hot tears slid unchecked down her cheeks. She felt it all over again—the terror, the powerlessness. She pressed into the memories, the emotions, recalling the unbelievable. It was all coming back now—clear and unquestionably true. All the while Jude stood by her side.

"When she pounced on him, Daddy fought back. I grabbed Luc's hand. I was so scared. Daddy used the snow to make a weapon to fight the woman. I didn't know if I was dreaming or if what I was seeing was the real thing. I had never seen my father like he was at that moment. Then a man came from the sky." She looked at Jude in wonder. "He was glowing like you, and he said something to my father. I don't know what he said but when he disappeared, Daddy..."

"What Lily...what did Eli do?"

"He looked at me. His eyes were sad. He must have known what was going to happen next. He told us to run. But I couldn't leave him. When the beautiful woman let her black beasts knock him down, I screamed. All I could think of was getting to him. I had to help him. But Lucas—he ran away. He left us there. I must have blacked out because I don't remember anything else."

She rocked back and forth. Gut-wrenching sobs shook her. Jude held her until she was spent. "I couldn't save him. And Luc left—he didn't even look back." Lily pushed back out of his embrace. "Where were you, Jude? Everyone left me...I was completely alone."

"But you weren't alone, Lily. Let me show you. Close your eyes. You need to see what you could not before." He placed his warm hands on either side of her face.

She closed her eyes and saw herself holding Lucas's hand in the clearing. The events she had just recounted played again, but this time she saw something different. She gasped. Encircling the clearing behind the beautiful ones were rows of golden soldiers with shields and swords. They stood quietly like sentries, ignoring the taunts the beautiful ones flung at them.

When the glowing man appeared next to Eli, the golden warriors snapped to attention.

She suddenly recognized him. It was Dr. Gable. He looked nothing like she'd seen before. He spoke to Eli then left him in a flash. But why did it have to happen like this? Why didn't Dr. Gable or the golden warriors help her father? They outnumbered the beautiful ones three to one. She opened her eyes and demanded, "How could they just watch my father die and do nothing? Why didn't they fight?"

"We wanted to. We grieved when Eli fell. But, Lily, it was his time, Eli's destiny. He sacrificed himself so that you could get away, Lily. He knew you must live."

"But why?"

"The Light within you and Lucas had to be protected. Your father knew you and Lucas would do what he could not."

"The Light within me? What are you saying?"

"Your dreams, Lily. Your dreams mean something. They are a prophecy of what will come.

Elohim never allows suffering without a purpose, Lily. He will never waste your pain."

Suddenly, four glowing figures catapulted from the sky and formed a ring around her and Jude. She had to put up her hand to shield her eyes from the blinding light emanating from their bodies. Immediately, the figures burned a little less bright as if they sensed her discomfort. Their enormous wings sounded like low rumbles of deep thunder. She decided these terrifyingly gorgeous angels must be the Dìonadain Council. Jude's rigid stance and bowed head only confirmed her thoughts. The creatures surrounding her were so epic in their proportion and appearance, she was afraid.

"Fear not, Lily. You are safe with us," Nolan spoke, sensing alarm.

"Recite your oath, brother," Hila commanded.

"The Dìonadain will guard and defend at all costs, never intervening in the life of humanity unless he is called upon," Jude said reverently.

Andreas, the largest of the council members boomed, "You disobeyed our oath, brother."

"Jude." Othiel, the most fiercely beautiful of the council said, "You took a great risk in bringing her to this place."

"I understood the risk but I believed she was ready. Lily is strong. It was time for her to unlock the truth of her past. The Council knows we are running out of time. Scáths are everywhere and getting closer by the minute."

"This decision was not yours to make. Did she ask you to help her remember?" Nolan questioned.

Jude shook his head. "She did not ask. I acted alone in this."

She could hold her tongue no longer. "I may not have asked for his help in so many words but Jude knows my heart, my feelings. I needed to remember. For so long, I have denied the truth of what happened here. I won't any longer. Please, I owe Jude my life as well as my thanks for allowing me to accept my gift, today," Lily pleaded.

"What's done is done, brothers. Jude was impulsive and acted without our permission; however, his motives were pure and his actions have helped Lily to recognize the Light within her," Nolan admonished. "Jude, take Lily home. We have other matters to attend."

Nolan and the rest of the council flew away. Before following his brother, Andreas promised, "We will deal with your insubordination, brother."

Jude picked her up and held her close to his warm glowing form. "I know remembering broke your heart all over again today. I am truly sorry for causing you such great pain."

Lily placed her fingers against Jude's face and said, "I'm not."

CHAPTER 26

Trials

• • •

LUCAS USED THE ENTRANCE IN the old church to make his way to his training lessons with the Dìonadain. Before coming to Cleveland, training sessions with Nolan were conducted in secret in whatever city the Quinns were living. Over the last seven years, Lucas had matured in his gift. He could now experience, process, and understand any number of sensory messages without becoming overwhelmed. He had learned so much. But even still he doubted sometimes if he was worthy of the Light within him.

Lost in thought, he ran right into the back of a Dìonadain. Although he had never seen her, he knew exactly who she was. When he was a young boy in training, Nolan had told him stories of her great beauty and strength. She had once been the fierce protector of Joan of Arc, the young girl who led French armies and saw supernatural visions. Nolan's stories hardly did the angel justice.

"Careful, young man," Agatha warned.

She was extraordinary. Lucas couldn't find the words to speak.

She smiled slightly. "Hurry along now. Nolan is waiting."

Lucas went quickly into the training chamber beyond the Great Hall. It was a large three-story room with solid rock walls. Opening off the main circular space were smaller rooms hewn into the stone. Everyone else was already there. A curt nod from Nolan was all Lucas needed to understand this better be the last time he arrived late to a training session.

"'Bout time you got here, man," Rafe muttered under his breath.

"Just catchin' up on my beauty sleep," Lucas quipped.

"Hmm, no wonder I was here on time—I don't need it," Rafe bantered.

Nolan's stern look quickly ended their conversation.

"For Zoe, Beni, Daniel, and Rafe, we begin the next phase of training today, the Light Trials. Lucas has already gained great control over his gift. Now, it is your turn," Nolan said. "Please enter a chamber and join your guardian."

"Here goes nothing," Rafe grinned. "Wish me luck."

"You got this," Lucas encouraged. "No pain, no gain!"

"That's what I'm afraid of," Rafe replied before entering a chamber.

Lucas was thankful he had already mastered this stage of training. It wasn't going to be easy for any of them. The Light Trials were incredibly demanding. Each light-bearer would be required to use his gift while remaining keenly focused, having relentless control over mind and body, despite significant pain and fear. Lucas knew his friends and his little sister would now be challenged in a way they had never experienced before. Perseverance was the true test.

Taking a seat beside Nolan outside of the training chambers, Lucas asked, "What's that sound?"

"The hum you hear is the sound of the force field created by the Dìonadain warrior. The training chamber is sealed."

"So we can see them but they can't see us? Like a two-way mirror?"

"Exactly," Nolan replied.

Lucas focused on the first training chamber. Inside, Rafe was seated at a small desk. Kiefer was next to him.

"On the desk in front of you is a cryptogram," Kiefer explained.

"A mind puzzle; yeah, I've solved hundreds of these. A block of text is rendered unreadable through the use of a substitution cipher or key. Figure out the cipher. Solve the puzzle. Got it, chief."

"Exactly, but this one is quite old. Focus the Light within, Rafe."

Lucas watched his friend bow his head before he started to manipulate the cryptogram. If he hadn't been looking at Kiefer, he would have missed the warrior wave his hand slightly. Within moments, Rafe started to shiver. The temperature in the chamber must have dropped dramatically because frost was forming on the glass. Soon, Rafe's body was shaking in response to the extreme cold. He pressed on.

"I have two letters. Working on the third," Rafe chattered.

"By wisdom, the Light laid the earth's foundations; by understanding, He set the heavens in place; by His knowledge, the depths were divided. You can do this," Kiefer encouraged.

When the frost began to melt, Rafe's body relaxed. "I have the third and fourth letters in the sequence."

It wasn't long before the increasing temperature forced Rafe to wipe the dripping perspiration from his face. Lucas was fascinated. The metal table Rafe was working on started to glow with heat.

"I have the fifth letter," Rafe called out. "But I can't focus—the table is too hot."

"Solve the puzzle," Kiefer commanded.

Rafe placed his hands back on the table but recoiled in agony. "I can't. My hands are burned."

"You can do this, Rafe. Press through the pain!"

Lucas was concerned for his friend. The burns must be excruciating. He cringed when Rafe jerked away from the table, howling.

Hundreds of bugs were suddenly everywhere, creeping across the puzzle, the table, and the chamber's walls. Vile creatures with black horns crawled up his arms and legs, across his face, into his clothes. Rafe growled in disgust and winced when the creatures' dagger-sharp stingers pierced his skin. Still, he didn't give up.

"It's done!" he screamed and fell from his chair.

The bugs disappeared instantly. The room was quiet. No cold, no fire, and no bugs.

"Well done, Rafe. You gained much strength and focus today." Kiefer grinned.

"Next time, I'm wearing gloves and bringing a blow torch," Rafe responded ruefully.

Now, it was Beni's turn. Lucas was glad Beni hadn't seen what had just happened to Rafe or he might have run from his training chamber. Asher instructed Beni to interpret the languages that appeared before him in written form.

"The key to wielding your gift, Beni, is complete focus. Elohim has given you the ability to speak in known and unknown languages, as well as the ability to interpret what is being said. Trust your gift," Asher challenged.

Lucas could see single words and phrases floating in the air around Beni. All were unfamiliar to him. It didn't take long before Beni was reading and then translating the foreign words and phrases aloud. Lucas could see and hear Beni's confidence growing with each interpretation: Hebrew, Gaelic, Russian, Ancient Egyptian, and Latin.

"Excellent, Beni—remain focused," Asher instructed.

Lucas heard a voice speaking an unknown tongue in Beni's chamber. Beni translated immediately. Soon, more and more voices were speaking different languages simultaneously; some were loud and sharp, while others were soft as a whisper. He knew Beni was trying to decipher at least ten to fifteen languages at once. And he was doing it!

Lucas felt his friend's anguish when the next language echoed from the chamber. Its sound caused all the warmth to drain from Lucas's body. The high-pitched screeching cacophony was unbearably painful to listen to. He had heard this cursed language before. He watched Beni collapse and curl into a fetal position, trying to no avail to block out the tormenting sound of it. It was clear that whatever the words meant, the message was paralyzing Beni. Lucas felt his friend's fear.

Asher knelt by Beni. "The spoken Word of Elohim is like a powerful sword in your mouth—use it!"

Beni rolled on his back and shouted at the ceiling, "His light is within me. I am not afraid!"

Suddenly, the chamber was silent.

Asher rose and began to sing. The entire chamber was filled with music so pure and divine, it stirred Lucas's soul. Asher's voice rolled like the waves of the ocean, rhythmic and peaceful. It was the most beautiful melody he had ever heard. Beni must have agreed. He was kneeling with tears of joy streaming down his face. When Asher finished his song, Beni whispered in awe, "I have never heard anything more wonderful in my whole life."

"The language of the Dìonadain is unknown to man. Soon, you will be strong enough to understand my song and have the gift to speak my language, wielding its comfort and power."

"But what of the cursed one?"

"The Scáths language is so cold and painful it fills the soul with fear. We do not speak it for it brings destruction. But using the Light within, Beni, you banished fear from your soul and from the room. You leashed its darkness."

Lucas knew Zoe would be next. He had to admit he was afraid for her. Rafe and Beni had both been faced with extraordinary and sometimes painful obstacles. Zoe, of course, was totally oblivious to the potential challenges of her session. Her focus was on her Dìonadain teacher, Tov. Lucas was thankful this soft-spoken gentle warrior would be with Zoe.

Tov directed Zoe to the center of the third chamber. Inside, the room was alive with activity. The bright sun suspended in the clear sky warmed the soft carpet of green grass. Birds chirped in the lush shade trees. Bees buzzed, flitting from flower to flower, in the colorful garden. Zoe looked happy and content.

"This is amazing, Tov. I could live here forever," she said.

Tov passed his hand over the flowers surrounding Zoe. Lucas watched each one wither.

"Make them bloom, Zoe."

His sister studied the flowers around her. She touched the petals of the roses, and Lucas grinned when the blooms flashed their pink, yellow, and red hues once again.

"Well done, Zoe. Now let's try something else," Tov encouraged.

A bird flew from its perch in a tree and across his sister's line of sight. Tov threw a rock at the bird and knocked him to the ground. Lucas knew Zoe would waste no time helping the bird. She loved animals. She picked up the bird and placed her hand on its broken wing. Again, almost immediately, the wing was mended and the bird flew away. Zoe giggled with pride.

Lucas, expecting to see pride on Tov's face, was shocked to see the angel struggling on the other side of the chamber with two Scáths. How did they get inside? He quickly realized the demons were not real because his senses had not responded to danger. But there was no way Zoe would know that. His sister screamed when the demons shot their fiery darts at Tov.

Zoe screamed. Beni burst through the door. Before he could reach Zoe, one of the Scáths knocked him to the ground and shot a wicked blue dart through his heart. Beni crumpled, grabbing his chest, his breathing labored. Zoe was obviously in shock, frozen to the spot. The Scáths continued to pummel Tov in the corner.

"Help me, Zoe," Beni groaned, reaching for her.

She knelt beside him and placed her hands on Beni's heart, willing him to live. Her head shot up when she heard a hiss. One of the Scáths was coming toward her. Tov was still struggling with the other one against the far wall.

"Please, he's dying," she cried to him.

"You can do this, Zoe," Tov managed.

Lucas prayed for Zoe's strength. She must overcome her fear and focus. When she spoke, he knew she was digging deep for the courage to do what she needed to do. Turning away from the approaching enemy, she placed her hands on Beni once again.

"Protect him and save his life, Elohim. Make him whole."

As he watched, the Scáths disappeared from the room, and Beni sat up, his injury gone. She had done it! Lucas was so proud of Zoe. He knew she must be reeling from what had just happened to her, but he also knew she had gained undeniable strength and confidence today. They all had. Except for Daniel. The chamber he had entered earlier had remained shrouded in darkness throughout the Trials of Light.

"What about Daniel?" Lucas asked. "Is his trial complete?"

"Look for yourself." Nolan waved his hand and light illuminated Daniel's chamber.

Lucas gasped. Daniel was kneeling on the stone floor. His body was soaked with perspiration; his hair matted and damp from what must have been a punishing amount of exertion. Blood dripped freely from his nose. His arms were painfully extended, bound on either side by thick iron chains. The effort it must have taken Daniel to lift his shackled arms into a posture of prayer was almost inconceivable. Lucas knew his tortured muscles must be strained to the point of ripping in two. Eyes tightly shut and mouth moving wordlessly, Daniel still prayed. When Ira moved his hand over Daniel's bent form, the chains broke. He slid to the floor completely spent. Ira gently picked Daniel up and carried him from the chamber.

"The Believer is willing to go where others will not," Nolan said quietly.

"Incredible," Lucas whispered.

CHAPTER 27

Stars

• • •

LILY HAD FOUND WHAT SHE considered to be her "place" in her new home. In the heart of downtown Cleveland was a quaint little café that served tea and scones in the afternoon. Outside on the sidewalk small tables and chairs were set just waiting for someone to sit down with their favorite book. She had always loved to read. Besides running, it was the thing she liked to do most.

Today, she was reading *Pride & Prejudice* for what must have been the twentieth time. She knew Mr. Darcy didn't exist in the real world, but it was still nice to imagine what life might be like if he did. She was a closet romantic to be sure. Lucas would have teased her mercilessly if he ever found out. Lost in her book, she didn't notice the black sports car that pulled up in front of the café.

"Hello, sweetness."

Startled, she looked up and came face to face with the last person she had expected to see. "Aiden, what are you doing here?"

She wished she had worn something else today. Her ponytail, athletic shorts, t-shirt, and flip-flops were hardly going to impress the young man standing in front of her. Even though he was dressed casually in jeans and a grey t-shirt, Aiden still looked like he had just stepped off the page of *GQ* magazine.

He took his black sunglasses off and looked her dead in the eye. "I came to see you, Lily. I went by your house and your mom told me you might be here."

Aiden drawled in the southern accent she had come to distinguish from all others in a crowd. His hands were jammed in his pockets and he rocked back on his heels. If Lily didn't know better, she would have thought he was nervous.

"Would you come for a drive with me?" Aiden asked. "I'd like to show you something."

"Umm, I don't know," she stalled, trying to calm her fluttering nerves. Why did this guy always have this effect on her?

"Please," Aiden implored. "It would mean a lot to me if you would come."

Her curiosity got the best of her. "What do you want to show me?"

"It's a surprise. We won't be gone long, I promise. You could text your mom and let her know if you like."

He looked so earnest and sweet she couldn't think of a reason to say no. Making her mind up in a moment she said, "Okay, I'll go with you."

Aiden's brilliant smile made her weak in the knees. She had to get control of herself and her reactions to this guy—the quicker the better. When Aiden took a blue bandana out of his pocket, she about lost her nerve. "What's that for?"

"Trust me, Lily? It will be worth it," he said.

After she sent her text, she tied the bandana securely over her eyes. He led her to his car. He buckled her into the seat and then joined her. Pulling away from the curb, Lily almost made Aiden stop the car.

"I hope you know what you're doing, Lily Quinn," she said to herself. "You are definitely playing with fire."

On the other hand, Aiden was devastatingly handsome and he seemed to truly want to get to know her better. Quickly weighing the pros and cons, Lily settled back in her seat and tried to focus on anything else but the butterflies that were her becoming her constant companions. Unconsciously, her knee began to bop up and down, keeping time with the music playing on the radio. They drove in companionable silence for a while and then Aiden slowed the car.

He announced, "We're here."

"Where is here exactly?"

"You'll see. Stay put and I'll be back to get you in a sec, okay? No peeking, Lily," he laughed.

"Okay, okay, no peeking."

She listened intently to Aiden's footsteps disappear.

"Get a grip, Lily Quinn," she muttered to herself.

Despite her frustration with the blindfold and the whole idea of being surprised, Lily couldn't deny the rush of excitement she was experiencing. Of course being near Aiden always made her feel that way. She questioned her good sense again.

Before she could think anything else, Aiden opened the car door.

"Give me your hand," he said.

She put her hand in his and followed his lead. They traversed some fairly uneven ground before climbing a few stairs to what felt like a metal floor. She had absolutely no idea where she was.

"I'm going to take your blindfold off but you have to keep your eyes closed until I tell you to open them, okay?"

Slowly Aiden untied the blindfold and removed it from her face. A warm breeze blew through her hair and she smelled honeysuckle.

"Open your eyes, Lily."

The sight that met her eyes was truly lovely. She was standing in an abandoned railway car in the middle of a beautiful field of summer wildflowers. Behind her was an old three-story textile warehouse. The Old Woolen Mill was vacant, just a mass of bricks and broken windows. Graffiti decorated its exterior and large metal doors. It was striking, haunting, empty, and rich, all at the same time. The summer sun was beginning to set and its red-gold and purple hues streaked the sky, reflecting off the water in the small pond beside the mill. On the floor of the rail car was a blanket. Small candles, ready to be lit, were set all-around. Lights hung from the ceiling and along the open door frames.

"This is amazing Aiden."

"You like it? Really?"

Catching the insecurity in his eyes, she replied, "It's perfect. But, I thought this place was private property."

"It is. But, I've got a connection with the owner," he said with a smirk.

Lily laughed, "Let me guess? Your dad?"

"Yes ma'am, guilty as charged."

Turning in a circle and surveying the view, she continued lightheartedly, "I bet this has been a slam dunk with all the girls you've brought here."

"I've never brought anyone else here, only you. I hoped you would like it. Your favorite things all in one place, the outdoors, the stars in just a few minutes, and of course, what would a picnic be without tacos!"

She couldn't help but giggle. "Who told you I love tacos?"

"Well, I may have asked your little sister. And you know how Zoe likes to talk," he smiled.

They laughed and talked while they ate their simple dinner. As afternoon faded into night, Lily relaxed and truly enjoyed Aiden's company. The string lights were glowing softly overhead in the rail car. The moon was beginning its ascent into the night sky. Still they talked—about anything, everything and nothing at all. It was so easy—like they had known one another forever. Before tonight, she had thought Aiden was so very different from her but she was realizing they had more in common than she knew—likes, dislikes, goals, and dreams. When they spoke of the parents they had both lost, she discovered in Aiden a sensitive heart and compassionate spirit. He continued to surprise her.

"Thank you for a lovely picnic, Aiden. You really know how to impress a girl."

"You're the only girl I care about impressing, Lily."

She couldn't help but blush. Maybe she had been wrong. Maybe there were men like Mr. Darcy in the world.

Aiden reached into the basket. His fingers shook slightly as he gave her a single white lily. She looked up into the eyes of the young man who had no idea that he had just turned her whole world upside down. Gone was the perfection and nonchalance of his practiced expression. Gone was the mask he wore everywhere he went, the one he believed protected his heart. In its place was the earnest and unguarded face of a young man who yearned to be loved.

She touched the cool softness of the white bloom. "It's beautiful, Aiden. I don't know what to say. No one has ever given me flowers."

"Remember the first day we met? I'll never be able to forget the way you looked or how I felt. I could barely breathe, Lily."

"Aiden…"

"Everything just fades to black and it's just you."

He gently touched a strand of her hair.

"When I see you, Lily, it's like the whole world comes alive. Everything is brighter, warmer, better. Every time, it's like that for me. Since I met you, I wake up everyday trying to figure out what I could do or say to make you smile or laugh. It's crazy but I get jealous when someone else beats me to it."

"Aiden, please, you don't need to say these things."

"Don't I? I'm not sure I can explain it, but when I'm with you, I'm different. I feel like I could do anything, be anything.

I know this is happening fast, Lily, but I want you to know what I'm feeling."

Lily put some distance between herself and Aiden. "This isn't easy for me. I've tried for a very long time to be in control, to never let my emotions get the best of me. But when I see you, I have to fight myself not to feel one hundred things at once."

"I feel the same way," Aiden returned.

He reached for her hand but she stood up and walked a few steps away from him. She looked up at the stars twinkling brightly in the sky.

"I've tried to ignore you, to avoid you even, and standing here right now with you I'm not so sure I want to do that anymore. But I need time, Aiden."

Aiden moved to stand beside her. He put his hands in his pockets and rocked back on his heels. He said softly, "Take all the time you need, Lily. I'm not going anywhere."

They both stood silently. Lily was a riot of emotion and thought. Strange—she wasn't scared—she was hopeful. Moments ticked away before Aiden took her hand in his. She turned towards him. He was gazing at her so intently as if he needed to find an answer in her eyes. When he whispered, "Give me a chance, sweet Lily."

She knew she was lost. He must have known it too because a heart-stopping smile broke across the hard planes of his face. He lifted her hand to his lips for the barest whisper of a kiss.

"Let's get you home, young lady. You've got some thinking to do," he winked and picked up the blanket.

She shook her head a little disconcerted by his quick change of mood. One thing was certain—Aiden Talbot was full of surprises and time with him would never be boring!

CHAPTER 28

Masquerade

• • •

Lucas waited at the bottom of the stairs, impatient. He hated to be late, but apparently the women in his life didn't share his feelings. Tonight was the Masquerade Ball at the Museum Center. Under protest, he had consented to attend the benefit with Mia and Lily. After putting on his black tuxedo, he had decided fancy parties might not be so bad after all. Catching his reflection in the mirror, he had to admit he looked pretty good. He held up the mask Audrey had given him to wear. She had purchased it, as well as the ones Lily and Mia would carry, on one of her trips to Venice, Italy.

"You look so handsome," Audrey said from behind. His aunt wore a simple yet classic black gown. The pearls around her neck were her only adornment. As always, his aunt was lovely in every way.

Lucas turned around with a grin. "A real heartbreaker, huh?"

"Come over here, Romeo, and let me straighten your tie."

Lucas allowed her to set him aright.

Zoe whistled from the top of the stairs. "You clean up real nice, bro. James Bond's got nothin' on you."

His little sister wasn't so little anymore. Her emerald-green party dress and heels made her look much older than he liked. His protective instincts kicked in.

"Wow, Zoe, you look so pretty. I'm gonna have to watch out for the guys tonight, aren't I?" He winked.

"Well, I hope so," Zoe teased.

"Are mom and Lily ready yet?"

"Almost. They both look like they just stepped out of a fairy tale."

"Come on, Zoe, the gala starts soon and we need to pick up Beni," Audrey urged. "Your mom is a bit jittery, Luc, so stick close, okay?"

"Sure, Aunt Audrey, I got it all under control," Lucas promised.

"We'll see you at the museum."

Lucas opened the front door and walked out on the porch. He inhaled the sweet scent of honeysuckle in the night air. He knew Nolan and the Dìonadain would be close tonight. He was confident they would be safe. When a sleek black limousine stopped in front of the house, he grinned.

"Thank you, Mr. Talbot. The Quinns will be riding in style tonight."

Lucas considered his mom's association with Talbot Industries and the great man himself to be a real opportunity. Even though he had been spending a lot of his free time with Aiden the last few weeks, he hadn't been around Mr. Talbot much at all. He hoped he would have the opportunity to talk with him tonight. He could learn so much from a man like him.

Lucas greeted the towering African who slid from the driver's seat of the limousine. "Good evening, Mr. K."

"Mr. Talbot sends his regards, Master Quinn. Is your mother ready?"

"Just a minute, please." Lucas shouted. "Mom, Lily, the car is here!"

"Coming," Lily answered. She was a vision in midnight blue. The simplicity of the shimmering satin dress with its scooped neckline, cinched waist, and flowing skirt complemented her figure and coloring perfectly. Her thick blonde hair hung in waves around her shoulders. Her pearl and ivory mask was in place but he recognized the insecurity in her eyes. Lily needed approval but would never ask for it. He knew she didn't see what everyone else readily saw. She was beautiful. He wished she thought so too.

"So what do you think?" she asked nonchalantly.

"You look stunning," he said with meaning.

"Thank you, Luc. Wait 'til you see mom."

He turned as Mia descended the staircase in her strapless sequined crimson brocade floor-length gown. The beautiful silver Venetian mask she wore accented her elaborate up-do. His mother was beaming.

"You look amazing, mom," Lucas offered her his arm. "Shall we?"

"Oh my, I didn't realize a car would be picking us up," Mia exclaimed when she saw the limousine waiting at the curb.

Mr. K opened the car door. "Mrs. Quinn, if you please."

Lucas settled into the limo with Mia and Lily for the short drive. When they pulled up to the museum, he felt his mother squeeze his hand.

"It's okay, mom. Everything is going to be perfect tonight, you'll see."

Mia squared her shoulders. Lucas knew she had worked so hard to make this evening a success and now it was time to enjoy the fruits of her labor. The entrance to the museum was lit with thousands of sparkling lights. The lobby was alive with costumed street performers and acrobats reminiscent of the formal Venetian masquerades. The ballroom itself was picturesque in silver and white. White silk covered the walls while tall silver candelabras held shimmering candles.

Large intricately carved ice sculptures adorned the tables of food and drink. An orchestra played while the masked attendees swirled around the room in a dance. It was dazzling!

Once inside, Mia said, "You guys have fun. I'll be around if you need me. Now, I've got to go make sure everything is lined up for the silent auction later." She walked off into the crowd.

"Look out, here comes Zoe and Beni," Lucas said. "Is there anything about those two that I should know about?"

"Shh, Luc, they're just good friends," Lily winked.

"Mom really knows how to throw a party," Zoe remarked when she joined them. "Lily, doesn't Beni look handsome?"

"Stop it, Zoe," Beni said sheepishly, his cheeks flushed with discomfort.

"Zoe's right, Beni. You look very dapper in your suit and tie," Lily complimented.

Wanting to change the subject, Lucas said, "Let's all be on our best behavior and not embarrass mom. She..."

"Ooh, look, it's a chocolate fountain," Zoe interrupted.

Beni's eyes widened. "A chocolate fountain? Are you serious?"

"Let's go, Beni," Zoe urged tugging on his arm.

"I love America," Beni said with conviction, following Zoe to the dessert table.

"Those two are so funny," Lily remarked.

"Yeah, I guess so. Do you want some punch or something?" Lucas asked.

"Truth? I do but I'm so nervous I'm afraid I'll spill it all over me. Don't laugh," she warned.

"Come on, Lily. I would never laugh at you. Okay, maybe I would?" He smiled. "Here comes Aiden. Maybe he can show us the ropes?"

"Hey, dude. You don't look half bad, brother," he teased and then turned to Lily. "And Lily, you're as captivating as a star."

Lucas noticed Lily's blush at Aiden's compliment. He was torn—frustrated because he wasn't comfortable with the idea of Aiden and his sister together, but he was also happy. He wanted Lily to feel pretty and knew that a few words from Aiden had done just that. He decided some time alone for these two might not be such a bad idea after all.

"Watch yourself, Talbot," he warned good-naturedly and walked away.

Lucas got something to drink and scanned the crowd. There was Daniel, as expected, standing solemnly against the wall, looking as if he would rather be anywhere but here. It was no surprise to him—Daniel wasn't exactly the party type. Now, it was time for him to find a certain woman he hadn't been able to get off his mind and ask her to dance. He had rehearsed it all in his head. Unfortunately, Rafe had beaten him to the punch. His friend was in a corner chatting up the woman of his dreams, Lysha Talbot, drop-dead gorgeous in a skin-tight red dress—so much for practicing his opening line in the bathroom mirror. Time for Plan B, also known as winging it!

Lucas looked down at his drink and knew exactly what he was going to do. He walked up behind Rafe, turned his head ever so slightly, and proceeded to run right into him. Red punch ran down Rafe's shoulder, soaking his grey suit jacket. Just as Lucas had hoped, Rafe was startled. His friend spun around immediately, with a few chosen words hanging in the air.

Lucas was only too happy to smirk and say, "Oh man, I'm so sorry. I bet if you get some water on that jacket right away, it won't stain."

The realization that he had been beaten at his own game slowly dawned in Rafe's eyes.

"Okay, dude, I'll get right on that."

"Don't worry, I'll entertain Lysha while you're gone," Lucas called out.

"Impressive, for a college-boy," Lysha smiled. "But I think your mother is looking for you, Lucas. She's out on the patio." And with that, she simply walked away.

Lucas was dumbfounded. He wasn't used to a total crash and burn! Deciding he would have to think about that later, he went to find his mom. She probably needed his help with the fireworks that were scheduled to go off later in the evening. He made his way through the crowd and opened the French doors leading to the outdoor patio. He was surprised to see Mia standing close with Flynn Talbot in the moonlight. He moved into the shadow of a yew arbor and listened to their hushed conversation.

"Come away with me, Mia. I'll take you anywhere you want to go," Mr. Talbot insisted.

"I can't, Flynn, at least not right now. The children are just settling in, and my new job…" his mother responded. "I love being with you, I do. But I think maybe things are moving a little too fast. I'm not ready for a serious relationship yet."

Lucas was relieved when Mia pushed lightly on Talbot's chest to put some distance between them. He was shocked and angry. How could she have feelings for another man?

"I understand, Mia. I really do. I loved my wife very much, just like you loved your Eli. I truly believed I could never feel passion for another woman. But then I met you. I knew our paths were meant to collide. Meeting you was no mistake. I feel alive again. Tell me you feel it as well?"

Talbot took her hands in his and pressed them to his chest.

"I do, Flynn, and it scares me. I just need some time."

"You will have it then. I am a patient man. But Mia, you should know, I don't give up easily."

When Talbot bent his head toward Mia and she leaned into his kiss, Lucas exploded.

"Get your hands off my mother," he yelled, storming across the patio.

Mia broke away from Talbot's embrace. Her embarrassment at being caught by her son was plainly on her face. "Lucas, what are you doing here? And keep your voice down!"

"The better question, mother, is what are you doing?"

"Lucas Elijah Quinn, you will not speak to me in that tone."

"Excuse me, Mia. You and your son have some things to discuss," Flynn retreated quietly.

Lucas didn't spare Flynn a look. He only had eyes for his mother.

"How could you? You don't even know him."

"It's not for you to say what I should or should not do, young man. You know nothing about my relationship with Mr. Talbot."

"Oh, I get it. So now it's a relationship? How long has this been going on?"

"Nothing is going on, Lucas."

"So why exactly were you kissing him, if nothing is going on? How could you just forget about dad? And you know what we are up against. We are in a fight for our lives and you want a boyfriend? Please, make me understand, mom."

"I am a grown woman, Lucas. My choices are my own. Don't forget I am your mother. I would think I have earned your trust and respect by now."

"Obviously Flynn Talbot has the greatest respect for you," he said sarcastically. "Can't you see he is taking advantage of a lonely widow?"

His face stung from her slap. Mia looked at her hand and then at her son's face. She reached for him. "Luc, I'm so sorry."

He turned on his heel and walked away, leaving Mia alone on the patio.

The
Masquerade Ball

ANNUAL
FUND RAISING GALA

VENETIAN GLASS
EXHIBIT

CHAPTER 29
Chivalry

• • •

"So, princess, have you been thinking about me?" Aiden whispered in her ear.

She was almost afraid to breathe. It had been two days since their picnic at the Mill and all she had done was think about him. Was this really happening to her? She felt like the heroine in her very own fairytale. Here she was on the arm of the most gorgeous guy in the room. He made her feel special, like she was the only girl he could see. Aiden's black tuxedo, open collar white shirt and pirate mask only added to the magic.

Lily's blush was evident below her mask but she continued his question with some sass. "Patience is a virtue, you know."

Aiden responded with a woeful grin and put his hand up to his heart like it was a pretend dagger.

"You're killing me sweetness. But, I'll play by the rules— for a little bit longer," he stressed.

Lily smiled brightly and changed the subject, "I've never been to a party like this before."

"Well then, we must dance. May I?"

Lily took Aiden's hand. The pirate swept the princess onto the dance floor, turning her expertly around the room. Lily was suddenly very thankful for the dance lessons Audrey had insisted on this past week. The music swelled and the candlelight cast a warm glow on the couple as they danced.

"You're smiling again, Lily. I'd like to think it's because of me."

"Well, you do make me smile. But I was actually just thinking about my mom. I'm proud of her."

"You should be. I've been to quite a few of these fundraiser galas and this one is the best we've ever had," Aiden remarked. "Your mom definitely knows what she's doing when it comes to parties."

"Lucas and I have been worried about her. She's worked so hard—long hours. But it definitely paid off. Everything is truly lovely."

"I couldn't have said it better, myself."

"Look, there's Lucas." She nodded toward the end of the ballroom. "What is he doing?"

"Flirting, I'm sure—and with my sister I bet," he grinned.

"Ridiculous. No way would your sister give him the time of day."

"Hmm, you might be surprised. Unlike myself, Luc has got some serious skills when it comes to charming women."

"Whatever! You're as bad as he is," she giggled.

When she and Aiden circled back around the room again, she blurted out, "Look at that! Lysha just walked away from him. I told you. And Lucas is just standing there with his mouth hanging open. Epic fail!"

Aiden laughed, "You two have that whole brother-sister love/hate thing going on, don't you?"

"We sure do and we're very good at it. But, seriously, I don't know what I would do without him."

"You're secret is safe with me. Lysha and I have our moments too. Half the time she can't decide if she wants to be my mother or my big sister. But I wouldn't trade her for the world."

Lily was disappointed when the music stopped. When they were dancing, it was like it was only the two of them in the room.

"May I fix you a plate, my lady?" Aiden asked playfully.

Lily smiled. "Yes, please."

Aiden circled the buffet table, filling a plate with all sorts of sweets. Watching him, she thought how lucky she was. Since their time at the mill, she felt closer to him. Aiden was quickly becoming rather important to her. The walls around her heart were showing a few cracks now that he was in her life. She didn't know where it was going to lead but she definitely liked the path she was on.

"I wouldn't look so smug if I were you. It's not as if you mean anything to him."

Lily turned around to see Reese Pooley resplendent in a fuchsia-pink strapless dress that hugged her every curve.

"What are you talking about, Reese?"

"Don't play dumb blonde with me. You've been after Aiden since you came to town. But, you're pathetic plan isn't going to work."

"Reese, there is no plan. Aiden and I are friends. Even if we were more, it wouldn't be any of your concern."

"Everything about Aiden is my concern. Don't you get it?" Reese's shrill voice was garnering people's attention. "You're just a plaything—not even a pretty one at that!"

Lily closed the distance between her and Reese. She lowered her voice and looked directly into Reese's vindictive eyes.

"Seriously?" Lily asked with frustration. "Keep your voice down. You're making a scene. Why are you being so rude anyway?"

"The fact you're breathing is enough for me. But don't get too comfortable. Your new girl scent will wear off soon. And Aiden Talbot will only be a memory. You're family is nothing and you're nothing."

"Okay, that's enough," Lily said.

When she tried to walk away, Reese grabbed her arm and twisted it back hard. When she tried to regain her balance, Lily tripped on the hem of her gown and fell to the floor. Humiliated, she looked up into the laughing faces of Grayson Lee and Marshall Cooper who stood on either side of a triumphant Reese.

"Poor little Lily. She just doesn't know her place," Reese drawled triumphantly.

Lily wanted the floor to just open up and swallow her. Her magical evening had turned into a nightmare. Reese's theatrics had drawn a crowd. They were all looking down at her. She couldn't decide which was worse—their pity or their amusement. She was fighting hard to keep her tears at bay when a strong warm hand took hers. Aiden helped her from the floor gently. When she was standing, he raised her hands to his lips for a soft kiss. His dark eyes were full of concern.

"Are you okay?"

"Yes, but my pride stings a little."

"Not for long," he promised. When he turned on his friends, his warm expression was gone, replaced by cold fury.

"Enough, Reese! You're the one who doesn't know her place."

"Aiden, honey, we both know she's nothing to you," Reese coaxed.

"Wrong again! And I don't think this is the place you want me to tell you what I think you are?"

Reese's face went white. Her eyes flashed dangerously at Aiden. When she turned her murderous glare toward Lily, Aiden warned, "Don't even think about it."

An incensed Reese left the room in a whirl. Lily didn't think it was possible but the gaze Aiden turned on Gray and Marshall was so icy she shivered.

"Who do you think you are? I thought you two of all people would be above something like this. Reese has always been malicious. But you?"

"Come on, Aiden. We were only having a little fun. Like we all used to do before she came," Marshall nodded at Lily.

"No harm, no foul, dude! She's just a girl," Gray quipped.

Aiden lunged at Gray. His momentum was halted when Lucas grabbed his arm and pulled him back.

"Shake it off, man," Lucas urged. "They aren't worth it."

Aiden nodded. "You're right." He straightened his jacket and looked directly at Marshall and Gray. Lily could see both young men squirm a little at Aiden's meaningful glare.

In a clear cold voice, emphasizing every word, Aiden commanded, "Get out of here or I'll have you thrown out!"

As if on cue, the monstrous form of Mr. K appeared behind Aiden and Lucas.

"No need," Marshall said deliberately. "We were just leaving anyhow, weren't we Gray?"

"Yeah, this party has become tedious," Gray responded never taking his eyes from Aiden's. "This isn't over, not by a long shot."

After his so-called friends left the room, Aiden turned back to Lily, "I am so sorry, Lily. Please forgive me."

"Forgive you? Are you kidding? You saved me," she said. "If you hadn't come back when you did, I'm pretty sure Reese would have had another go at me."

"She's right, you did. I owe you, man," Lucas said. Then he grabbed her shoulders and squeezed. "And if Reese Pooley ever comes near you again…"

"Don't worry, big brother. I'll be ready for her next time," Lily responded with a grin.

"Are you sure you're okay, Lily?" Aiden asked again earnestly.

"I promise. I'm fine. Now, how 'bout my two favorite men take me to get some punch?"

"I think I'm partied out. Time for me to head home," Lucas said.

Lily noticed her brother's preoccupation. Maybe Lysha's rejection earlier had thrown him for a loop.

"Lucas, are you sure?" Lily asked. "It's still early—there's lots of pretty girls that would love to dance with you."

"Next time, maybe. Enjoy the night, Lily," Lucas said and gave her forehead a quick kiss. "Take care of her, Aiden."

Lily watched Lucas walk away. She was torn. Maybe she should go after him and find out what was wrong? Or maybe he was just tired and needed some time alone?

"Give him some space," Aiden urged. "I'm sure it's nothing."

"You're right," Lily agreed. "I just worry about him."

"He's lucky to have you," Aiden returned. "What would you like to do now, princess?"

She looked at Aiden and smirked playfully. "Well, considering what just happened, I think you owe me a dance, mister."

"Happy to oblige and I always pay my debts," Aiden said before twirling her onto the dance floor.

CHAPTER 30

Diamonds

• • •

LILY WAS THANKFUL FOR THE peace and quiet as she sat down on the couch in her favorite sweatshirt and pants with a big bowl of popcorn to watch *Star Wars*. She needed some alone time. So much had happened in the last several weeks that she needed to process. Everyone was busy doing something tonight so she had the house to herself.

When the doorbell rang, Lily thought she just might pretend no one was home. At the second ring, she gave in and got off the couch.

"I'm coming. Give me a sec." She flung open the door. "Aiden, what are you doing here?"

Ugh! Why did she have the most rotten luck? Here she was again, surprised by Aiden, and dressed in the worst outfit imaginable: Lucas's old sweatshirt and leggings.

"I just wanted to come by and see what my favorite girl was doing?" Aiden grinned. "It's been a week since the masquerade. I was kinda hoping you had been missing me?"

She knew she was blushing. "Okay, well, I was just watching a movie."

"Want some company?"

"I'd love that. Come on in."

She waved him into the den and then joined him on the couch. Sitting close to him, she felt the hum of electricity between them. She didn't think she would ever get used to it. And maybe she didn't want to.

"*Star Wars?* It's on my top ten list of favorite movies of all time," Aiden said. "I didn't take you for a sci-fi fan."

"I've got some surprises up my sleeve too, ya know?" She teased. "It brings back good memories. When Lucas and I were little, we used to pretend we were Luke Skywalker and Princess Leia. I loved it as much as he did."

"Sweet!" He grinned and grabbed a handful of popcorn from the bowl. "Since we're talking about favorites—this right here is the snack of champions! There's never not a good time to eat popcorn."

"I'll make sure to put that down on my list," she joked.

"You're making a list?" Aiden asked, wide-eyed. "Well, now, sounds like you might be thinking some about what I told you at the mill."

Playfully, she pushed on his arm. He caught her hand and intertwined his fingers with hers. After a quick and meaningful look into her eyes, he turned his head back toward the action on the television screen. Lily slowly laid her head on his shoulder and relaxed against him.

After a few minutes, he said, "So you know I'm leaving tomorrow for family vacation."

"Yes, Montana right? Your ranch?"

"Yeah, I love it there. The mountains are incredible, fantastic fishing and riding, and you haven't lived until you've seen the stars in a Montana night sky."

"I bet," she said wistfully. "You must be looking forward to time with your dad and sister?"

"It's the only time we're all together, no distractions. It will be good. My dad told me he has something special planned for me this time."

"That's really great, Aiden. How long will you be gone?"

"Dad said today we would probably stay for three weeks. So I won't be back until school starts. Our place is in the middle of nowhere, so I don't have good cell service. I've never minded it before, at least until now..."

"Don't worry, Aiden. Lucas won't do anything remarkable while you're gone," she teased. "You won't miss a thing."

"It's not Lucas I'm worried about."

Aiden was looking at her so intently—her face flushed. He was looking at her like she was the only girl in the world. She couldn't tear her eyes away from his. She had the sensation of sliding down a slippery slope.

"I don't understand."

"I think you do, Lily."

Aiden reached out, taking a strand of her hair and gently twirling it around his finger before letting it fall back into place. She caught her breath. Was this even really happening? And then he leaned in and kissed her, gently at first, but then more insistently. When he leaned back, she was so lost all she could do was stare at him, mute.

He must have been pleased by her stunned expression because a heart-stopping smile broke across the strong planes of his face. "I just wanted to give you something to think about while I was gone. I'll see myself out."

When he stood up, he placed a small blue box on the table in front of her. And as quickly as he had appeared, he was gone. Riotous thoughts crowded Lily's mind. Staring at the box, she touched her lips, still tingling from his. Scared but excited nonetheless, she picked up the box and opened it. Inside the box was a hand-written note lying on top of some tissue.

Lily,

Do you remember the night up at the river after your accident? You told me that night the stars reminded you of your father. And that when you looked up at them, you knew he was with you. You should have the stars with you always.

Aiden

Lily pulled back the tissue and looked at the sparkling diamond stud earrings in the box. She was overwhelmed.

Unknown to her, a lone figure, unseen to the human eye, watched intently from a distance. His beautiful glowing face was taut with strong emotion.

"Your anger is displaced, brother," Tov admonished gently from the darkness.

"She is making a poor decision. He is not for her. I'm sure of it," Jude said.

"It is not for us to judge or interfere, you know that."

"It's my duty to watch over her," Jude answered hotly. "I won't stand idly by while she gives her heart away, only for it to be broken into pieces when he tires of her."

"She must make her own choices, Jude. Good or bad. The council forbids otherwise. Remember, we are Dìonadain, not their friends or even their family. We can only intervene when they call upon us."

Tov moved next to Jude, willing him with his closeness to calm down.

"I will not see her hurt," Jude vowed, watching Lily.

Tov watched a single tear slide slowly down Jude's face. He knew the deep emotions that were coursing through his brother's being could not be held in check for long.

"I know your pain, Jude. I have felt it as well."

CHAPTER 31

Nightmares

• • •

LILY PEERED INTO THE MIRROR in the foyer and admired the diamonds in her ears. It had only been two weeks but she still couldn't stop thinking about him. Aiden was a chameleon. Most of the time he was charming, confident, and well-spoken, a wall with no cracks. But on the two occasions they had been alone together, he had been different. He was vulnerable, sensitive, and compassionate.

Who was the real Aiden? And did she really want to risk finding out? What did he see in her? She wasn't gorgeous like Reese. She wasn't alluring like his sister Lysha. She wasn't anything remarkable at all. How could a guy like him be interested in a girl like her? She was quickly working herself into an anxiety meltdown.

She climbed the stairs slowly wishing the stillness of the house would somehow flood into her being. Lately, she had started to hate the hours of the night because it meant only one thing: dreaming. She had reluctantly accepted the truth of who she was and her gift of visions only after Lucas had shown her the star-shaped sign on the skin behind her ear. She could no longer deny that she was a light-bearer. Her dreams were coming more often now and they frightened her. Nolan had told her to expect them to grow stronger each time. Every night, every ounce of energy was drained from her. It was like her dreams were a thousand pounds of chain wrapped around her body, heavy, cold and unforgiving. She was bound to them and their hidden secrets. Until she solved the mystery of her visions, the meaning of the images that visited her each night, she would never be free.

She got in bed and closed her eyes, willing herself to sleep. She longed for a deep dreamless sleep. Unfortunately, a few hours later she woke up screaming, her nightgown drenched in a cold sweat. She got out of bed shivering, barely able to stand on her own two feet. She fought for control as she walked unsteadily to Lucas's room. He was sleeping on his stomach, burrowed deep beneath the covers.

"Lucas, wake up—it happened again."

"What?" He rolled over and rubbed his eyes. "The same dream?"

"Yes but it was different this time. It was stronger, more vivid. I felt so cold and powerless."

"Lily, you're shivering." Lucas sat up and put a blanket around her shoulders. "Better?"

"Yeah, thank you."

"How was it different?"

"I was running down a long hallway. But it wasn't dark this time. I could see things that were hidden before. I think I was in an art museum. Paintings were hanging on the walls. People were standing around looking at the art. They were silent. When I asked them for help, they just ignored me."

"That's super weird. What about the little boy?"

"He was there. This time I grabbed his arm and he looked up at me. His eyes were pitch black, just deep empty holes in his face. He smiled at me and I felt my skin crawl. His eyes flamed hot blue and I ran. He chased me and when I looked back, he turned into an enormous two-headed green dragon."

"Wow, that's intense."

"You have no idea. It was so real. I screamed and tried to run away. But I stumbled and fell. I could feel the dragon's hot breath on my neck. I got up and started to run again. Then the girl shoved me out of the way when the dragon spit flames at me."

"The same Asian girl from the other dreams?"

"Yeah, but I still have no idea who she was. She gave me a small red bag and pointed me to another passage. This time you were there, Lucas, waiting on me with Daniel and Rafe. When we heard the woman again, moaning dreadfully like she was writhing in pain, we all followed her voice. The passage twisted and turned. It must have been going deeper underground because I was getting cold. The passage was a dead-end. And there it was..."

"What was it, Lily?"

"A large painting stood against the wall. It was moving, black swirls crawling all over the canvas. When I stopped in front of it and reached out, it exploded with blood. More and more blood kept pouring out, filling the space. I couldn't breathe. My nose was full of a sticky sweetness that made me want to vomit. Then I woke up."

"That's horrible. Do you have any idea what it means?"

"No, not really. But I'm pretty sure something bad is going to happen, and soon. I wish I understood it but I can't make sense of it. Shouldn't I be able to figure it out?"

"You have the power within you, Lily. You just need help to unlock it. We need to talk with Nolan. He will know what to do."

"I'm scared, Lucas. I think someone is going to die. Someone I love."

"Lily, we can't be sure what your dream means yet."

"But you can't be sure I'm not right. I keep thinking about what Nolan told me in training today. He said my vision is waiting for its appointed time; it hastens to the end and it will not lie. If the vision seems slow, then I must wait for it, for it will surely come. But what if it's terrible? What if I don't want to know what it means?"

"We've got to try." Lily was thankful for her brother's warm hug. "Hey, as long as we are both awake, we might as well go find him now. It's almost dawn anyway."

"Alright, give me a minute to get dressed. I'll tell Mom where we're going."

She went back to her room and put on jeans and a t-shirt. She pulled her unruly hair back in a ponytail and looked at her reflection in the mirror. The diamonds in her ears sparkled against the paleness of her skin. If only her dad was here. He would tell her to pull herself together and figure it out. She sighed, "I'm trying, Daddy. I'd appreciate a little help though."

"Come on, Lily. Let's go," Lucas whispered from the hall.

"Right, did you tell mom?"

"No, I thought you did. I hate to wake her so early, but she will be worried if we don't let her know where we are."

She knocked faintly on Mia's door. When her mother didn't answer, she slipped inside quietly. Mia's bed hadn't been slept in.

"That's weird," Lucas mused. "Mom never gets up this early."

When she looked up at the oil painting hanging over her mother's bed, she swayed abruptly. Lucas reached out and steadied her. It was the painting from her dream. The ornate black script shown against the red background of the canvas. She knew she had seen the painting before but hadn't been able to remember where. Now, here in her mother's room was the key to her vision. Aunt Scarlet had painted the picture for her mother when she and Lucas had been born. The Chinese letters spelled "mother." Fighting the waves of nausea rising from the pit of her stomach, the mystery of her dreams unraveled before her eyes.

She pointed to the picture and cried, "Oh no, Luc, I think Cain has mom!"

• • •

She watched the Quinn woman slowly awaken
and survey her surroundings. The delicate blue
silk-covered walls, the magnificent crystal chandelier
hung from the high ceiling, the dark wood four-poster
bed covered in blue satin, all foreign to the wretched woman.
Keket grinned when her captive sat up in confusion.
Sheer panic played across Mia's pale features. Hidden
in the dark recesses of the room, she watched Mia
walk quickly across the room and put her ear against the door.
Her smile widened when Mia turned the knob and cracked
the door just slightly so she could hear the voices outside.

"Why did you bring her here?" a woman's voice asked in frustration.

"Lower your voice, love—you will wake our guest," a deep voice
answered.

"Don't call me that. We haven't been that to each other
in a very long time. Answer me, Cain—why is she here?"

"I need her. Without Mia, the future cannot be known.
I will not let you interfere."

There was silence and then the woman spoke again,
this time more softly. "You never loved me, did you?
All the years I have given you, all I gave up for you? It was
meaningless."

"*I wouldn't say that. You did give me a perfect child, my first-born.*"

"*I thought when you killed her husband it was finished.*"

"*You were always a little slow, my love. It was our child, our perfect Keket,*
who killed Eli. Haven't you learned anything from your time with me?
Soon, my children, the Mescáths, will take this world for me."

"*No!*" *the woman wailed. "You have crossed the line. I am finished. I refuse…*"

The woman never finished her sentence. A loud slap echoed
through the crack in the door followed by the pitiful whimpering
cry of the woman. Mia closed the door and sank to the floor.
Keket moved from the shadows then and stalked toward her captive.
She imagined Mia was paralyzed with fear, her eyes wide and unblinking.
She was going to enjoy this!

CHAPTER 32

Brothers

• • •

"MIA QUINN HAS BEEN TAKEN. It happened quickly—her guardian had no time to warn us," Nolan reported to the Dìonadain Council.

"We must get her back," Othiel urged. "If we lose her, her children will be torn apart. If they lose faith now, Simon's key will remain hidden."

"It is not our task, you know this. The Sorcha must find her, rescue her," Nolan offered.

"They are not ready," Andreas boomed. "Cain will squash them like little bugs."

"We have a visitor," Asher announced from the entryway.

Agatha walked into the council chamber, holding a Scáth bound in glowing restraints. She bowed her head, curtly acknowledging the members of the Council. The Scáth stood silently, showing no signs of struggle. Dìonadain and Scáth had been enemies since the beginning of time. So to stand there and not seek to destroy required the utmost control. Nolan was very curious indeed.

"He came to us at the Centenary boundary. He says he has a message, Nolan," Agatha announced through her clenched jaw.

Nolan commanded the Scáth, "Well go ahead, speak!"

"My master extends an invitation. He wants to meet you and only you," the Scáth hissed.

"We don't take orders from you or your master!" Agatha spat.

"Where is Cain?" Nolan asked, his gaze never leaving the smoldering blue ones of the Scáth.

"My master said you would know," the Scáth answered.

"Escort him beyond our boundaries," Nolan commanded. Instantly, Agatha disappeared with the Scáth, leaving the council behind.

"You cannot mean to do this, Nolan," Hila said.

"It is most certainly a trap. A Scáth cannot be trusted," Othiel implored.

"I have no choice," Nolan announced. "Too much is at stake."

Andreas said, "I agree; however, watch your back. Cain is after something."

"Indeed. And I intend to find out exactly what he wants."

Nolan left his brothers behind to watch and wait. A flash of light and a thundering boom announced his arrival. The ground shook when he landed, his mighty wings imbedded with eyes waving in the cold wind. He was alone on the tor. The sky was grey and ominous—rain fell softly. This haunting place—frozen in time—was the same as it was the day Simon had been executed. Nolan grimaced and remembered.

The crowd mocked him. They circled Simon who was lay-ing in the mud. His clothes torn and his face battered. They kicked him again and again. Spitting curses and screaming for death. The crazed villagers drug him up from the mud and pulled him into the circle of giant stones. There they pushed him down on the altar. They tied his outstretched arms above him to a wooden pole. The same was done to his legs. Simon didn't resist although the extreme pulling of his muscles must have been excruciating.

Nolan stood silently outside the stone circle. His heart grieved for the light-bearer. But he knew as well as Simon did, a martyr's death was his cup to bear. Nolan spied the object of his guard-ian mission in the crowd—Amhlaid—Simon's son. His face was partially obscured by his rough wool cloak and hood—his body rigid—his eyes fixated on the center of the stone circle. Nolan knew Amhlaid would never desert his father. He would be with him until the very end. The boy was brave, loyal and unswerving in his devotion to his father and the light.

Nolan felt hot anger flash through him when the executioner entered the circle. The crowd roared in approval. Simon's lips moved silently in prayer. The executioner appeared as one of the villagers, garbed in black, but looks were deceiving. It was no human who would deliver death to Simon—it was Cain—his brother—his friend—the betrayer.

"Kill him, kill him," the crowd chanted loudly.

Cain raised a wicked steel saw in his hand. The blade was long and thick—its teeth jagged and sharp. A hush fell over the once frenzied crowd. Nolan watched as Cain laid the saw across

Simon's midsection. Simon's lips were still moving in prayer—his eyes wide open.

"Darkness has been waiting for you, light-bearer."

Before his first pull on the blade, Cain's eyes flashed cold blue. The blade cut raggedly into Simon's gut. A bright light burst from his belly. The people fell back shocked and afraid. Simon's body was cut through in a single stroke. No blood, no gore, no suffering. Simon's face was peaceful and at rest. Cain raised the blade and scowled at the etchings of light that now covered the saw. Nolan looked at Simon's son. His eyes were grave but his lips curved in a slight smile before he turned away and moved quickly into the forest surrounding the stone circle. Nolan followed knowing his mission had just begun.

Nolan moved instantly into his battle stance ready to counter any attack when he heard the crack of lightening. Across the windswept moor, the stunningly beautiful figure known as Cain exploded through the clouds and landed with a thud on the grassy plane. Nolan knew Cain's great beauty disguised the abhorrent evil residing in his black soul. His folded his monstrous leathery wings behind him and strode deliberately toward Nolan. Cain halted a few paces from him.

"Fitting, don't you think, brother?" Cain asked. "I thought our first conversation in a millennia should take place where it all began. You remember the stone circle. It still stands unlike Simon of course."

"We are not brothers, Cain. When you made the choice to join the Prince of this World, you marked yourself for ruin. Your greed and betrayal sicken me."

"Ha—so many empty threats, Nolan. Who could destroy me? Not you and surely not your precious little light-bearers. You've always underestimated me. It was your mistake with Simon, and even now your naiveté and unbending loyalty to Elohim blinds you to what you could have and to what you could be."

"Why am I here, Cain?"

"I want to offer you the world, brother. We have been at odds with each other for far too long. You will never unite the Sorcha; you must know this. The task is beyond you. I have thwarted you at every turn. This time will be no different, Nolan."

"The uniting will occur. I vow I will not allow you to kill any more Sorcha."

"Oddly enough, I agree with you. I don't want to kill any more light-bearers. It is truly a waste of their extraordinary potential. I have decided the power they possess is invaluable. Whoever can harness and use it will be undefeatable. Imagine it, Nolan—you and I, together. Through the Sorcha, we can wield the most powerful force this world has ever known."

"And Abaddon? He has approved your plan?"

Cain smiled slightly, "My prince has underestimated me as well."

"I would never join you, Cain. You are a deceiver, a traitor and a murderer. Soon, I will see you bound!"

"Pity. I don't know why I ever expected more from you, Nolan."

"What of Mia? Why did you take her? She is of no value to you."

"My plans for the Quinn woman are not your concern."

When Nolan spoke, his body flamed hotter with pulsing light. "Hear me, Cain. Your plan will never come to fruition because you have underestimated me and the overwhelming purpose and power of Elohim's Light. I will find the twelve no matter the cost. They will unite."

Cain's eyes flamed blue as he hovered in the air. "So be it. Remember, what happens now to you, to them could have been avoided. The burden is yours to bear."

Nolan found himself alone, looking out toward the distant waves crashing against the jagged cliffs. The situation was dire indeed. No longer was Cain just in service to Abaddon. He now imagined himself capable of ruling both the forces of good and evil. Nolan knew he could not allow it. He needed to consult with the council. Flying into the air, Nolan understood wherever Mia was, she was not a pawn in Cain's game of chess. Mia was the queen.

CHAPTER 33

Red

• • •

Lucas paced the den floor, impatient for Nolan's arrival. It had been less than an hour since he and Lily had discovered their mother was gone. He put his hand lightly on Lily's shaking leg as he walked by the chair she was sitting in. His sister was more agitated than he had ever seen her. He couldn't blame her. He didn't want to think about all the awful things his mother might be experiencing right now either. He had to stay calm and keep a cool head.

Everyone had gathered together, anxious for news about Mia. Beni and Zoe were on the couch, Jack settled between them. Rafe kept vigil by the front door, hoping Mia would return at any moment. Daniel stood by the window, praying quietly. Aunt Audrey was making phone calls to anyone who might have seen Mia before she disappeared.

"Lucas, please come and sit down. Nolan will be here soon. He'll know what to do," Zoe urged.

"I was such a jerk at the gala. If anything has happened to her, Zoe, I'll never forgive myself," he said.

"Don't say it! We have to believe we're gonna find her. I need my big brother now to tell me everything is going to be alright."

He wrapped his arms around his sister and hugged her tightly. "You're right, Zoe. We will find mom and bring her home."

"He's here," Rafe announced.

When Nolan walked into the room, Lucas blurted out the one question that had been burning in his mind for the last hour.

"Have you found my mother?"

Nolan ignored his question and turned to Audrey instead. "Any news?"

"Nothing," Audrey said desperately. "I talked to Mrs. Bradley at the historical society—no Mia. I contacted Della's, the park, even the library on campus and no one has seen her. Her car is still in the garage. I even took a long shot and called Flynn Talbot."

"What did Mr. Talbot say? Did he have any idea where she was?" Lucas asked.

Audrey shook her head. "None. He said he hadn't talked with her since yesterday. He was very concerned though and wanted us to let him know the moment she turned up. He told me he would call the Sheriff's Office immediately and file a missing person report."

"She was with him last night, wasn't she?" Zoe asked. "Did Mr. Talbot notice anything strange?"

"No, he said they had a lovely dinner and then he brought her home. When I talked with her before she went to bed, she was fine," Audrey answered.

Frustrated and dissatisfied, Lucas asked, "Nolan, do you know what's happened to my mother?"

"I believe I do," Nolan answered calmly.

From across the room, Daniel asked, "Cain has her, doesn't he?"

"I'm afraid you're right, Daniel," Nolan responded.

"But why?" Lucas demanded. "If he's after this generation of the Sorcha, why would he take her?"

"Cain's purpose is not yet clear," Nolan said. "But if he can succeed in filling your hearts and minds with fear, he knows you will lose your focus. I do believe Mia is in great danger."

"We have to find her before he has a chance to hurt her," Lucas insisted.

"Luc is right. Nolan, can you help us find Mia?" Rafe asked.

"The Dìonadain are combing the globe looking for any clue to her whereabouts, but Mia's location is still a mystery," Nolan answered.

"If the Dìonadain can't find her, how will we ever be able to?" Zoe said miserably and leaned her head into Beni's shoulder.

A heavy silence filled the room.

"Wait a minute!" Lucas exclaimed. "Lily, you can find mom."

"What do you mean, Luc?" Lily asked.

"You dream about what is to come, right? You dreamed about Mom being taken. So maybe Mom's location is in your dream as well."

"It's true, Lily, your dream might be the only clue we have to finding your mother," Nolan encouraged. "You see and can understand what is to come. Think—was there anything you might have missed?

Lily took a deep breath. "Last night my dream was more vivid than ever before. When I walked into mom's room this morning, I looked at the painting hanging over her bed and it all just clicked. But maybe I did miss something. I wrote it all down. Here, look." She picked up a piece of paper and showed everyone what she had drawn.

They all studied the curious symbols, words, and pictures Lily had drawn.

"Okay, spit it out. Tell us everything—the whole dream," Rafe suggested.

"Go on, Lily, you can do this," Beni urged.

Lily closed her eyes to concentrate. "In my dream, the long hall and the paintings hanging on the walls must be an art museum. The Chinese symbols on the painting that gushes blood are the same as the ones in the picture in mom's room. They mean "mother." I think the blood means pain or death. The woman moaning is mom."

"That's good, right? She's moaning so she's alive," Audrey offered.

"I agree with Aunt Audrey. She may be hurt but there's still hope we can find her," Lucas said.

"Keep going, Lily," Zoe urged.

"In the dream, when I'm searching, I ask the people standing around the museum for help, but they just ignore me. So I believe mom is hidden in a public place and nobody notices the evil right there in front of them."

"That makes sense," Rafe interjected. "But it doesn't narrow the location down for us."

"There was a little boy—I know he was a demon, I'm sure of it. When I got close to him, he looked up at me. His hollow eyes flamed blue so I ran. He ran after me, hissing, and I felt his breath hot on my back."

"That is horrible, Lily," Daniel said, gently laying his hand over hers. "I imagine you were very frightened."

"Way to go, Einstein!" Rafe said sarcastically. "Of course she was scared, Daniel, seriously?"

"Rafe, we don't have time for this," Lucas admonished. "Finish it, Lily."

Lily continued, "When I looked behind me, the boy shape-shifted into a monstrous two-headed green dragon. It happened so fast. He spit flames at me, but out of nowhere this Asian girl appeared and pushed me into another passage. She gave me a red purse and told me I was going to need it. You were there, Lucas, waiting on me. And so were Daniel and Rafe. I'm not sure what the dragon means yet. But I do know where we need to start our search for mom," she finished.

"Where exactly?" Lucas asked.

Everyone looked at Lily, a mixture of anticipation and dread on their faces.

"Chinatown, New York City," Lily said confidently.

Lucas stared at his sister in disbelief. "You're sure?"

"The Asian girl that rescued me from the dragon was wearing a Yankees baseball cap. In the painting, mother was written in Chinese script. Isn't it obvious?" She smiled.

His sister's confidence was contagious. For the first time, he felt like he could bring his mother back home. Turning to the others, Lucas said, "The time for talking is done. We need to act."

"We aren't ready, man. You are way ahead of us. We can't fully control our gifts yet," Rafe said.

"Rafe is right, there has to be another way," Daniel said.

"Tell him, Nolan. We aren't ready. The Dìonadain can rescue Mia," Rafe insisted.

Nolan looked intently at each one of the Sorcha. "I wish there was another way. But there isn't. You must trust in yourself and in each other. You can do this. Believe me, you are all ready. And remember, you only have to speak our name if you need our help."

"But what about me and Beni?" Zoe asked.

"Neither of you were in Lily's dream, Zoe. Her vision is prophetic so we must honor it if we are going to find mom," Lucas said.

"Please," Zoe stood up with her fists clenched by her sides. "You may need me. If Mom is hurt, I can help her."

Lucas tipped his sister's angry tear-stained face up to his. "We'll bring her home, Zoe. I promise."

"Alright then, I'll trust you. But don't take too long," she said bravely.

Lucas turned to Nolan and asked, "How are we gonna to get to New York City?"

Nolan smiled when Daniel answered, "I know a way, and it's very fast. Let's go outside."

Lucas and the others followed Daniel to the backyard. He lifted his head and said four simple words, "Elohim, make a way."

The ground trembled beneath Lucas's feet. A lightening bolt cracked across the clear blue sky. Five very familiar winged men radiant with the power of Elohim landed in the yard. Oddly enough, Lucas barely flinched when he recognized Jude among them. He noticed right away his sister wasn't surprised by Jude's appearance.

"Are you kidding me?" Rafe cried. "Jude? We all thought you were just Lily's nerdy tag-along. No offense, man."

"None taken," Jude replied.

Lucas looked at his sister and his friends. He knew they were headed into the fight of their lives—untried and largely unprepared—but he also knew the power of Elohim's Light would lead them. It was time for courage, for perseverance, and for trust.

"Your Dìonadain guard will transport you to the city. You'll be moving very fast through space and time. So hold on and keep your eyes open, okay? Believe me, it will help you with the queasiness," Nolan commanded. "Asher, you know what must be done."

Asher nodded. "Lucas will be with Kiefer, Rafe with Tov, Daniel with Ira, and Jude, you will take Lily."

"You can do this," Nolan charged. "Trust your senses, Lucas. Be mindful of the signs in your dream, Lily. Stay focused and sharp, Rafe. Keep your mind clear. And Daniel, keep them balanced. They will need your powerful faith."

Kiefer laughed. "Hold on, Lucas! This is gonna be the ride of your life."

CHAPTER 34

Purses

• • •

"What the heck just happened?" Lucas shouted.

The Dìonadain had flown them within moments from Audrey's yard in Cleveland onto a subway train barreling through a dark underground tunnel. Lucas looked around at the others who were all trying to get their bearings while fighting to remain balanced and upright on the fast-moving train. The car they were in was empty except for them.

Kiefir grinned. "Wicked ride, yeah?"

"I feel like I'm going to puke right now," Lily moaned.

"Breathe, Lily. It will pass in a moment," Jude assured.

"Man, I can't even feel my toes," Rafe swore to no one in particular.

The train stopped and the doors slid open. People filed out of the other subway cars onto the platform. Canal Street was emblazoned on the brick wall across from him.

"Okay, Lily, where do we go from here?" Lucas asked.

She stood staring at the open door.

"Lily, do we get off here or not?" Lucas insisted.

Lily exhaled loudly. "Yes, this is it, Chinatown."

Lucas exited the train with the others behind him, up the stairs and through the turnstiles into the main area of the subway station.

"Sorcha, we must part ways. We will be near, watching. Remember, call upon us if you need help," Asher said.

The angels, now dressed as normal men, followed Asher up the staircase and disappeared.

"Well isn't that just great? How are we supposed to do this without our guardians?" Rafe asked.

"It's up to us now. All of us," Daniel said. "We can do this. We are the Sorcha."

"Oh, the man can speak more than one sentence! Why don't you keep it to yourself, Daniel? I'm supposed to be the smart one," Rafe said sarcastically.

"We won't ever find Mia and get back home in one piece if we don't start trusting our gifts and each other," Daniel said.

"Are you guys done? We have a job to do. Come on, this way," Lily said.

Exiting the station, Lucas was assaulted by the sights and smells of Chinatown. It was like he had just entered a different country. Located in the lower portion of the island of Manhattan, Chinatown was an assault on the senses. Home to one of the densest populations of Chinese immigrants in the western hemisphere, Chinatown was bustling with activity. Street vendors were selling everything from hotdogs to perfume to ancient Chinese herbs. People crowded the streets headed to work or to the many shops, restaurants and businesses populating the area.

"Dude, what a gnarly smell!" Rafe crinkled his nose in distaste. "Atlanta's not anything like this."

"You wouldn't last long in Mosul, that's for sure," Daniel commented dryly.

Lucas followed Lily to a small grocery on the corner. She was quiet, observing everything around her. He knew she must have been revisiting her dream, looking for clues as to where they should go.

"I think we need to go shopping," she said suddenly.

"Shopping, are you kidding me?" Lucas questioned.

Lily looked directly into his eyes and said, "We need to buy a purse."

Rafe must have been just as dumbfounded as Lucas was when he said, "Come on Lily, a purse? Are you sure? What does that have to do with finding Mia?"

"We need to listen to Lily. She is the Dreamer. Let her use her gift," Daniel encouraged.

"I'm sorry, Lily. I won't doubt you again," Rafe assured.

Before Lily could respond, a young woman walked up to her and asked, "Hey, lady, you want Gucci or Prada?"

Lucas couldn't believe his eyes. Could it be? He looked at Lily and knew instantly from her huge smile this was the girl from his sister's dream. She was petite with long dark hair. She was wearing a New York Yankees baseball cap. She held a cell phone to her ear. She cut her eyes toward him and asked, "How 'bout Coach for you? I take you to secret place, no cops. Follow me?"

Lucas responded immediately, his heart racing, "Yes!"

The young woman nodded and waved them to follow her. She weaved in and out of the crowded streets, leading them farther away from the hustle and bustle of Canal Street. She walked quickly, turning around often to make sure they were following.

"Hurry now, not far," she encouraged.

"Are you sure this is a good idea, Lucas?" Rafe questioned. "I grew up in the city. A quiet neighborhood is trouble."

"I don't sense any danger but stay alert."

They followed her to the corner of Crosby and Howard Street. A kid dressed in jeans and a cheap "I Love New York" t-shirt was waiting for them.

"He will take you. Follow him to the pretty purses," she said and hurried back the way they had come.

"Okay, this is a little weird," Lily said.

"No kidding," Rafe agreed. "I think we just got passed off."

"Come on, let's keep moving," Lucas said.

Everyone followed the kid into a small storefront. When Lucas stepped inside, his nostrils burned with the smell of incense. Behind the counter was an old woman smoking a pipe. She looked like she was a hundred years old, with wispy white hair and deep grooves lining her leathered face.

Chinese umbrellas hung from the ceiling. Little Buddha statues, tea sets, and colorful embroidered clothes were on display. Stacked on shelves on the back wall were dozens of pairs of shoes. Lucas was unnerved when the kid they had followed stuck his hand in one of the shoes on the end of the fourth shelf. Pushing a concealed button in the shoe, a door in the wall to the right slid open.

"Quick now, you go in," the kid pointed.

"This just keeps getting better all the time," Rafe whistled, following the rest through the door.

Lucas and the others were now in a room about the size of a small closet. When the door in the wall behind them slid shut, another door opened opposite them. A small woman with eyes that disappeared in her chubby face motioned them forward into the dark space. The small light bulb hanging from the ceiling provided the only light. They followed her down a long metal staircase and stopped in front of another steel door. The woman rapped on the door three times. Immediately, the door cracked open and a man peered out. Bright fluorescent light beamed through the small opening. The man and woman exchanged a few words in Chinese. Then the man opened the door wide to let them in.

The small windowless room was brightly lit and stacked floor to ceiling with hundreds of counterfeit purses, bags, and wallets. Coach, Gucci, Louis Vuitton, and Prada in every color and design filled the room. Several shoppers in the room were oohing and aahing over the impressive array. Others were bartering for a good price with two Chinese women working in the room.

"Jackpot," Rafe announced. "Now which one do we buy, Lily?"

Lucas whispered, "Mom's close. I can sense it."

"Where?" Lily asked. "In this room?"

"No, I don't think so. The feelings are faint. But she is near," he answered.

"You buy? You stay. If not, you leave," one of the small dark-haired women said to Daniel.

"Well, figure it out, we don't have much time," Daniel suggested and walked toward the far row decorated with Louis Vuitton purses and asked, "How much for this one?"

"Look around, see if there's another door somewhere besides the one we came in," Lucas urged.

Rafe, Lily, and Lucas searched the space, pretending to look at the bags and purses. But they found no other entrance or exit.

"There's nothing here, Lucas," Lily whispered dejectedly. "The clues in my dream have led us here. I must be missing something."

"There!" Lucas pointed to a small crawlspace door just visible behind a row of handbags on the floor.

"Time you go. Must make room for others," the man announced.

"If we leave now, we'll never get back in," Rafe said.

"We don't have a choice. We'll just have to figure out how to get back in later," Lucas said.

He was frustrated. He was sure Mia was near. Would they get to her in time? Walking out of the store, he passed the old woman again at the counter.

"You find what you looking for, pretty boy?" she rasped.

"No, ma'am, not yet."

"You wait, pretty boy, it will come," she promised. She sat back in her chair, closed her eyes, and puffed on her pipe.

She was very strange, he thought. What had the old lady meant?

"Lucas, come here!" Lily motioned excitedly.

He jogged down the street to join the others. They were standing in front of a five-story structure adjacent to the storefront. It was dark grey and trimmed in crimson. Marble bas-relief faces topped every window. Painted in gold letters on the front door as well as the street-level windows was Dragoni Ltd, Antiquities and Fine Art. Peering through the windows, Lucas saw statues, vases, large columns, and paintings; all looked very old and expensive.

"Look, up there," Lily whispered.

Following his sister's gaze, he drew in a shaky breath. Emblazoned on a sign hanging over the door was a two-headed green Chinese dragon.

"It's the dragon from my dream," she said.

"Mom's got to be in this building," he said. "That's why I could feel her presence when we were in the basement of the store next door."

"Hey, kids, you need to move along," a burly police officer said from behind them. "Police business. We need to clear the area, now."

"We passed a coffee shop around the corner. Let's wait there 'til we can come back," Daniel urged.

"Agreed," Lucas said. "We need to plan our next move anyway."

They made their way to the coffee shop and sat at a table by the front window.

Lucas asked, "Lily, any other clues from your dream that might help us?"

"No, at least nothing that makes sense right now."

"Let me get this straight: We lost Mia. We took a vomit-inducing thrill ride in the arms of an angel. We followed a girl who probably speaks three words of English into a sketchy store in what might as well be another country. We entered a room, illegally, to buy a purse. We then leave without a purse and without Lucas and Lily's mom. Wow, I am so proud of us," Rafe said dryly.

"As hard as it is, we need to be patient and wait. Our path will be revealed to us a step at a time," Daniel said.

"Easy for you to say, man. It's not your mom being held and possibly tortured by demons at this very moment," Rafe responded hotly.

"Arguing isn't going to help us find mom any quicker," Lucas said pointedly. "We know where she is, so let's put our heads together and figure out the best way to get back in that building."

Rafe shook his head. "I can't believe I'm gonna say this, but I'm sorry Daniel, you're right."

"Apology accepted, my friend," Daniel said seriously.

"We're going to need help though," Rafe offered. "We need Asher."

The bell on top of the coffee shop entrance jingled. Asher walked through the door.

"You guys never cease to amaze me. That was brilliant," Rafe exclaimed.

Asher offered a quick smile and sat next to Lucas. "How can I help?"

"We think we know where mom is being held," he said.

"You are correct. She is being held on one of the upper floors in the Dragoni building. Scáths are everywhere. You will need to find a way to enter the building undetected," Asher answered.

"Most of these older buildings should have their floor plans on file," Lucas mused.

Rafe pulled his laptop from his backpack. "I'm on it."

While Rafe's fingers moved deftly across the keyboard, Lucas looked out the window. He noticed the same young woman from before leading another group of people down the street. She happened to look at him as she passed. He thought he saw a trace of anxiety in her eyes. He felt the same way.

He turned back to the group and said, "We need to make our move tonight. I'm afraid to wait any longer."

"I got it," Rafe announced. "The Dragoni building is built on top of some underground tunnels that were never fully developed by the city transit system. If we can get in through one of those tunnels then we can get to Mia."

"Rafe, memorize those plans, every nook and cranny," Lucas asked.

"Done." Rafe stared at his computer screen.

"Lucas, why are you smiling?" Lily asked.

"I think I know how we can get in."

He watched the girl with the Yankees cap run by the window. He wasn't surprised to see the burly officer from before chasing right behind her.

"Asher, come with me."

Lucas was out the door with Asher right behind. He ran down the street in the direction of the police officer. He couldn't see the girl ahead but he knew he had to get to her before the cop caught her. She was their ticket into the Dragoni building. When he saw three familiar figures dressed like cops join the chase, he grinned. Kiefer yelled at the burly cop and pointed down a side street. The cop didn't hesitate and followed Kiefer away from the main street. Ira and Tov barreled across the street after Kiefer. Asher pointed down a nearby alley and disappeared in the crowd. Lucas edged quietly into the shadowy space between the tall buildings. Trash littered the street. Clothes hung from lines that were strung overhead between the buildings. Lucas paused by a fire escape ladder.

From behind a battered green dumpster, she lunged. Knocking him to the ground, she hopped up, ready to run. But he was too quick. He grabbed her ankle and pulled her back down. He rolled over on top of her and pinned her to the concrete.

"Stop struggling! I'm here to help."

Her movements stilled and she looked defiantly at him.

"The cop chasing you will be here any moment. I'm the best shot you've got."

For a split-second, he thought the girl would not comply. But a slight nod of her head was all the agreement he needed.

He released her and they ran to the end of the alley. A taxicab was waiting.

"Get in," Asher ordered.

The taxi pulled away just as Kiefir and the burly police officer ran into the alley.

"I owe you, whoever you are," she said. Her broken English was gone replaced by a perfectly American accent.

"'You're welcome," Lucas replied. "And don't worry, I have an idea of how you can repay me."

CHAPTER 35

Tunnels

• • •

"LUCAS, WHERE HAVE YOU BEEN?" Lily asked anxiously.

His sister, Daniel, and Rafe were waiting with Jude and Tov in front of a four-story walkup in the heart of Chinatown.

"Good, you're all here," he said. "Everyone meet Wei Sung. She's going to help us get inside the Dragoni building."

Wei asked, "All of them? You didn't tell me there were so many."

"No, just the four of us. The other two men won't need to be shown the way."

"You're all crazy. There is evil in that place," Wei announced. She paused, doubt written all over her face. "But I always repay my debts. Let's go, we need to talk to my grandmother."

"We will wait outside," Tov said.

Lucas nodded. He and the others followed Wei to the fourth floor. A sweet cloying smell intensified the higher he climbed. His eyes started to burn.

"It's incense. My grandmother loves the stuff." Wei unlocked the door at the top of the stairs and went in.

The young boy from the souvenir shop greeted her. He cocked an eyebrow and asked, "Who are they?"

"Just some friends. This is my little brother, Junjie."

"Hello, pretty boy."

Lucas recognized that voice. When he turned, he wasn't surprised to see the same old woman from the store sitting in a recliner in the living room of the small apartment.

"I see you found what you were looking for."

"How did you know?"

"I know many things, pretty boy."

"Nainai, this is Lucas Quinn. He helped me get out of some trouble today. This is his family."

"Thank you for saving my Wei. She is a smart girl, been working the streets since before she was a teenager. Now she is in charge of our little business." She turned to her granddaughter and asked, "How will you repay the young man for his service to you?"

"He wants me to help him get into the Dragoni building."

"No! I will not allow it." Her face paled. "Remember the promise."

Lucas interjected, "Mrs. Sung, I believe my mother is being held captive somewhere in the building. I have to find a way in and rescue her. If I don't get to her soon, she might die. I need Wei's help."

Lucas watched while Mrs. Sung studied the group around her. She must have seen something in them that communicated to her their desperate need. Lucas knew when she had made her decision.

"Sit down, my children," Mrs. Sung commanded gently.

Everyone did as she asked, finding places around the small room.

"There is a path. But it is very dangerous and I am not sure where it will lead. Wei knows the place, a small door in the room where we keep the purses. We keep it locked. It leads down into the bowels of the building, but we dare not venture there. Long ago, my family promised to never enter or we would be killed."

"Mrs. Sung, believe me, I wouldn't ask if there was any other way," Lucas said.

"Yes, I see that. When I saw you walk into our store today, I knew the time had come. We can no longer keep our promise."

From around her neck, she pulled a long chain. Dangling from it was a key. "Take this," she said to Wei. "Be watchful, little one. Evil lurks in dark places."

"Yes, Nainai. I'll be careful."

"Thank you, Mrs. Sung," Lucas bowed gratefully.

Back outside, Lucas shared their plan with Tov and Jude.

"What you are about to do, it will be dangerous," Tov said. "Don't hesitate, be quick and sure. Mistakes will get you killed."

"I understand," Lucas said. "We all do."

"If you need us…" Jude said looking directly at Lily. "You know what to do."

Tov and Jude walked down the street and disappeared into the night.

"Well, that's it then. This is really going down," Rafe said seriously.

Lucas looked around at the others. There was no mistaking the fear in their expressions, but they were also clearly resolved to doing what had to be done. "We can do this," he stated deliberately.

"We're not going to do anything if we don't get a move on," Wei urged impatiently. "Ready?"

"Ready," they echoed.

In the darkness, Wei led them through the empty streets back to her family's store.

"I thought this was the city that never sleeps," Rafe whispered, the edge in his voice apparent.

Wei whipped her head around and glared at Rafe. Putting a finger to her lips—the unmistakable sign for "shut up." Lucas and the others followed her into the dark store. They made their way down to the room full of purses.

Wei paused, holding the key, and said, "After I unlock the door, you're on your own, okay?"

"I understand. Thank you, Wei, for bringing us this far." Lucas took her hand and gave it a slight squeeze. When he tried to move his hand, she held on to it.

"We're square now, Lucas," she said quickly. "And if you make it out of this alive, you know where you can find me."

Wei dropped his hand and turned to the small door. Crouching down she slipped the key in the lock and turned it. The door popped open, releasing a cold blast of air.

"Okay, guys, stick close," Lucas urged.

"Can I come too?" a small voice asked from behind them.

"Junjie, what are you doing here?" Wei snapped. "Go home now!"

"I won't," Junjie refused. "You can't make me."

Wei moved deliberately towards her brother.

"Be still!" Lucas shouted.

Wei and Junjie froze responding to the direct command.

"What is it? What's wrong?" Daniel demanded.

Lucas's whole body tensed. Shrieking sounds pierced his hearing and ghastly smells filled his nostrils. All of his senses were magnified, in overdrive, the same way it had been in the clearing so long ago. Speaking to no one in particular, he said, "They're here."

"Who's here?"' Wei demanded.

"I can smell them. They're upstairs." He exploded into action. "Get in the crawlspace, now!"

Rafe dove through with Daniel following behind.

"Come on, Lily," he insisted. His sister was paralyzed with fear.

"There's no time, Lucas," Daniel shouted.

He grabbed Lily and shoved her through the door. He looked at Wei and her brother who still stood by the far wall. Their eyes were large and filled with panic. The shrieking was getting closer. He held out his hand.

"Wei, you have to trust me," Lucas said and held out his hand.

Wei pulled Junjie to the door and pushed through. He slammed the door behind him. He had crawled about twenty paces when the crawlspace dipped, opening up into a large tunnel. When he joined everyone, he was glad to see Lily was herself again and standing close to Rafe and Daniel.

Lucas commanded, "Rafe, lead the way."

Rafe ran down the tunnel with everyone close behind. He never paused, anticipating every right and left turn. Lucas knew his friend had memorized the schematics of the underground tunnels. Rafe paused at a fork in their path.

"They're coming, Rafe. I can still smell them. They're close," Lucas urged.

"Who's coming?" Wei asked.

He answered simply, "Death."

Junjie whimpered, "I want to go home."

"Lucas, you're scaring him," Daniel admonished. "Like it or not, Wei, you and Junjie are in this now. You can't go back the way you came. If you want to help your brother get back home then we have to keep moving forward."

"Promise me Junjie will be safe?"

"I will take care of him," Daniel promised.

Suddenly a cold wind blew down the tunnel. Lucas grimaced. The stink was overwhelming. He looked behind and recognized familiar silver lights twisting and writhing, hurtling at great speed through the tunnel.

"Which way, Rafe?" he yelled impatiently.

"Relax, man." Rafe pointed to his head. "It's all right here."

Rafe took the left passageway at a dead run. The demons were gaining. The air was so cold it was difficult to run. The tunnel rumbled with thunder and the Scáths awful shrieks pierced the shadows rolling around him. The path snaked to the right and ended suddenly. It was a dead-end. Their escape was halted by solid concrete block wall.

"I thought you knew where you were going?" Lucas admonished.

"I do. This wall wasn't in the schematics. It must have been put up after they were drawn," Rafe answered.

"Those things are almost on us," Wei cried.

Junjie whimpered from the shelter of Daniel's arms.

Lily shouted, "There's no way out. We're trapped."

"There must be a way," Lucas yelled. "We just need to get through this wall."

"Last time I checked people couldn't walk through concrete walls," Rafe retorted.

"Please, please, don't let us die." Wei slammed her hand against the wall and it disappeared into the concrete.

Lucas stared at her missing hand and the concrete wall that was now shimmering and fluid like liquid. Wei didn't even notice. Her head was bowed and her lips were moving furiously in Chinese.

"Whoa!" Rafe exclaimed.

"Put both hands on the wall, Wei," Lucas commanded.

Wei looked at where her hand should have been and inhaled sharply. Without hesitation, she put her other hand against the wall. Again, her hand passed through, creating a soft shimmering space.

"Focus on getting us through the wall," Lucas urged.

Wei concentrated on the wall. A large circle opened in the center where her hands were.

"That's freakin' amazing," Rafe whispered in awe. "You did it."

Daniel grabbed Junjie and jumped through the wall. Rafe and Lily followed. The silver lights had arrived. Right before Lucas' eyes, the lights exploded into two beautiful silver-masked Scàths. Lucas grabbed Wei, throwing them both through the opening she had made. It immediately closed behind them.

"Don't let them pass," Lucas directed.

Wei lifted her hands and created a golden shimmering barrier between herself and the wall. When the Scàths came through the wall, a pulsing golden light prevented them from coming any closer. Screaming, they disappeared back through the wall.

He grabbed Wei's arm and lifted her from the floor. "We gotta move!"

Wei was in shock. Her pupils were dilated in her dark eyes. Her arms hung limp by her side.

"What happened to me?"

"We don't have time, Wei. The Scàths are coming back. We can't stay here," Lucas said.

Wei stared back belligerently. "I feel like I just got a swift kick in the gut. My whole body is buzzing with electricity and I have no idea what just happened. So I'm not going any further until somebody talks."

When she wavered, Lucas gripped her shoulders to steady her.

"I think we've just found our Wielder," Lily said.

Rafe nodded his head. "Good, we're definitely going to need her to get out of this."

"What?" Wei asked.

Lucas explained, "The Wielder. It means you can do the impossible, the miraculous, like the hole in the wall. Look, I know you are scared. I am too. Wei, I believe our paths crossed today because we were meant to. But if the Scáths get to us, they will kill us."

"I am freaking out right now!" Wei exclaimed. "I'm in the middle of a very bad dream."

Junjie grabbed his sister's hand. "But you saved us, Wei."

Lucas squeezed her shoulders insistently.

"Okay, but once we're out of here, you all have a lot of explaining to do," she said.

Moving away from the pulsing light barrier Wei had created, Lucas realized they were no longer in a tunnel but in a dimly lit hallway.

"If my calculations are correct, and they usually are, we are now in one of the sub-basements of the Dragoni building," Rafe boasted.

Lily said, "This is the hallway in my dream. You found it, Rafe."

"Which way, Lily?" Lucas asked.

To his left was a stairwell leading to who knows where and to his right a series of metal doors, keeping what lay beyond each a terrifying secret.

Before Lily could answer, the fluorescent lights overhead sparked and faded, plunging the hallway into absolute darkness.

"Grab someone's hand. We can't get separated," Lucas ordered.

"I don't know which way to go," Lily whispered. "I can't see."

Lucas focused his senses on his surroundings and made a choice. "Follow me—don't let go."

He turned right and inched down the hallway, running his hand over each metal door he touched. He tried each door but each one was locked. When he reached the last door, he paused. Lily squeezed his hand as if she sensed her brother's uncertainty. He squeezed back.

"No matter what happens, whatever might be behind this door, don't you dare let go of my hand, do you understand? Nobody lets go!"

"We're right behind you, boss," Rafe assured.

Lucas turned the handle slowly and entered the unknown.

CHAPTER 36

Twins

• • •

"Finally! Mia said you would come."

Lucas gasped. Standing in front of him was a carbon copy of his mother but yet it wasn't her. This woman had the same face and body, but instead of Mia's pale blonde hair, she had fiery auburn hair. Her long black dress only accentuated the paleness of her face and willowy frame. Purple bruises mottled her lower jaw and shadows smudged her stormy blue eyes.

"Who are you?" he asked suspiciously.

"I'm your Aunt Scarlet, Lucas, your mother's twin sister."

"But you're supposed to be dead," Lily scoffed.

She smiled faintly. "I'm afraid I am very much alive."

"How do you know who we are?" Lily asked uneasily.

"Your mother has a picture of you in the locket she is wearing. I guess seeing her again gave me hope. I managed to escape the room I was in and made it down here. We need to get Mia out of here before the worst happens."

"What do you mean? The worst?" Lucas questioned abruptly.

Scarlet looked directly at him and said, "He wants your mother to bear him a child."

"A child? That's just crazy." Lucas couldn't wrap his mind around the idea. "But Cain is a demon—is that even possible?"

"The joining of a Scáth and a Sorcha can produce a child of such great power and strength, he is virtually invincible. A child born of the union of light and dark is known as a Mescáth. Cain is creating an army of Mescáths, his children. This is the reason he took me and why he wants your mother now."

Lucas swore. "I'm not gonna let that happen. He's not laying a hand on her. Where is she?"

"Cain moved her to the training arena. There is only one way in and out of the room. He knows you're here and my guess is he's using Mia as bait."

"So I guess a surprise rescue is out of the question, then?" Rafe smirked.

"We don't have any other choice," Lucas said with resolve.

Scarlet smiled slightly and said, "Alright then, stay sharp. Scáths are crawling all over this place."

She led them out of the storage room and down a short hallway into an elevator.

"Hold on," she suggested as the elevator plummeted to its destination.

The doors slid open to reveal a long dark tunnel lit by torches. The air was cool but to Lucas the smell of Scáth was distinct.

"Stick close, everyone. I can sense them all around us," Lucas said. "Remember, the battle is real."

"This way," Scarlet motioned.

They followed her through a gate into a large circular arena surrounded by ten terraced rows. It looked like a coliseum from ancient times where spectators would come to view the bloody fights of seasoned gladiators. There was no visible ceiling—they could have been outside now in the deepest darkest night he had ever seen for all he knew. A single light bore down on a spot in the center of the arena floor. Lucas broke into a run when he saw his mother standing within the light. She was chained to a tall wooden pole.

"Mom!"

"Stop, Lucas," Mia screamed. "Don't come any closer."

Right in front of his feet, cold blue flames erupted, encircling the space around Mia. The flames burned so high he couldn't cross. When he caught sight of the ugly purple bruises on her arms and neck, he shuddered with rage. He quickly studied the blue flames looking for any gap that he might get through.

"Mom, I'm going to get you out of here."

"You shouldn't have come, Lucas. Cain is too powerful."

His eyes never leaving his mom, he ordered, "Wei, find a way through these flames."

"You can't be serious! I can't do that, Lucas."

"Just like before. Focus on what you need."

Daniel added insistently, "Elohim's light is within you, Wei. Use it."

Wei concentrated on the flames, extending her hands toward them, but nothing happened. If anything, they only appeared to get higher and stronger.

"It's not working," she shouted.

"Keep trying. You can do this," Daniel urged.

"He's coming," Scarlet breathed softly.

"I know. I smell him," Lucas said. "Hang on, Mom. I will not leave this place without you."

The air in the arena grew suddenly colder. Thunder rumbled and echoed low and angry. Ominous black clouds formed over the arena, whipping up the cold air. Silver-white lightening cracked and a cloaked figure walked towards him across the arena's dirt floor. His long flaming crimson hair waved around the silver faceplate he wore. He stopped across the flaming circle opposite the Sorcha.

"What a touching family reunion." The man's icy voice sliced through the air like steel. "It almost brings me to tears, really."

Knowing he must not panic, understanding he must now live everything he had been taught and all he believed to be truth, Lucas announced bravely, "We don't fear you."

"Many before you have made the same mistake. Young Quinn, so much like your father, quick to defend and protect. Isn't he, Mia? Will you die with as much bravado as your father did?"

Lucas answered, "You forget you are standing in the presence of the Sorcha. Light obliterates darkness. Now, let my mother go."

"Arrogance is the folly of youth, Lucas. I count only five light-bearers. Without the twelve, your power is no match for mine."

"Why hide behind a mask? Show yourself, Cain," Lucas challenged.

"With pleasure," Cain crossed the flames separating him from Lucas. His stench was overpowering, a sharp contrast to his beautiful perfection. Towering over Lucas, he slowly removed his silver faceplate.

Lucas gasped. He couldn't believe his eyes. Behind the mask was Flynn Talbot.

"You're surprised? Well, of course you are, pitiful Sorcha. The truth was always right in front of you but you were too blind to see it. And, of course, Nolan let you come here without knowing the truth. Don't you wonder why?"

"You're just one, and we are many. Looks like the odds are in our favor," Rafe boasted.

"I've been remiss. Let me introduce you to my brothers."

Swooping down out of nothingness, hundreds of Scáths landed all around the arena. Their shrieking chant caused Lucas and the others to grab their ears to muffle the painful sound. Daniel tried to shield Junjie from the beautiful and terrifying demons hissing at them.

"What do you think of the odds now, Mr. Rafferty?"

"We can't beat them. There are too many of them," Lily said desperately.

"Your sister is correct. Listen to her, Lucas. You are weak and defenseless. Did you really think you could waltz right in and take your mother from me? Did you think you could best me?" The demon raised his arms and thundered, "I am Cain, commander of the demon horde, the deliverer of darkness!"

The Scáths answered their master with frenzied shrieks. Lucas fought hard to stay focused and not let his riotous senses overwhelm him.

"Let my mother go or you'll have a fight you won't soon forget."

Cain threw back his head and laughed. "I'll take that as an invitation."

He unhooked the clasp of the long shimmering cloak covering his body to reveal a perfectly muscled physique, amazing in its vitality and strength. Dark green markings writhed across his exposed chest, arms, and head. His eyes flamed cold blue when he began his hideous chant.

"I think you riled him up pretty good," Rafe exclaimed.

"Now, Lucas," Lily urged. The Sorcha joined their hands with him and stood courageously in the face of the enemy.

Daniel prayed, "Great and mighty Elohim, out of the belly of the beast we cry, and we believe you will hear our voices."

Cain raised his hands and the Scáths hissed in recognition. Hundreds of flaming blue eyes pierced the darkness of the arena. When he dropped his arms, signaling the attack of his Scáths, Lucas and the Sorcha bellowed, "Dìonadain!"

Instantly, hundreds of glowing winged warriors thundered into the arena, surrounding the Sorcha in an orb of golden light. Swords and shields drawn, they took their battle stances, prepared for the onslaught of Scáths. Darkness met light, exploding in thousands of white-hot sparks.

Blue flames shot from the Scáths hands as they tumbled and flew through the air. The Dìonadain, perfectly in sync, deflected their advances, using their weapons like warriors of old. The crash of Scáth on Dìonadain was deafening.

Asher appeared within the impregnable fortress the Dìonadain had secured around the Sorcha, followed by Tov,

Kiefer, Ira and Jude. They drew their gleaming swords and drove them simultaneously into the ground around the flaming blue circle surrounding Mia. The flames died instantly and Lucas ran to his mother.

Looking to Asher, he said, "Help me get her out of here."

"Jude and Tov will lead you from the fray. Ira and Kiefer will guard the rear. We will take care of things here," Asher instructed before running back into the frenzied mob of Scáths.

"Let's go already!" Rafe yelled.

"Jude, what are we waiting for?" Lucas shouted.

But Lily's guardian wasn't listening. Lucas watched the golden warrior reach his hand out and lightly touch Lily's face.

"I've got you," Jude said solemnly. Then he turned to Lucas, his sword glowing hotly and commanded, "Follow me."

Lucas knew the power of the Light encased in a Dìonadain warrior's sword was the only thing able to bind a Scáth. He grabbed Lily and motioned for the others to follow. Jude and Tov charged through the golden orb, cutting a path through the hissing Scáths barreling toward them. He marveled at the precision and skill of the Dìonadain warriors. Kiefer and Ira acting as the rear guard, kept the pursuing Scáths at bay. Exiting the arena, the Sorcha and Dìonadain ran down the torch-lit tunnel back to the elevator.

"We made it," Junjie whispered.

Lucas was about to agree when a sense of dread settled in his gut.

CHAPTER 37

Betrayed

`• • •`

THE ELEVATOR DOORS SLID OPEN to reveal another threat even more deadly than a room full of bloodthirsty Scáths.

"Aiden," Lucas whispered painfully, rocked to the core.

Lucas couldn't believe what he was seeing. His best friend stood defiantly with his beautiful sister in the elevator. Both Lysha and Aiden were dressed in supple black leather. Dark green tattoos twisted around their exposed arms. Their eyes were glowing blue orbs and their palms were crackling with blue flames. Mescaths!

"I've been dreaming of this day, little Sorcha," Lysha taunted.

When she stepped from the elevator, the Dìonadain moved instantly to protect. Lucas stood immobile, trying to get a grip on reality. Lysha circled the group slowly.

"I've waited so patiently for you, Lucas. Since the day I killed your pathetic daddy in the snow. The beasts feasted on his flesh but I was the one who took his life. He was my first."

Cold rage coursed through Lucas.

Lysha caressed the crystal vial hanging around her neck. "I wear your daddy's blood. It reminds me of the glorious victory to come when Elohim and His Light are extinguished forever."

He sprang toward Lysha but Kiefer restrained him. He swore, "I'll kill you myself, demon."

"Don't tease, little Sorcha. I am both light and dark joined in one body. I am more powerful than you can imagine."

"Do something, man," Rafe urged Jude. "This is gonna get outta hand."

Lysha continued circling the group, spitting her taunts. "Your guardians are weak, pitiful really. Did you know a Dìonadain cannot attack unless he is provoked? I would have to hurt one of you before they would even move."

Lysha stopped in front of Ira. "Isn't that right, Dìonadain? Is it control or fear keeping you silent? Your race doesn't deserve to be called warriors!"

"Lysha, stop this. Your father has blinded you with his lies," Scarlet implored.

"Don't beg, mother," she said with contempt. "It shows your weakness."

"Mother?" Lucas whispered under his breath.

Was it possible? Her father a demon and her mother a light-bearer? What about Aiden? Was he as evil as his sister? He wouldn't accept his friend's betrayal without a fight. The noise of the ongoing battle in the arena stormed closer. The Scáths were drawn to the Sorcha like moths to flame. Lucas knew they were running out of time. Desperately, he looked to Aiden standing silently in the elevator. He was the one he had trusted above all others, the one who had unlocked his sister's heart.

"Lysha, my sweet girl, please, let us pass," Scarlet cried.

"I am not Lysha. I am the darkness before midnight. I am Keket!"

"No! You are my Lysha, my little girl," Scarlet pleaded. "I believe there is good in you because you are a part of me."

Lysha's livid face crumpled. Her body shuddered. "Mother, please forgive me," she sobbed.

Scarlet ran to embrace her daughter, a relieved and thankful smile beaming on her tear-stained face. Lysha looked into her mother's eyes and said, "I love you, dearest mother."

The crack of Scarlet's neck snapping in two echoed throughout the tunnel. Lucas watched in horror as his aunt's limp body slipped to the floor. The look of pure and unadulterated satisfaction on Keket's face rocked him to his very core. She was cold, violent, without remorse—everything he abhorred. She was pure evil.

Mia screamed in disbelief. Lucas turned to comfort her but Daniel was already there. He held his mother, soothing Mia with soft words while her body was racked with sobs. A terrified Junjie held Mia's hand. Lucas looked back at his friend standing in the elevator. For just a moment, Aiden's expression showed his confusion and disbelief. A tiny chink in Aiden's armor of evil was all Lucas needed.

"Aiden, come on, man. This isn't you. You can make a different choice," Lucas urged.

"Please, Aiden, do it for me," Lily begged, tears flowing freely down her face. She reached out her hand towards Aiden. "You're breaking my heart."

Keket warned, "Remember who we are, brother."

Aiden met his sister's challenging gaze. Lucas watched his friend's eyes flame intensely. In that moment, Aiden was gone, a vile demon left in his place. Thunder boomed. Keket and Aiden spun wildly around the group. Sister and brother burned fiercely, their violent spin creating an ear-piercing hum. Grabbing his ears, Lucas fell to his knees. He writhed painfully on the floor. His agony so excruciating he felt his brain cells start to implode. Desperate, he cried out, "Elohim, help me."

Suddenly, the pain disappeared and the debilitating hum became a dull echo. When he opened his eyes, everything was moving in slow motion. Like viewing a movie frame by frame, he watched the Talbots spin and the Dìonadain track their movement. Aiden and Keket stopped suddenly on opposite sides and flung fiery darts at the Sorcha. Lucas was instantly jarred back into real time.

Tov, Kiefer, and Ira deflected the fast and furious shots while Jude, never leaving Lily's side, thrust his sword deeply into the stone floor creating a glowing defensive barricade around the Sorcha. He swung his armored shield in an arc over his head, sending bolts of white-hot light toward the Talbots. Keket and Aiden jumped in the air, turning and contorting their bodies, narrowly missing the powerful blasts.

"You will pay for that, Dìonadain," Aiden threatened Jude.

Keket threw a lightening bolt toward Jude's glowing shield. When it exploded, smoke blinded Lucas for a moment. When his vision cleared, Aiden stood in front of him. Smiling wickedly, Lucas knew he was amping up for an even more powerful attack. Aiden's palms roared with purple-blue flames and he flung them toward Lucas. But Ira was there to deflect the darts with his monstrous shield. Lucas was knocked back into a corner when Mr. K ran from the arena and pummeled into Ira.

The impact of their bodies shot sparks all around. The Sorcha were now vulnerable, their rear guard engaged in one-on-one combat with Mr. K. Jude moved to take Ira's place, dragging Lily along with him. From his vantage point, Lucas could see Mr. K was much larger than Ira. The Dìonadain had the clear advantage. He was quicker and deflected the Mescáth's blue bolts easily, even gracefully. Swinging his radiant sword, Ira brought Mr. K to his knees. When he moved to bury his sword in Mr. K's dark chest, the Mescáth jumped and whirled behind Ira. The glowing Dìonadain warrior was too late to repel the attack. He was struck from behind by Mr. K's flaming blue darts. Ira crumpled to the ground.

"No," Lily screamed in horror.

Lucas couldn't stop his sister when she ran from Jude's protective presence toward Ira who lay outside the glowing shield. Jude was busy deflecting Aiden's forceful attack and turned too late to stop her flight. When she reached Ira, she tried to drag him back into the protective shield. She had no idea how vulnerable she was. She couldn't see the danger. Mr. K had moved in for the kill.

Jude roared in anguish as deadly blue flames shot from the Mescáth's eyes. From out of nowhere, Aiden catapulted in front of Lily, receiving the full force of Mr. K's lethal attack. He fell moaning at Lily's feet. Jude rushed to Lily's side, flinging two gleaming daggers toward the hulking black Mescáth. Pinned to the wall, Mr. K screamed in agony as the daggers burned hot and deep into his shoulders. When Lily reached out to Aiden, Jude picked her up and whisked her back into the protective guardian shield.

For a moment the fighting ceased, everyone staring in disbelief at Aiden lying motionless on the stone floor. A mighty roar of thunder clapped and Cain appeared. He rushed to gather his son in his arms. His eyes flamed cold.

"Finish them," Cain ordered his daughter. And then they were gone.

Keket screamed in rage. Her entire body consumed in blue flame. The Dìonadain moved to repel her vicious onslaught.

Lucas grabbed Wei's hand. "Can you stop her? Even for just a second, so we can get out of here?"

Wei nodded her head, determination in her dark eyes. "I'll try."

"Rafe, you and Lily join hands with me. Focus all your energy towards Wei. Daniel, start praying."

"Hurry," Jude yelled, circling the Sorcha and reinforcing the shield.

Tov and Kiefer were in the fight of their lives, trying to hold off Keket's renewed attack. Mr. K had managed to rip Jude's daggers from his body. He roared into the fight once again alongside his sister Mescáth. The Dìonadain sheathed their glowing broadswords, their shields at their backs. They changed tactics and weapons for fighting in close quarters. Kiefer brandished two golden tomahawks, repelling Keket's blue darts while Tov, wielding a pair of bladed sai, blocked and parried with Mr. K.

"Do it now, Wei!" Lucas shouted.

Wei's whole body buzzed with electricity. Lucas watched her extend both hands toward Keket, channeling the light within for a singular purpose: to stop this foul creature from wreaking any more havoc. Lucas, Rafe, and Lily focused on nothing but Wei. Instantly, Keket froze. She couldn't move, bound by the energy flowing through and from Wei. Without his sister, Mr. K was easily bound by the efforts of Tov and Kiefer.

"It's working," Rafe encouraged. "You got this Wei."

"Stay focused," Lucas commanded.

Wei moved one of her hands and placed it on the wall beside her. Just like before, she created a small opening big enough for the Sorcha to pass through.

"Go, go! Move it!" Kiefir cried, leading Mia, Daniel and Junjie.

Lucas looked at Keket, bound and powerless in Wei's net. He held her gaze and said with conviction, "This is not over."

"Far from it—this is just the beginning, Sorcha," Keket vowed before she disappeared with Mr. K. Lucas bent down to Wei who was crumpled on the floor. Rafe and Lily were already at her side.

"Are you okay?" He brushed back her hair from her face.

"I will be when you get me out of this mess," she retorted weakly. The wall that had been opened just a moment before was now closed.

"The Scáths are bound...but not for long. We need to get clear of the building," Asher announced as he charged into the passage. He looked at Ira who came forward deliberately. The glowing blue wounds covering his body were slowly disappearing. "Brother?"

"I'll make it," Ira said. The warrior released his golden sword from its scabbard ready to fight.

"What are we waiting for?" Lucas shouted. The violent screeching sounds of the Scáths were growing louder. Asher was right, it wouldn't be long until the demons were free and upon them. "Let's get outta here!"

Lucas charged down the tunnel along with the others. He knew they were running for their very lives.

Epilogue

• • •

Every moment brings us closer to our destiny.

The others must be found quickly for the uniting of the twelve has been foretold.

Evil will not give up his hunt.

We have seen his face and wrestled with him.

No matter the cost or risk to us, we must find the key and unlock the secret of Simon's Book.

Our quest continues.

Elohim (el-o-heem)
Creator and Judge; He is the one and only true God; Elohim is the Hebrew word for God that occurs 2000 times in the Old Testament. It also refers to the plurality within the Godhead. (Genesis 1; Deuteronomy 4:39)

The Light
Elohim came to earth in human form in the embodiment of His son, The Light; He chose twelve to follow him and be His light unto the world. (John 3:16; John 8:12)

Dìonadain (di-o-na-dane)
Gaelic word meaning one who guards; legion of angels created by Elohim; act as watchers, guardians, messengers and warriors of the Light. (Psalms 91:11; Matthew 26:53)

Simon the Zealot
One of the twelve original Sorcha chosen by Elohim; tradition says he was martyred with a saw in Caistor, Lincolnshire, Britain around 61 A.D. (Matthew 10:2-4; Mark 10:2-4)

Sorcha (sor-sha)
Gaelic word meaning light (not dark); twelve human beings, possessing supernatural gifts, created by Elohim and chosen to embody the power of His Light in each generation (Genesis 1:26-28; Matthew 5:14-16; Matthew 10:2-4; 2 Peter 1:19-21)

Gifts of the Sorcha
The Dreamer (Daniel 1:17; Acts 2:17)
The Crafter (Exodus 31: 1-11; 2 Chronicles 2:12)
The Perceiver (1 Corinthians 12:10; 1 John 4: 1-6; 2)
The Believer (1 Corinthians 12:9; Hebrews 11:1)
The Healer (Acts 3:1-10; 1 Corinthians 12: 28)
The Wielder (Acts 5:12; Acts 19:11)
The Knower (Psalm 119:66; 1 Corinthians 12:8)
The Leader (2 Chronicles 1:7-12; Romans 12:6-8)
The Speaker (Mark 16:17-18; Acts 2:1-12)
The Warrior (Judges 13:24; 16:28; Philippians 4:13)
The Exiler (Mark 9:29; Luke 10:17)
The Psalter (2 Chronicles 20:21; Psalm 68:25)

GLOSSARY OF SHADOWS

Abaddon (ab-ah-don)
Hebrew word meaning destroyer; a fallen angel who rebelled against Elohim; the Prince of Darkness; roams the Earth seeking to destroy Elohim's creation, His Light, and the Sorcha. (Revelation 9:11; Isaiah 14:12-15; 1 Peter 5:8-9)

Scàth (skahth)
Gaelic word meaning shadow; fallen angels who rebelled with Abaddon against Elohim; warriors of destruction; demons and malevolent spirits (Ephesians 6:12; Jude 1:6; Revelation 12:9-11)

Mescàth (me-skahth)
Beings produced by the union of Scàth and Sorcha; at war with what lives within them, light and dark. (Genesis 6:4)

"This is War" by 30 Seconds to Mars.
If the Sorcha could have a theme song this would be it—It's our anthem

"Undisclosed Desires" by Muse.
Demons are beautiful—they deceive

"You Are My Sunshine" by Civil Wars.
Eli's song to his kids

"Marchin On" by One Republic.
*Lucas's song

"Misguided Ghosts" by Paramore.
*Lily's song

"Drag Me Down" by One Direction.
Perfect for Zoe & Beni's wonderful friendship

"No Worries" by the Robert Glasper Trio.
*Rafe listens to jazz in his headphones to keep himself focused

"The Violet Hour" by Civil Wars.
This song takes you to the clearing—haunting and lovely (Candy's mood music)

"Guardian Angel" by The Red Jumpsuit Apparatus.
   All the Dìonadain really

"A Sky Full of Stars" by Coldplay.
   The way Lily sees Aiden—had to include a song from
   Coldplay (Lesley's favorite)

"Only by the Night" by Kings of Leon.
   *Keket's song—the darkness before midnight

"Fearless" by Group One Crew.
   *Daniel's song

"Warriors" by Imagine Dragons.
   Song for the Light Trials

"I Won't Give Up" by Jason Mraz.
   *Aiden's song for Lily at the Mill

"Awake and Alive" by Skillet.
   Battle in NYC

"Oceans" by Hillsong United.
   Every morning before writing—meaningful on so many
   levels—to me and to every light-bearer out there (Susan's song)

"Hall of Fame" by Script.
   We all have gifts—let's use them for good

"You Make Me Brave" by Amanda Cook & Bethel Music.
The song in the heart of every light-bearer

DIVE INTO THIS SNEAK PEEK OF

UNITE

VOLUME 2 OF THE SORCHA

He opened his bloodshot eyes and groaned. His mouth was dry—his head pounding. He rubbed his face feeling the roughness of his day's growth of beard. He didn't know how long he had been passed out on the king-size bed in the luxurious hotel suite. He didn't really care. Even though too much living and too little rest were taking its toll, Aiden needed to lose himself in the blur. He had only been in Ireland for a week, the fourth stop on his spree of destruction across Europe. It had been two months since the battle in New York and no matter how much he tried to forget, the events of that day would be forever etched in his mind.

He grabbed his phone to look at the time—8:00pm. He would have to hurry if he was going to make the fight. He rolled out of bed and headed for the shower. The hot water cleansed his body but not his mind. He was already jazzed up for what was to come. His jeans, t-shirt, boots and supple black leather jacket complemented his dangerous mood. He left his room—the predator ready for his prey.

Outside the hotel, he climbed on his motorcycle and roared through the dark streets of Dublin heading toward the outskirts of town. When he arrived at the old abandoned distillery, a rush of adrenaline coursed through his body. His senses were heightened—his anticipation growing. He entered the building through a heavy metal door. He descended the steps into another world.

"It's about bloody time! The crowd is restless," the beefy man in the woolen cap reproved.

Aiden's dark look silenced any further quarrel even though the man was twice his size.

He walked down the dimly lit hall removing his jacket and shirt. He tossed them nonchalantly at the burly man trying to keep up with his long strides. He was focused, deadly calm—ready to begin. He flung open the double doors and was met by thunderous applause. He strode purposefully through the wild crowd towards the iron cage. Some people were taunting and cursing, while others whistled and bellowed his name in wicked glee. Aiden had made quite a name for himself in Dublin's underground fight circuit these last two weeks. He was now the one to beat; he was the sure bet. His lethal skill and cunning strength were an unbeatable combination, especially when there were no rules. Tonight, like every other night, it would be a fight to the death. And Aiden felt right at home.

He removed his boots and stepped into the cage. It was a boxing ring inside an impregnable fortress of thick iron. The door was slammed shut and chained behind him. It was literally a death trap. In the cage, fighters could use a mixture of martial arts to take down their opponent. It was full-contact combat.

Stadium bleachers, for spectators, circled the cage. Their cheers were deafening. Aiden turned slowly in a circle giving the crowd what they wanted—a better look at him. He was the main event! Their attention only sharpened his focus. Then, he sized up his opponent.

He had the look of an Irishman born and bred on the streets of Dublin. He was fair-skinned, reddish-blonde hair, about 6' 2" tall, lean and brawny in an understated way. He was tough as nails. Aiden knew immediately that this man would be a worthy adversary. His steely green eyes were full of determination and something else Aiden couldn't quite put his finger on. When his opponent exchanged a meaningful glance with a fresh-faced young man with curly red hair, standing outside the cage, Aiden knew. The boy's eyes and face were so similar to the man he was getting ready to fight, Aiden decided the two must be brothers. He sensed something was definitely wrong. The young boy was held firmly despite his struggle between two hefty and intimidating men. That could only mean one thing—his rival was fighting for a cause and that made him dangerous. Aiden smiled—this was gonna be fun.

The bell rang signaling the beginning of their deadly dance. The crowd vanished—their shouts silenced. For Aiden there was only the Irishman and nothing else. He wasted no time in his frontal attack. He was quick but the Irishman was methodical taking his measure, deftly dodging his jabs. Aiden pushed ahead striking with an incredible combination kick. The Irishman stood his ground. He returned Aiden's attack with an outside left kick and then a jab to the midsection. Aiden laughed—finally—a challenge. The two warriors fought returning blow for blow.

Aiden took the Irishman by surprise and drove him up against the cage. When the Irishman spared a glance toward his little brother, Aiden went in for the kill. He muscled the Irishman down to the mat trapping him in an unbelievable chokehold. The Irishman strained against Aiden's death grip to no avail. Aiden knew his rival's strength was spent—he had run out of options. A sweet sense of victory filled Aiden's dark soul. Death was so liberating. Death was his savior.

The Irishman turned his eyes toward his little brother outside of the cage. The boy was yelling. The men holding him drug him out of the room through a thick metal door. Aiden looked at the Irishman, his eyes full of pain. He had failed himself and Aiden figured even more the Irishman had failed his little brother. It meant nothing to him! Aiden squeezed applying a tremendous amount of pressure to his fallen opponent's throat. When the Irishman's eyes rolled back in his head, Aiden jumped up and raised both arms in victory. The crowd roared violently.

A huge hulking force slammed into him from behind knocking him flat to the ground. The Irishman had risen. Aiden cursed himself for not finishing the job. He wrestled with the Irishman but was quickly overpowered. But not before, he saw a telltale symbol behind the Irishman's ear. He sucked in his breath. He gave no recourse when the Irishman picked him up and threw him bodily across the cage. Then the Irishman went to the thick iron bars and pulled them apart with his bare hands. The crowd roared in disbelief. Aiden watched the Irishman exit the cage and run to the heavy metal door his brother had been taken through. He ripped it off its hinges and threw it easily aside and disappeared. Things had just gotten very complicated.

About the Authors & Illustrator

• • •

The Alford sisters grew up listening to their grandparents' real-life stories of angels and demons and the unbelievable power of spiritual gifts. *Sorcha: Awaken*, their first novel, grew from this fascination.

Susan Alford is a published author and popular speaker who loves the written word. She started writing in fifth grade. Today she is a psychology professor at Lee University and lives in Cleveland, Tennessee with her two daughters.

Lesley Smith is an author, accomplished producer and singer, and an acclaimed photographer. When not writing and capturing life with her camera, she is immersed in being a wife and mother of two in Atlanta, Georgia.

Candace Alford is a freelance artist, illustrator, and graphic designer. Always interested in the arts, she enjoys music but her passion is creating visual art. She resides in Cleveland, Tennessee with her son.

50685725R00195

Made in the USA
Lexington, KY
25 March 2016